CW01095485

FAMILY
DOCTOR

BOOKS BY J M DALGLIESH

Homewrecker

Blood Runs Cold

FAMILY DOCTOR

J M DALGLIESH

Bookouture

Published by Bookouture in 2025

An imprint of Storyfire Ltd.
Carmelite House
50 Victoria Embankment
London EC4Y 0DZ

www.bookouture.com

The authorised representative in the EEA is Hachette Ireland
8 Castlecourt Centre
Dublin 15 D15 XTP3
Ireland
(email: info@hbgi.ie)

ISBN: 978-1-83525-843-9
eBook ISBN: 978-1-83525-842-2

PROLOGUE

I'm hit by a gust of salt-flecked wind as I get out of the car on the quayside. The pitch of the engines on the vessel coming into port lifts as the pilot brings her into the dock. Fastening my coat up to just below my chin, I turn myself away, sweeping my hair away from my eyes.

Mum doesn't want me to leave home. She feels like she nearly lost me that day two summers ago and I understand, but the truth is I'm suffocating. I've been distanced from all my friends and Mum walks on eggshells around me. Yet nothing that happened was my fault and I need to move forward, somehow.

Walking to the edge of the dock, the swell is clashing against the stone of the harbour wall.

Then approaching footsteps startle me. I didn't realise anyone else was here.

I turn to see a lone man, his face hidden by a thick scarf and a beanie.

'Can I help?' I ask. He's looking at the rear of my car and the hairs on my neck are standing up. 'Is something the matter?'

He says nothing, just pointing at the car. I approach but he moves another step away and I still can't see his face.

Rounding the back corner of my car, I see the light cluster is broken and there's a bright white light. 'Damn. I hadn't seen that. I'll have to get it fixed. Thanks.'

He says nothing and I'm starting to feel a chill, all over my body. I have the urge to get back into my car or move to where the ferry's crew can see me.

'What's the capacity of the boot like?' he says suddenly.

'No idea,' I say. 'Look, I don't know what your deal is, but I have to go.'

'Okay,' he says quietly, looking down at his feet.

'No listen, I'm sorry,' I say, placing a flat hand on my chest. 'I don't mean to be rude. I have a lot on my mind right now, you know?'

'That's okay.'

I make to leave.

'One more thing,' he says brightly.

I turn back. 'What?'

He gestures towards my car. 'Do you think you'll fit in there?'

There's something about him, something almost familiar. Is it his eyes or the voice?

'In... where?'

'In the boot.'

The last I recall is the feel of the cold against my cheek, the damp tarmac of the quayside. I hear a solitary blast from the horn of the vessel on its final approach, but I'll never get to see it dock.

ONE

DAY ONE

KELLY

The window frame rattles, buffeted by the wind coursing through the Sound of Jura, the narrow stretch of water separating us from our larger Hebridean sister, Islay. On the east coast of Jura, we are at least offered some protection from the Atlantic winds by our neighbour, but not much. The mainland is visible across the water as I look out the window, for now, until the weather front crosses the island and it disappears into the mist. I'm wondering how Lauren is getting on. It'll likely be a rough crossing, but she'll cope I'm sure.

'So, what do you think it is, Doctor Kelly?'

My eyes drift towards my patient, Ashleigh, a pretty twenty-something, and I sigh before offering her the usual reassurances. Then there's a knock, right on time. The door cracks open and Ava MacLeod, my partner in crime, pokes her head through.

'I'm sorry to interrupt, but you have a video consultation with a patient in less than three minutes.'

'Thanks, Ava.'

I'm the only medical practitioner on the island, which makes me the first port of call for any standing ailments as well as any emergency situation. But with only one road on the island, one town, one pub and a single hotel, there isn't much that passes for an emergency on Jura.

The locals, outnumbered by the deer who roam freely, are largely kept in employment by the five private estates that carve up the island between them, or in one of the three operating distilleries, whisky, rum or gin. Pick your favourite. I try not to drink anymore, despite the trauma in my not-too-distant past, and I'm doing well.

I watch Ashleigh leave my consulting room, Ava holding the door open for her before stepping inside. Not only is she a very competent receptionist and my solitary, dependable member of staff, but Ava is so much more than that. She knows everyone and keeps her ear to the ground. How she manages it, I don't know, but she's abreast of everything that's going on.

'It's almost the anniversary of her mother's passing,' Ava says, lowering her voice as if someone could overhear us.

'Yes, it is,' I say. 'Barely a fortnight away.'

'The poor thing, put her own life on hold.' Ava's gaze drifts to the window. 'It's amazing what people will do for the ones they love, isn't it? Ashleigh, staying on the island to care for her dear old mum, and now she feels she can't leave.'

'The fear of letting go of the past. It's powerful.'

'I suppose so,' Ava says. 'Much better to live in the present, wouldn't you say?'

'Absolutely.'

'Would you like a cup of tea?'

I turn to her. 'Oh, that would be lovely.'

'I'll be right through with it,' Ava says. At the door, she pauses and looks back. 'Your next appointment has been cancelled, so you have a bit of time.'

'Cancelled, why?'

'Some kind of issue with the engines on the ferry, so I'm told. No one's going anywhere at the moment.'

'Thank heavens Lauren set off early then.'

'Lauren?' Ava asks. 'Was she heading over to Islay?'

'Only to catch the first sailing to Kennacraig—'

'Oh, that's right. It's her interview today.'

I nod glumly. Don't get me wrong, I'm incredibly proud of my daughter and St Andrews is a wonderful university. She had to defer her place twice and, for some reason that I fear is related to what has happened in my life these past couple of years, the admissions team have called her for an interview. Provided she makes a good impression, I think it's now or never. But that doesn't mean I want her to go.

'It will all work out as it's meant to, Doctor Kelly. Don't worry.' I look up at Ava, forcing a smile. 'That's better,' she says and leaves me, the door slowly closing behind her.

Scooping up my mobile I check for messages. There's still nothing from Lauren.

I check the time. She'll be docking at Kennacraig soon enough. I shouldn't worry. If she hadn't caught the earlier sailing she'd have let me know, wouldn't she?

Shouting outside draws my gaze back to the window. Blair, my main contractor, is barking out an instruction to his apprentice, who is also his son. The benefit of having the surgery attached to my home makes it easy to keep up with renovation progress, but also leaves me with no escape from the noise. That reminds me, I need to speak to Blair. Grabbing my house keys and with my mobile still in my hand, I walk out into reception. I don't have a video consult, that was simply the ruse Ava and I concocted to ensure that I didn't spend the entire morning with Ashleigh, who is a very sweet and lovely young woman, but suffers from the worst case of hypochondria I've ever witnessed.

'I've made you tea!' Ava calls, stepping out from the small kitchenette that caters for us in the medical centre. A centre is a stretch. It is three rooms attached to the south side of the old croft house I live in with Lauren, our new home. When we first came the whitewash on the stone was flaking off and mould grew on the exposed interior walls where the roof had failed. Stone built, once roofed with thatch, Blair has laid new slate tiles and repointed the stonework prior to a fresh coat of white paint. The previous occupant of my role retired to the mainland and I am the latest addition recruited by the Highlands and Islands Enterprise Council.

'I'm just ducking home to have a word with Blair. I'll not be long,' I say over my shoulder, pushing open the door to the outside. A gust of cold wind cuts through my blouse and I'm already regretting not bringing my coat.

Folding my arms across my chest, I hurry around the building to my home with my head down. I'm grateful to have been able to move into the main house now that most of the building work is finished. The summer in the caravan, a very Scottish summer as it turns out, was okay but as autumn set in we were pleased to move into our home.

'Blair!'

A head pops up from above the ridge line of the house, tartan beanie pulled down to his ears, and Blair McInally looks down at me, a hand-rolled cigarette dangling from his lips.

'Oh, hey there, Doctor Kelly. You all right?'

'The shower in the main bathroom is still backing up. Can you look at it for me?'

'Aye, leave it with me.'

'Thanks, Blair.'

'Nae bother,' Blair says absently and I duck into the house, keen to make sure neither Lauren nor I have left anything in the bathroom that we'd rather Blair or Donnie didn't see. This is a small community and I'm well aware that people talk.

The bathroom needs only a cursory tidy up. Happy, I soon

head back through the house and prepare to face the elements again, looking forward to that cup of tea, when my phone beeps.

It's a message from Lauren. I open it immediately, but there's nothing but a short link and two words.

Open this.

If it hadn't come from my daughter I would never open a random link, but without hesitation I tap on it and the screen changes.

I'm expecting a video of the ferry ride, the approach into Kennacraig. But it appears to be a live video feed.

It's dark and I can't make much out, just some movement. Instinctively I increase the volume and I can hear breathing. Short intakes, laboured.

The camera zooms out and I see a cheek, then a chin and something is in her mouth, a rag or material of some kind. She flinches, trying to look away from the camera, the bright light illuminating her features whilst dazzling her. I hear her muffled scream.

There's a sharp pang in my chest, but I'm transfixed. It's the slow-motion car crash that you cannot look away from. It is unmistakable though. I would know her anywhere.

My baby. My Lauren.

'What—'

The feed ends, and I'm fumbling with my phone to replay it when a message flashes up.

Pay attention, Kelly. You must do exactly as I say. There are three rules.

Rule One. You have seventy-two hours – three days – to murder one of your patients.

I gasp, raising a hand to my mouth. This is a sick prank. What the hell is going on?

Another message comes now, pushing the former off the screen.

Rule Two. You must not tell another soul.

Rule Three. You must not be caught.

And then they come, the words that will forever be imprinted on my brain.

If you break these simple rules, your daughter will die.

This is a joke. It must be. Before I can even begin to process it all a call comes through, from Lauren.

I answer immediately, feeling a flash of anger course through me.

'Lauren, what the hell—'

The voice is digitally manipulated, distinctively monotone and authoritative. 'Do you understand these rules, Kelly?'

'Where's my daughter?' Terror permeates my voice. 'I want to speak to Lauren, now!'

Silence.

I hear scraping in the background, wooden chair legs on stone or tiles, perhaps, and I listen intently. I'm holding my breath. Where is she? More movement and then breathing.

'Mum?' she whispers. 'It's me...'

It's Lauren; her speech is stilted. I know my daughter, she's terrified. I recognise every sound she makes. 'Baby, it's me. I'm going to—' She screams and I'm out of my body, detached from reality. *My child.* 'Lauren!'

Silence.

My chest feels incredibly tight. My throat is constricted. I can't breathe. I want to speak, to tell her everything will be okay, but all I can manage is a whimper. 'L-Lauren... baby?'

That voice again.

'Lauren understands these rules, and why I've chosen her. Do you understand, Kelly?'

'I-I...'

'Focus, Kelly. The rules. Do you understand?'

'Yes. *Yes*, I-I understand the rules.'

The call ends.

'Lauren!' I scream into the phone, staring at the screen. Sinking to the floor, clutching the mobile to my chest, I'm hyperventilating. *My... baby.* Someone has my baby.

TWO

SIX HOURS EARLIER

Lauren is buzzing around in the kitchen, picking up items she's left lying around and may or may not need on her trip. People say that we are so alike, my daughter and me. If that's true, am I this annoying when packing for a trip? Possibly. Lauren calls it the *Kelly faff*, the action of bringing everything together at the last minute, a whirlwind of activity that, with the benefit of hindsight, need never be quite as chaotic as it always is, I'm sure. And, for the record, I know who she got that description from. *He who must not be named.*

We pass one another like choreographed dancers, failing to touch as we navigate the space. Lauren to add her hairbrush – why is this in the kitchen? – to her bag and me to switch on the coffee machine. I can't function without my regular morning caffeine hit and at five thirty, I need it today more than I do on most days.

It's dark outside. Mind you, in the bleak midwinter on the Inner Hebrides it will be dark for much of the day, perhaps brightening for a few hours either side of midday, if we're lucky. As overcast as it is, with sleet coming down almost horizontally as I glance out of the nearest window, it is a day that promises little by way of brightness.

Lauren is throwing items into a travel bag, then hesitates as she spies something on the counter. The newspaper, with the article I don't want her to see. She reaches for it and quick as a cat, I snatch it from her grasp.

'What?' she asks.

'You don't need it, do you?'

'Well, actually, my trainers were wet through after getting caught out in the rain yesterday. I was going to pack them with paper. They'll be dry by the time I come to wear them this evening.'

'Oh, well I'm still reading it—'

'Mum! It's... like... a month old,' she says, rolling her eyes. 'If you haven't finished it by now—'

I shrug. 'I am still going to read it, so I'll just get you another one from the recycling box. Is that okay with you?'

'Whatever.'

'Remind me again,' I ask as I'm rooting through the old cardboard and plastic tubs in the recycling, searching for something paper that's suitable, 'why you didn't want to travel across yesterday?' Passing her another old newspaper, I turn my attention to the coffee machine, knocking out yesterday's grind from the filter head. The sound hurts my head but not as much as when the grinder kicks in. To think, I used to experience this with a hangover as well. In the mornings I wake with the sensation of overdoing it but not so much as a dram has passed my lips since we came to the island. Maybe it's residual muscle memory, like athletes, only for recovering alcoholics.

Not that I was ever an alcoholic. I just needed... something, to get me through the day. For a while anyway. They say doctors make the worst patients, and that I can wholeheartedly attest to.

'Remember?' Lauren says, pausing for a moment to arch her

eyebrows in that way I used to do to her when she was seven or eight and pushing the boundaries on what was acceptable. 'I wanted to travel the day before, but *you* wouldn't let me. So, *now*, I have a very long day of travel ahead of me with an interview that I really need to go well at the end of it.'

I frown. The conversation certainly rings a bell. 'Why did I say that?'

'Because Dad was going to be out of town last night, and you didn't trust me not to meet up with—'

'Oh, yes! That's right. I didn't.' I nod slowly, reassuring myself that I made the right call. 'Still, nothing focuses the mind more than having a lot to do with not enough time to do it in. Right?'

Lauren looks at me, and I know she wants to be angry, but we have a great relationship. An honest relationship where we don't keep things from one another. Wishful thinking, perhaps. She is a teenager after all, and I never had that sort of relationship with my mother. That's probably why I'm seeking it. Or maybe it's just the guilt I'm carrying over the last two years. She exaggerates a sigh and purses her lips. 'Right.'

'You'll be fine. Your interview is at three o'clock. You will have plenty of time to get there and prep. Not that I think you'll need to do much.'

'No?' she asks, stopping again and glancing at me. Not for the first time I see my image reflected back at me. She has my eyes, pale blue, finely sculpted cheekbones and classic jawline, and all framed by dark shoulder-length hair. Models would kill to have lines like my daughter's.

'No,' I tell her honestly. 'You're a shoo-in. I guarantee it.'

She smiles. 'You think so?'

'Yes, I do.'

Lauren pushes her bag aside and crosses the kitchen to me, throwing her arms around me. I hold her, then tighten my grip around her, bringing her closer. 'Thanks, Mum,' she says, her head resting on my chest. I'm still taller than her, but not by much. Easing her off me, I keep my hands on her shoulders.

'Is everything all right?'

She nods. 'Yes, why?'

'You seem... I don't know, but whatever it is, you seem it.'

Lauren laughs, shaking her head. 'I guess it's a lot to take in.'

'I know. But it will be okay, darling. You're nineteen, nearly twenty years of age. With everything that's happened these past' – I shake my head; I can't quite believe it, but it has been that long – 'two years, you've had so much to cope with. Now it's time you started making some of your own life decisions rather than taking the lead from a dinosaur like me. Now, what time is your sailing?'

Lauren's forehead creases. 'I'm booked onto the first crossing back to Askaig, and then the CalMac ferry sails at seven. I'll be on the mainland by nine o'clock.'

The coffee machine finishes grinding and I grab a cup, setting it below the filter head before pressing the start button to commence the extraction process. 'Plenty of time to get across to Edinburgh.'

Lauren exhales. 'I'll look a mess by the time I get there.'

'You'll look the same as you always do, gorgeous! Just like your mum,' I say, looking over my shoulder and winking.

Lauren bursts out laughing. 'Thanks, Mum.' I give her another hug and then I gently slap her backside as I glance at the clock.

'Come on, if you miss the first ferry your day will be totally screwed. Get a move on!'

'All right, I'm pretty much set.'

'You'll keep me updated on progress?'

'Yes.'

'You promise?' I ask. Lauren tilts her head to one side.

'Yes!'

'Say it.'

'I promise I'll keep you updated.'

'Good luck,' I say, leaning in and kissing her cheek, stroking her arm as I do so. 'I love you.'

'I love you too, Mum,' she says, gathering two bags in her arms and hustling to the back door, her bags clattering against the kitchen units in the confined space. These old croft houses were never designed with modern family life in mind.

The door closes and I'm alone. I guess I'd better get used to this feeling. At one time all I had to think about was myself and what I wanted to do. That changes when you have a child. I've come to learn that everything becomes about them, and I am a distant second. What will I do when there is only me again? What is my purpose then? Our little house, one that feels cramped most of the time, is going to feel much, much larger.

THREE

NOW

I don't know how long I've been sitting here on the floor of my kitchen. I can remember every detail of that conversation with my daughter's kidnapper. I have no need to read those messages again. I could recite them word for word.

Snapping into focus, I look at my mobile and dial Lauren's number. I desperately want to believe this is a hoax, some sick prank she's playing on me. Pressing the phone to my ear I listen to it ring until the call shifts to voicemail.

No, I'm not going to leave a bloody message. This can't be happening. It's unbelievable.

It's approaching midday. Lauren should have made it to Kennacraig almost a couple of hours ago now. So... she could be anywhere between here and the coast of Argyll and Bute. That's a massive tranche of the west coast and islands.

There's a problem with the ferry though, Ava said so. Did Lauren even leave the island? She must have, otherwise she would have come home or be sitting in her car at Feolin just like everyone else waiting on either side of the crossing point.

That wasn't Lauren siting in the darkness, bound and

gagged, surely? It couldn't be. I've imagined it. I'm losing my mind.

Scrolling through my contacts, my hands shaking and struggling to breathe, I call the only person I can think of. He answers, his suave, Edinburgh Morningside accent altered only slightly by his surprise at my call.

'Kelly? This is unexpected—'

'Yes, I know... I mean, I'm sure it is,' I say, stumbling over my words and talking over him. 'Listen, have you spoken to Lauren?'

'Today? No. Why?'

'Oh, I was just wondering, you know?' I say, failing to keep the tension out of my voice, my free hand pressed against my forehead.

What else can I tell him? Nothing. *Do you understand the rules, Kelly?* Only too well.

'Kel? Is something wrong? What's happened?'

I try to swallow but my mouth is dry. Tears are streaming down my face but I can't swallow. What the hell is going on? I look up at the ceiling – I'll find no answers there – wiping my face with the back of my hand, trying hard not to wail like a child. Like my child.

'Nothing's happened,' I scoff, my voice breaking as I force a laugh. 'Of course nothing's happened, it's just, you know, I worry—'

'I'm seeing her this evening. It's a good job you called and reminded me, I've been so busy with work, I might have forgotten.'

'You're seeing her tonight?'

'Aye, that's correct. After her interview at—'

'Yes, yes, of course. I-I didn't know you were seeing her, that's all.' Lauren hadn't told me she was meeting him, but I regret the admission immediately. 'I mean, I forgot. It slipped my mind, you know?' I grimace.

Why did I call my husband, of all people? I've been avoiding him for months, but I have no one else to reach out to in an emergency, not anymore.

'She told you then?' he asks. There it is. They were keeping it from me. That's just great. What else were these two keeping from me? I guess it doesn't matter. All that matters is I get my daughter back, regardless of whether they are sneaking around behind my back. 'Look, I know it's a difficult situation—'

'Um... yeah, this is not really the time, Niall. Can we get into this another day?'

'Sure. Any idea when you might be able to squeeze in a phone call with me?'

'Please, Niall. Not today,' I say, hearing my voice crack.

'Kelly. Are you sure everything is all right? You sound—'

'I'm fine, I promise.'

'Okay, if you're sure?'

'I am. Only, I'm not sure whether Lauren is going to be seeing you later.'

'Come on, Kelly. I haven't seen her in months as it is, hardly at all since you moved to the other end of the earth—'

'It's Jura, Niall, not the Antarctic colonies.'

'It may as well be! And now you won't let me see her when she's—'

'No, it's not that. She's sick, that's all.'

'Oh, right. Nothing serious, I hope?'

'No, no, just a tummy bug or something. She'll be right as rain in a day or two.'

'What about her interview?'

'They'll reschedule it.'

'Right. Can I speak to her?'

'No, she's asleep. I-I don't want to wake her. She needs her rest.'

'Of course, no problem. I can call later.'

'Yeah, yeah, do that. Look, I need to get back to... um... work.'

'Okay,' he says, sounding disappointed. 'But call me if Lauren gets any worse, will you?'

'Um, yes. I'll do that, but don't worry. Everything's fine.' The reassurance sounds hollow. I'd never be successful in an elevator pitch or, as it turned out, in a coroner's inquest.

'If you're sure?'

'I am.'

'Okay,' he says and I sense he doesn't want to end the call, but I can hear someone in the background trying to get his attention, distracting him. 'I should go too.'

'Okay.'

'I,' he says, hesitantly, 'love you, Kelly.'

I hang up without responding. I don't know what to say to that. What the hell am I supposed to do here? I'm her mother, and I'm supposed to do what's right by my daughter, but I have no clue what that looks like.

I could call the police? That's what I should do. That's what anyone else would do, wouldn't they? Ian would listen. He's a good guy, but he's the only police presence on Jura. One man. And he's only a part-time special at that. There isn't any crime around here. There's nothing to steal and nowhere to sell or spend it if you did. There's one way off this island, and that's currently broken by all accounts.

But even if Ian could help, whoever has done this was insistent. If I tell anyone, if I go for help, then I won't see Lauren again.

He'll kill her.

Maybe this is all some twisted prank; I'll cling to that, but for now I have to take him at his word.

So no, I won't call Ian McLean. I won't tell anyone.

I have to handle this on my own. I'll get Lauren out of this.

Whatever *this* is. Somehow. I have to get her back to me. I've no idea how I'll do it but there has to be a way.

Hauling myself up off the floor, my hand firmly holding onto my mobile just in case he calls again.

Who would want to hurt my daughter? And why have they concocted this insane scenario, demanding I kill one of my patients? Why haven't they just blackmailed me? What could their motivation possibly be? He said Lauren *understands the rules* and why he chose her. So is this someone she knows?

Slipping the mobile into my pocket I make my way through the house to Lauren's bedroom. There is no upstairs to our home; it's small. Compact and cosy the estate agent described it as. Cosy it certainly wasn't, but it's better now since Blair has been on the project. We've made it a bit bigger than it was previously, but it's anything but large when compared to my former home in Edinburgh. These old crofts were functional at best, built to withstand the brute force of the Atlantic weather with few creature comforts. Imagine a modern home shoe-horned into a building a third of the size and you'd be almost there.

Entering her bedroom, I find it in the style of a rubbish tip, the usual manner that a teenager leaves behind. A cyclone of energy barely focused on picking up after herself, but still presenting an immaculate representation to the external world whenever she goes out.

Perching myself on the edge of her bed, I take in the room. It's not huge, way smaller than the one she had back in our house in Edinburgh. I can hear the clock on her bedside table, the second-hand ticking round. It feels oppressive, being this close to my daughter and yet so far removed from her.

Where does Lauren keep her innermost thoughts? We have a great relationship, although she didn't tell me she was going to see Niall. I can't really blame her for that. But if she wasn't going to tell me about that arrangement, then what else would she have chosen to keep from me?

Where are you, Lauren? I lift my legs onto the bed and lie back, trying to imagine I'm her. I feel close to my daughter in her bedroom, surrounded by her things.

I can work this problem, just like any other. There have been times these past couple of years where I thought I would break, that it was over and I should just end it all. But I didn't. That which did not kill me, only made me stronger.

No one is going to harm my daughter. I'll find a way. I always do.

Putting my arms above my head and beneath the pillow, my fingers brush against something cold and metallic. Heaving myself up, I flip over the pillow and there's an old tin tucked down the back of the bed between the mattress and the headboard. I have to lift the mattress up to get it out.

It's an old biscuit tin of some kind, with a Dutch-looking street scene printed onto the front, a mix of blue shades and white. I think this belonged to my father. It looks familiar anyway, and is a bit battered, with pits and dents to the top and sides.

Inside is a small notebook, or maybe it's supposed to be a diary, A5 sized, and a handful of old photographs. I didn't realise anyone kept physical photos now, not least a teenager. She's never posted any of this stuff to social media. I didn't know she had it. Why would she keep it secret from everyone? Well, I'm thinking from me, more than anyone else. Maybe the public persona she shares is just as fake as everyone else's on social media. Flicking through the pictures, they are something of a mixed bag. Some are photos taken in and around Edinburgh's old town, hanging out with her friends in the Meadows on a sunny day, whilst others are more thoughtful, and probably planned, landscape shots. We do get those from time to time, contrary to popular opinion. Seeing her smiling, messing around with her friends, it's all so carefree. But that was before. Before what I did, on that day when our world fell apart.

My vision blurs and I have to blink away the tears as I put the photos aside and lift out the diary.

Lauren was never a writer, but her counsellor taught her it was a good way to draw out the emotion. Lauren and I had similar sessions, from the little she shared with me. Glancing through the entries, there appears to be no structure to the passages she has written. No dates, no headers delineating subjects. It's all just a random jumble of words and phrases, emotions or sketches. None of it makes any sense. It's like a mood board, or the mind map of someone with multiple personalities. I can barely read most of the entries. It's gibberish.

I feel guilty about going through her things. If ever I was justified in snooping, in breaking that trust, then it would be today. I find many of the pages are actually blank as if she's given up on the process, or whatever this is, but I come across a photo wedged between the most recent scribbles. A strip of photos, the ones you get from the old-style photo booths at the supermarket behind the checkouts. And I don't care for it. Her hair is as it is just now, and it wasn't styled that way before we moved to the island.

Lauren is smiling, gurning comically in two of the images alongside *him*.

That boy. One of the reasons I insisted on bringing her to Jura was to get her away from him: Cameron Stewart.

She swore she'd had no more contact with him. She knows how I feel. I guess that's why she's kept it confined to the pages of her diary.

The boy who – if I'd allowed it – would have destroyed my daughter's life.

FOUR

TWO YEARS PREVIOUSLY

'She should be home by now.'

Niall looks at me, sitting on the sofa in the drawing room, one leg crossed over the other, nursing the glass of scotch in his right hand. His eyebrows dance momentarily as he looks away.

'What?'

He looks back at me, only this time one eyebrow raises in that rather James Bond-esque way Roger Moore made famous back in the 80s. He shrugs. '*What*, what?'

'You know full well what I mean,' I say accusingly.

'She's almost eighteen.'

'So?'

'It's Friday night. This is Edinburgh.'

'And, so what?'

'It's not even midnight,' Niall says disapprovingly. 'You're being—'

'What?' I ask, moving to stand over him and he looks away. I bat his dangling foot and he uncrosses his legs, looking up glumly. '*What am I being, exactly?*'

'All right, if you insist,' he says, downing the contents of his glass and banging the crystal tumbler down on the place mat on the table in front of him. 'You're being a little neurotic.'

'Is that right?' I'm standing with my balled fists on my hips, glaring at my husband. 'Lauren is out God knows where with that lowlife, and you accuse me of being neurotic.'

He shrugs. 'She'll be fine. She has a sensible head on her shoulders.'

'And what about him?'

'Cameron?'

'Yes. Do you think he is sensible?'

'No,' Niall says, sitting forward, resting his elbows on his knees and interlocking his fingers before him. 'He's not who we'd like her to be spending time with, that's obvious—'

'And you don't see an issue with him being out with our daughter until who knows when and taking her...' – I fling my arms theatrically in the air – 'taking her—'

'Who knows where?'

'Yes!'

Niall heaves a sigh as he gets up, retrieves his glass and crosses to the sideboard and the resident decanter, pouring himself another. 'There's a song in that phrase. I think it might already have been done though.'

'You're not taking this seriously.'

'No,' he says, turning on me. 'I'm not. She said she'd be home before midnight, and I trust her to—' He looks towards the bay window, car headlights making the turn into our drive. The sound of wheels on gravel follows. 'There you go,' he says, lifting his glass in salutation towards the window. 'And it's not even ten to midnight. She's early. Happy?'

My arms are folded tightly across my chest, and I forcibly loosen the grip on myself. 'No, I'm not bloody happy at all.' Hearing a key in the lock of the front door, I stalk out into the hall.

'Kelly, don't...'

The front door creaks open and my seventeen-year-old daughter stumbles in, practically held up by Cameron, who has an arm around her waist. She's giggling, and he's laughing as he hauls her upright and she throws her arms around his neck, leaning forwards and kissing him.

'Well, don't mind us!'

Cameron immediately withdraws from the kiss, but Lauren only looks my way, her lips parting as she rolls her tongue along her lower lip, before grinning wildly. 'Hello, Mummy!'

'And what time do you call this, young lady?' Niall comes to stand at my shoulder, hands thrust casually into his pockets, lips pursed. The warm night air, the follow on from what's been a beautiful Edinburgh summer evening, carries in on the slightest of breezes.

'*Night-time*,' Lauren says, before cackling and looking back at her boyfriend. He's a similar height to Niall, over six feet, but slightly built. I guess that's normal for a boy – because that's what he is, a boy – at the age of twenty-two. It's the stupid fade haircut he sports, combined with the battered-leather biker jacket and the tattoos stretching almost from wrist to jaw that bother me. And the fact that I think he's supplying drugs to his friends and God knows who else.

'I think it's time you went to bed, Lauren,' Niall says, taking a step forward and clearly trying to de-escalate the situation. Not this time, husband darling. I place a restraining hand on his chest. Lauren's gaze passes from Niall to me, and she smiles.

'Yes, good idea. Come on, Cammie. Let's go to bed.'

'Oh, hell no!' I say, stepping forward. Cameron instinctively releases any hold he has over my daughter and she stumbles back against the panelling of the hall, pouting at her boyfriend.

'I think maybe I should go,' Cameron says quietly, although he's not cowed by my anger. Quite the contrary, I think he's almost enjoying it.

'That's the best idea you've had today, Cameron. Goodnight!'

He inclines his head towards me, his eyes moving momentarily to Niall, who nods. Cameron leans into Lauren to give her a kiss goodnight and she pulls him into her, kissing him fiercely much to my disgust. Then, pushing him away, she smiles at me. 'Night, Cammie,' she says, winking at him.

'Give us a phone tomorrow then, aye?' Cameron says, backing away. Lauren blows him a kiss as he opens the door. Niall follows him, taking the door in hand and, once Cameron is outside, he closes it, wincing in my direction.

'Hello, Mummy!' Lauren says, grinning. She's intoxicated, certainly, but I can tell from the lack of pupil dilation that she's only been drinking. Thankfully.

'You have some nerve,' I say to her but Lauren only sneers at me.

'I can date who I want to.'

'Not while you're living under my roof—'

'It's his roof,' Lauren says, pointing to Niall, who lowers his gaze to the floor, hiding his grimace and I feel the anger rising in me.

'Where have you been?'

'Out! With friends, before you ask,' Lauren says, ambling towards the ornate, wrought-iron staircase that winds its way to the upper floors of this stone Morningside villa we've called home since I married Niall. She pauses at the foot of the stairs, grasping the newel cap and swinging from it, turning to face me. 'Having a good time. You know what that is, don't you? Having a good time, with friends?'

'Lauren, he's not good for you!'

'Says who?'

'Me, Niall... probably the police, too, if you asked them.'

'And I'm supposed to trust your judgement, am I?' Lauren

says disdainfully, looking between me and Niall. 'You two?' She snorts with derision. 'Please!'

'Lauren, I forbid you to see that boy—'

'Boy? He's a man!'

'He's twenty-two,' I tell her, 'and he knows nothing!'

'At his age, you already had me, Mum!'

'Yes, exactly.' I fold my arms defensively across my chest. 'So, I think I know what I'm talking about, wouldn't you say?'

'Hah! You could have a child at the same age, but he can't take me out for a few beers?'

'You're underage. It's the law!'

'Well... the *law is an ass*, so Mark Twain once said.'

'I'm pleased to see the expensive education has paid dividends.'

'No, someone wrote it on the toilet wall of the pub we were just at.' She grins at me, while Niall raises his eyes to the ceiling in despair.

'Lauren—'

'Goodnight, Mummy. See you in the morning for croissants,' she says, practising a wobbly curtsy before setting off up the stairs, almost missing the first tread and stumbling forward. Niall moves to support her, but she braces herself on the banister and waves him away. 'Probably best if you don't help,' Lauren instructs him. 'All things considered, eh?'

Niall backs away, sheepishly avoiding my gaze and doesn't comment. Once Lauren is on the landing she begins singing some rendition of a pop song she might have heard earlier in the evening. The lyrics tail off as she moves to the back of the house and into her room, slamming the door behind her. Niall runs a hand through his wavy hair and cocks his head in my direction.

'That could have gone better.'

'She's out of order.'

He winces. 'She's only doing it to wind you up.'

'Yes, well, it's working.'

Just then someone hammers on Lauren's bedroom door, and the memory fades as I'm jolted back into reality.

I thought I was alone?

FIVE

PRESENT DAY

'Who is it?' I shout.

'It's me, Blair.'

Reluctantly, I get up off the bed, close the diary and slide it into the rear waistband of my trousers. Crossing to the bedroom door, I pull it open and Blair is standing outside. He seems taken aback as he looks at me, glancing to his right and then back into the living room.

'I... er... knocked,' he says, thumbing in the direction of the back door, presumably. 'But... er... you didna hear me, eh?'

'No, I didn't. What is it?'

'About your drain,' he says, frowning. 'I've had a look at it—'

'I'm not really bothered just now, Blair, to be honest.'

'Well, hopefully it's something simple. Probably just a blockage. If so, then—'

'Whatever it costs, just fix it, okay?'

'Right you are, lass. Nae bother.' He looks at me with a queer look. 'Is everything okay?'

I meet his eye and shrug. 'Yes, why do you ask?'

'Oh, nothing.'

He has this way about him, does Blair McInally. He's a

middle-aged, beer-bellied man, who is something of a stranger to a razor, but he's a straight shooter.

'It's just, we thought – wee Donnie and me – that we heard a scream earlier, maybe ten or fifteen minutes ago.'

'Oh, don't worry. That was nothing.'

'It was you, aye?'

'Yes, I-I caught my hand,' I say, waving it around. 'On a cupboard door. You know how it is?'

'Trapped it like, eh?'

'Yes.'

'Painful,' he says and I nod.

'Yes.'

'Right, well, I'll have another look at that drain this week. It's probably just some gunk built up in the waste pipe. Don't worry, that's easy enough to fix, eh?'

I smile briefly. 'Great. If you say so.' I rub my hand across my mouth. 'I need to get on, Blair, so if there's nothing else—'

'No, no, you crack on, lass. I'll get on myself.'

'Thanks, Blair,' I say, checking my watch.

I have seventy-one hours to figure out what the hell is going on and to get my daughter back.

Will I really have to kill a patient to do so, or can I fix this some other way?

Blair sets off down the corridor and into the living room, heading for the kitchen and the back door.

'Oh,' he says, turning back to face me. 'I was going to ask, how's Lauren?'

I stop dead and look straight at him. 'Lauren? Why do you ask?'

He shrugs. 'Just something Donnie said is all.'

Donnie is Blair's son, and his building partner. Between the two of them, they are quite the pairing. A comedy duo of sorts, but that isn't necessarily a good thing.

'What did he say, exactly?'

'Just that he saw her the other night, and... er...'

'What?'

'Well, you know... kids...'

I move towards him and Blair instinctively gets out of my way. I yank open the door and step outside. At least the sleet has stopped falling but it's still a raw wind blowing across Craighouse towards us here on the outskirts of the town.

'Donnie!' I shout.

'Aye?' a voice says, and Donald McInally pokes his head out from inside the old byre across the driveway from the main house. We've been using it to store materials for the build, to keep them away from the elements. It's little more than an old stone building, non-mortared joints with corrugated steel sheeting for a roof, but it does the job.

'What have you got to say about Lauren?' I ask, marching towards him. He looks scared. He's in his early twenties, I think, but he has a baby face that's pockmarked with acne scars and fresh outbreaks that will produce more. His red hair is cut close to his scalp, but that is hidden by a tatty old beanie.

'Lauren? Nothing, honest.'

I come to stand before him. 'You sure?' He glances beyond me, at his dad, his eyes pleading.

'I was just saying, Donnie, that you saw Lauren the other night. That's all.'

'Ah right, aye. I did.'

'Where?' I ask.

'Out at the bothy, like.'

'The bothy?' I ask, narrowing my eyes. I don't know anything about a bothy.

'Aye, it's where we sort of hang out of an evening. You know, just for the craic.'

I shake my head. 'And Lauren?'

'Aye.' He nods. 'Every now and again.'

'And what is it you do while you're hanging out?'

Donnie shrugs. 'We just... you know?'

'No, I don't,' I say pointedly. 'Drinking? Taking drugs?'

'Oh, hang on a second, lass,' Blair says, coming to stand alongside me and raising a hand. 'There'll be none of that sort of thing going on around my boy.' He looks at his son. 'What do you say, Donnie?'

'Aye, right enough,' Donnie says, nodding vigorously.

'See,' Blair says, like he's proved his point. Perhaps they're right. I'm overreacting, but who could blame me? 'Are you sure you're all right?' Blair asks, watching me intently.

'Sure. Yes, I'm fine.' Though I've a pounding headache coming on, but I'm sure I have something inside that will take the edge off it. I need to keep my wits about me. 'Sorry,' I mumble, turning back to go inside. As I look back, Donnie is almost about to disappear from view. 'Donnie!'

'Aye?'

'Did... um... has anything odd happened out at the bothy recently?'

'Odd? Weird like?'

'Yes, anything strange... with Lauren specifically?'

He frowns. 'No. Why?'

'No matter, forget I asked.'

Donnie returns to whatever task he was doing and I can feel Blair's eyes upon me as I go back inside the house. Closing the door, I turn the lock and put my back against the door.

My hands are shaking and I squeeze them into fists to try to make it stop. Donnie and Blair are speaking but their voices are muffled. They're probably questioning what that was all about. They won't know. They can't, because neither do I.

SIX

My mobile rings and I answer quickly, without looking at the screen. 'Hello!'

Clearly taken aback, Ava is tentative. 'Doctor Kelly... are you all right?'

'Yes!' I wince at my snappiness, forcing myself to calm down. 'Sorry, Ava... I'm okay, it's just I'm not feeling well.'

'Oh no. Is there anything I can do?'

'No – actually, yes – can you cancel my appointments for the rest of the day, please.'

'Cancel them? What, all of them?'

'Yes, please. I don't think I'm up to it.'

'Um, yes, I suppose I can do that, but Mr Baird is already here waiting for you—'

'Yes, I'm sorry, but you'll just have to reschedule it for another time.'

Ava's voice lowers, presumably so Thomas Baird cannot overhear. 'I'm not sure that will go down very well, Doctor Kelly—'

'Well, he'll just have to manage, won't he?'

'Yes, of course,' she says. 'Sorry.'

'No, I'm sorry, Ava. It's just difficult. Okay? Can you manage?'

I can picture the reassuring smile on her slightly chubby cheeks. Ava is quite the mumsy sort; despite being only a decade older than me, she has a very maternal nature about her. 'Leave it to me, dear. I'll take care of it. You take yourself off to your bed. Don't worry.'

'Thanks, Ava. I don't know what I'd do without you.'

'That's what everyone says, dear.'

I hang up and take a deep breath. I can figure this out. I know I can. As I head into my bedroom my mobile beeps with a message; the notification chime is different with this communication app and I only use it with Lauren, having lost touch with all of my friends. I open it quickly.

You shouldn't be changing your routine, Kelly. It arouses suspicion.

Open-mouthed, my eyes sweep the room, falling on the window. Running across to it, I peer through the shutters scanning the exterior. All I can see is the machair stretching off up the hillside, until it becomes lost in the shroud of driving sleet, falling once more. My fingers curled tightly around the mobile, my eyes study every clutch of wild grass, shadow or boulder. He's out there, watching. Listening.

Holding my breath, I slowly turn and my eyes sweep the room. Nothing is out of place. Nothing has been moved as far as I can tell. The wardrobe door is ajar, and I'm certain I closed it this morning after I got dressed. At least, I think I did.

Walking slowly across the room, I come to stand before it. I'm breathing heavily now; a bead of sweat is forming on my spine, I can feel it. What will I do if he is in here? Scream? Will

Blair and Donnie hear me if I do? I can hear hammering outside, the roof repairs Donnie was going to be doing this week. Slowly, I extend my hand to the wardrobe knob and my phone beeps again. Releasing my hold, I open the message.

> *If you don't go back to the surgery, people will start asking questions. It will complicate matters. And none of us want that, do we, Kelly? Do you need a reminder of what is at stake here, Kelly? If you do, I can arrange it?*

Reaching for the knob, I throw open the wardrobe, several items of clothing perched precariously on the edge of shelving fall to my feet as a result. Aside from my clothes, the wardrobe is empty.

'Get a grip, for crying out loud, woman!' Exhaling, I close my eyes after opening my recent call list and dialling the reception. Ava answers.

'Is everything okay, Doctor Kelly?'

'Yes, it is. Is Thomas Baird still with you?'

'Aye, he's... not keen to give up his appointment—'

'I'll be right there.'

'But I thought you wanted me to—'

'I know. I've changed my mind. I think I need to be at work.' I blink away tears and desperately try to stop my voice from breaking as I stamp my foot on the carpeted floor, the only way I can think to release the tension without screaming. 'I'll be right there.'

'Okay. If you're sure?' Ava asks cautiously. 'Because, I can always—'

'No, it's fine. I'll be right over.'

I take one more look around the room, even glancing up at the ceiling, before checking my messages once more. I type out a quick reply.

I'm going back to work.

Thrusting my mobile into my pocket, I move to the bedroom door. How did he know what I was doing? I thought it might be Cameron, but he's not capable of all of this, surely? Who do I, or Lauren for that matter, know who could manage any of this? Doing my best to ignore the knot of panic lodged in my chest, I grab a coat for the short walk back to the surgery. Blair nods in my direction as I walk along the path and even Donnie glances at me. I swear he has the trace of a smile on his lips but he looks away when I turn my face towards him.

Heated voices carry as I open the door to the reception which doubles as a waiting room. Thomas Baird, possibly the most unsavoury character on my patient list, is standing at the counter berating Ava, who is as calm as ever. She is so well suited to this role. Measured and unflappable, she is calmness personified.

'Mr Baird, the doctor will be along directly—'

'I'm here, Ava. It's okay,' I say, entering, my eyes flicking to the red-faced Thomas Baird.

'Well, it's about damn time!'

'I'm sorry to have kept you waiting, Mr Baird—'

'You think I haven't got better things to be doing with my time than waiting around for you?'

I smile warmly, knowing full well the only thing he has to be doing, rather than waiting for me, lies inside a 70cl glass bottle. And it's probably half empty already. 'Would you like to come through, Mr Baird?' I say, gesturing for him to go through to the consulting room.

'About damn time, young lady!' he says indignantly, setting off in front of me. I follow, taking a deep breath and casting a sideways glance towards Ava, who rolls her eyes, silently mouthing the word *sorry*. Thomas enters the room ahead of me muttering under his breath and I don't get the chance to offer him a seat before he takes one.

'What can I do for you today, Thomas?' I ask, sitting down at my desk, to his left.

'The SS sent me to see you again.'

'Social Security Scotland?'

'Aye, who else? This isn't 1940s Germany, is it? Although,' he says, snorting derisively, 'it's starting to feel like it.'

I sit back in my seat, folding my arms across my chest. 'What is it they want you to get from me?'

'A certificate or something,' he says, avoiding my eye. 'To say I'm no' fit for work.'

'And aren't you?'

He glares at me, and I see a gleam in his eye. He's drunk but trying to hide it. He's good at it by now, to be fair. If I couldn't see it in his body language though, I can certainly smell it on him. No amount of mouthwash will hide the aroma that clings to the fibres of your clothes. I know.

'They want it all official. So, write up your little docket or whatever, and I'll be out of your hair.'

Thomas Baird. The island's recognised alcoholic. And in a place where heavy drinking is practically a leisure pursuit, that takes some doing. He'd likely be considered one of the lads if it wasn't common knowledge that he knocks his wife around most days of the week, worse if his football team loses on a Saturday.

I turn to my screen and look up the necessary paperwork. It is true that Thomas Baird isn't fit for work. Any job he could get he'd be sacked from within a day. That's if he managed to turn up sober.

I only know of one occasion where he genuinely tried to come off the booze, and PC McLean had to be called to talk him out of his house. He'd barricaded himself inside, screaming that a family of five were trying to take over his home. They weren't. They didn't exist, and he hallucinated the entire episode. Had he not started throwing bottles into the street, no one would have bothered, but in the end, all it took to settle him down was a bottle of scotch.

Some people are too far gone, even for the most patient of people. Even if Thomas wanted to help himself, he wouldn't succeed. It's just a pity he takes his wife along with him. Although, she drinks almost as much as he does. Two cheeks of the same backside, Ava says. At least, when she's in a momentary loss of professionalism. But that's a bit harsh. She has little option, no family and nowhere to go and no money if she did. If I lived with him, I dare say I'd drink like a fish too.

I hit return and the certificate starts to print from the little printer on the far side of my desk. I have to lean across and I'm aware of Thomas leering at me, and so I hurriedly sit back down. The dirty sod. I pass him the formal certificate. That will give him, and me, some breathing space.

'Thanks, Doc,' he says, holding the paper aloft and grinning, revealing tobacco-stained, scale-encrusted teeth. 'I'll be seeing you again soon enough.'

'I'm sure you will, Thomas.' He gets up and shuffles across to the door. 'How's Shona?'

He hesitates, holding the handle, before looking back. 'Aye, she's all right. Why do you ask?'

'I've not seen her for a while. Just wondering why that might be.'

He looks away, pensive. 'Aye, she's grand, right enough.'

'I was thinking I should stop by and see—'

'You should keep to your own affairs, that's what you should do,' he says. 'I'm sure you have enough going on in your own life just noo, eh?'

His gaze lingers on me, his upper lip curling into a sneer. I don't like how he's looking at me. 'What's that supposed to mean?' I can hear the fear in my voice and it surprises me.

'How's that wee lassie of yours?'

'What's that to you?'

He shrugs, then smiles. 'I see her about here and there. Pretty wee thing, isn't she? Looks a lot like you, only younger, eh?'

'Goodbye,' I say and his grin broadens as he turns away, leaving the room and allowing the door to slam behind him. Closing my eyes, I picture him still sitting before me. Why do good things happen to decent people and then someone like Thomas Baird gets to have his way? 'Now, if it ends up being you I have to kill—'

The door opens and Ava pokes her head around the door. I force a smile.

'Do you want that cup of tea now? You have a few minutes between appointments.'

'Yes, thank you. Tea would be lovely.'

'You know, you're looking a little peaky, dear. Are you sure you can manage today?'

I hold up a reassuring hand. 'I'll be okay, I'm sure, but thank you.'

'As you wish. I'll be back with your tea in a minute or two.'

'Ava?' I call as she makes to close the door.

'Yes, dear?'

'Shona, have you seen her about recently?'

'Shona Baird?' she asks and I nod. Thinking hard, Ava shakes her head. 'No, I can't say I have. Not for a few weeks. Thomas has probably been up to his usual tricks, I suspect.'

'She never usually hides away though, does she? I have tried, but sometimes I think I could do more to help her.'

'And what's that old saying, you can lead a horse to water—'

'But you canna make it drink.'

'Exactly. I'll get you that tea,' Ava says, closing the door gently.

Sitting back in my seat, my thoughts flit between Lauren and the rules her kidnapper has set for me.

He wants me to 'choose' the right patient to kill. Unless I can figure another way out of this, I'll be left with no option. And there is no question in my mind about who is most deserving of living, between my daughter and a man like Thomas Baird.

SEVEN

A knock on the door.

Why can't I be left alone? I don't want to see anyone until I have to, and even then, it's under protest. I ignore it, pretend I'm on a call or something.

Another knock, only firmer this time.

'Come in!' The door cracks open and a woman pokes her head through the gap.

'Sorry to bother you, Doctor Kelly,' she says meekly, glancing back into reception. 'I don't know where Ava is, but the door wasn't locked and—'

'It's okay, Amelia. Come in,' I say, beckoning her to enter and patting the seat of the chair beside me. 'We are closed for lunch.'

Amelia Allen walks into the room, clearly struggling with putting weight onto her left foot. A sheen of perspiration covers her face despite the cold and the wet of the outdoors. I glance out of the window and the sleet appears to have ceased falling again but for how long I don't know.

'Thank you, Doctor Kelly,' she says, lowering herself unceremoniously into the patient's chair adjacent to me. She sighs. 'Phew, that was a mission, I can tell you.'

'Did you walk here?'

She offers me a conspiratorial look, leaning forward. 'Aye, better not to tell anyone though, if that's okay with you?'

I lean towards her. 'Who would I tell?'

'Och, you know, people and the like.' She glances around, almost as if she fears being seen with me.

'There's only the two of us here, Amelia. What's up? Is your chest giving you trouble?' That wouldn't be a surprise. In her sixties now, Amelia is carrying more weight on her body than could be considered healthy and has a history of angina.

She waves the comment away. 'Always, but that's not why I'm here.'

'Then why are you here?'

Again, she looks nervously towards the door. Amelia is one of those highly strung, anxious people. Widely regarded as the longest-serving spinster on the island, gossip is rife among the younger generation that she is a closet lesbian and by the more mature of Jura's inhabitants as simply a little eccentric.

'I'm worried about my mother.'

'Mhari? The last I saw her she was doing fine.'

'She was, aye. But she's not herself now.'

'Okay,' I say, turning to my screen and looking up her medical file. Mhari has been hospitalised three times in the previous eighteen months, twice under my care, and due to her age, she always ends up in hospital on the mainland. A woman in her nineties is always going to have various complaints to manage, but Mhari is as tough as they come. The Scottish islands breed hardy folk, that's for sure. 'What seems to be the problem?'

Amelia shuffles in her seat. 'She's complaining about stomach trouble. Like before,' Amelia says. I notice her eyes drifting to the cling film wrapped sandwich on my desk. 'Are you not hungry?'

'No,' I tell her. I made Lauren food to take with her. I doubt she's eaten it, and I'd feel guilty about eating mine as a result. 'And is it getting worse or staying the same?'

'The same,' Amelia says.

'Is she eating and drinking?'

'Yes.'

'Passing water okay?'

She nods. 'I think so, but Morgan usually deals with that side of things. I struggle to lift her up onto the seat. He's much better at coping with her than me.'

'Nonsense,' I tell her. 'You do a great job with your mum. You're a saint.'

Amelia flushes and looks down, her hands cupped in her lap. 'I don't know about that but I try.'

'I think,' I say, sitting back, 'I need to see your mum. Can you bring her in to see—'

Amelia firmly shakes her head. 'No, no, I can't be doing that. Morgan has the car, and he is on the mainland.'

'I see.' I smile warmly. 'And when will he be back?'

'He left this morning, and I don't know when he'll be back.'

'He didn't say?'

She shakes her head again, her eyes momentarily lifting to meet mine before looking away again.

'Right,' I say, placing my hands on the desk. 'I'll need to come out to yours then.'

'Oh...'

I'm surprised. 'Oh?'

'Well, I just thought you could prescribe me some of those tablets that you did for her last time and... um... then I could be on my way.'

'You'll recall those tablets didn't work and your mum had to go into hospital.'

'Aye, yes. I remember. Okay. When?'

'Tomorrow,' I say, glancing at my appointment list for the following day. 'I have another house call that I have to make, so I can stop by yours on the way back. How's that?'

'Great,' she says.

I reach across and place my hand on the back of hers. 'Just to make sure. It'll be fine, don't worry.'

'Yes, of course. Thank you, Doctor Kelly.'

After she leaves, I go through to the reception and Ava looks at me inquisitively.

'I don't remember seeing her on the list for today.'

'She wasn't,' I say. 'Just walked in.'

'What did she want?'

'Mhari's ill again. I said I'd call in tomorrow on my way back from seeing Alistair Aitken.'

'That's right,' Ava says, her expression souring. 'You're heading over to see Alistair tomorrow, aren't you?'

'You don't like him, do you?'

Ava arches her eyebrows. 'It would be a dull world if everyone got on, wouldn't it? Did you eat your sandwich?'

'Not yet.'

Ava looks at me sternly. 'You need to eat, dear. It will make you feel better. And that's my finest garlic chicken recipe leftovers you have there. I don't want it going to waste.'

'I don't deserve you, Ava. I really don't. You'll make someone a lovely wife one day.'

'Hah! I've been there and done that. Never again, I tell you. I'll just have to waste my talents on you instead. You're my surrogate. The daughter I never had.'

'For which I am eternally grateful.' An image of Lauren jumps to mind, bound and gagged, sitting alone in the dark and sudden despair washes over me.

'Ava… earlier, when Thomas Baird was here—'

'Being his usual charming self.'

'Yes. Did anyone else come in? Or maybe someone phoned?'

'No, but I was on the phone to you at the time. Why?'

I know that whoever has Lauren is also somehow able to see and hear me. So they're either here in person or they're spying on me somehow. But who could manage that on Jura? I'm doubting my own logic now. The internet has changed everything. Someone on the other side of the world could spy on me with the right equipment, and never leave their own home. They could be next door or on the mainland. They could be anywhere. With or without my daughter.

'Are you okay?'

Ava's hand is on my forearm and she squeezes it gently. I lift my eyes to hers. 'Sorry, what did you say?'

'You drifted off there for a moment.'

This is impossible. I can't do this, acting normally. As if my life hasn't been turned upside down by a text message. As if my daughter isn't in terrible danger. 'I'm okay, I just...'

'You do look pale, dear.' Ava reaches up to touch my forehead and I recoil from her hand.

'I'm okay. I need to go home, I feel sick.' The thought occurs that this might be deviating from the rules, but I often finish early if I have house calls or few appointments. The island isn't very big after all, and I'm only rushed off my feet when a virus sweeps through the inhabitants. Thankfully, that hasn't been for a while now.

'Yes, I think that's sensible. You should.' Ava is concerned for me. I can see it in her face. 'I'll cancel your afternoon appointments. You've only two more anyway and neither is particularly important. We can rearrange those, no bother.'

'Yes, thank you,' I say. 'I'll just get my things.' Retreating to the consultation room, I feel eyes on me. Not only Ava's but someone else's too. My chest constricts, and I feel like I'm ready to burst into tears. Moving to the window, I stare out towards the centre of Craighouse but it is obscured by the weather.

He's close, and somehow I am certain he can see everything.

EIGHT

With my head down against the sleet, I hurry back to my house next door to the surgery. There's no sign of either Blair or his son, Donnie, which I'm grateful for. Blair's pickup isn't in the driveway, so they must have called it a day due to the weather. If I thought it wouldn't be diverging from normality in the kidnapper's eyes, I'd send them away for a couple of days. Until I get my daughter back. Because I *will* get her back.

In the corner of my eye I see my neighbour Hughie getting out of his car, but I pretend not to see him, and go into the back of my house swiftly, closing the door behind me. Standing in my kitchen, everything is quiet aside from the wind buffeting the building, driving sleet and snow at the window in strong gusts.

I've been so focused on questioning who would want to do something like this to Lauren. I thought of Cameron, but he's not capable of pulling this off. He's from a dark place, I'm sure, but this? It's far too enterprising. Why Lauren, and why this way? Could it be Cameron? But right now, with tears falling down my cheeks, I don't even care about who it is. All I want to know is where is she? How is she? Is she frightened? In pain? Does she trust me to come and save her? The thought of her suffering and scared to death makes me want to throw up. My baby girl.

A scraping sound.

What was that? It came from inside the house, I'm almost certain. Listening intently, I crane my neck as if I can see around the corner into the living room or through the walls to the bedrooms at the back of the house.

Nothing.

Maybe it was outside after all. I'm thinking about calling out, but I don't. If someone is here in the house, and they've come for me, then I don't want to hurry the process. Then again, he might take me to my daughter.

I step forward and someone hammers on the back door. I yelp in fright, leaping away from the door just as it opens.

A blast of bitterly cold air is sucked into the kitchen and Hughie smiles at me, squinting against the sleet driving into the side of his face. 'Hello, gorgeous!'

'Geez, Hughie. You scared the hell out of me!'

'Ah, sorry,' he says sheepishly, moving inside but not stepping past the floor mat sitting behind the door. He glances down at his feet. 'I'll no' come any further. I've just put the chickens away and been sorting out the pigs.'

Much of the ground on the island is solid, having been frozen for weeks now, but the recent rainfall has turned the muddy surface areas a little slippery underfoot. Hughie's boots are mucky and normally I'd chastise him for entering but a bit of shelter from the weather is understandable.

'This isn't a good time, Hughie.'

Hughie McIntosh is my next-door neighbour. He lives in an old stone-built cottage that was once a shooting lodge for one of the nearby estates. On the buildings at risk register for many years, the cottage fell into disrepair until Hughie bought it and invested the time, energy and, of course, the money into restoring it. It must have been one of the most imposing residences on the island back in the day. Much larger and more substantial than the black houses most islanders lived in.

'Aye, no bother,' he says, taking off his woollen hat and running his hand through his hair. Hughie is a little older than the men I've gone for in the past. His hair has a salt and pepper effect to it now; greying of the stubble is more pronounced though. He has something of the gentleman farmer about him, a pleasant way of carrying himself. He's not rugged with calloused hands, as most of the crofters I meet on the island are, but I know he works damned hard to make a go of it. 'I just saw you coming home. Finished early for the day?'

'Yes, I... don't feel well.'

'Oh, right.' He seems pensive, biting his bottom lip. 'Are we... um... still on for tonight, like?'

'Tonight?'

'Aye. Remember?' I look at him and I have to admit I've no idea what he's talking about. 'Lauren is away, and you and me... date night?'

'Oh! Yes, of course—'

'You forgot, didn't you?' he asks and I can hear the despondency in his tone. Although a blind man could see it in his face.

'No, I didn't forget...'

He wrinkles his nose in that knowing way, and nods. 'Aye, you did.'

'I did, it's true. I'm sorry.'

'That's okay,' Hughie says. 'As long as you didn't get a better offer?'

'On this island?'

His eyes narrow and he's gauging my humour, wondering if I mean it. He's a nice guy, Hughie. He's one of the good ones, and although we've only had a handful of dates he's never pushed it further than I felt comfortable with. Believe me, that's unlike anyone I've ever dated before. Unless you include James

Ingham, and I was only eleven when we were an item for that week at school. He was way too keen.

'So,' he says, pursing his lips. 'Still on for tonight—'

'Can we not, tonight—'

'No, no, of course not.' He frowns, looking at his feet. 'Don't be silly. You probably have something important to do.'

'No, it's not that,' I say, failing to formulate a suitable excuse in my mind. 'I just have a lot on my mind.'

'Sure, okay,' he says, his head bobbing. He shifts his weight between his feet, glancing over his shoulder. 'I guess... um... I'd better go and see to these pigs. Oh,' – he hesitates – 'I've already seen to them, haven't I. I-I meant the chickens.'

'Hughie,' I say, crossing quickly to him as he makes to leave and taking his arm to stop him. He looks at me, a faint trace of a smile on his lips. 'I really do have something important going on. I'm not brushing you off, I promise.' His smile widens and he nods.

'Aye, that's great. I thought for a second there—'

'No, it's nothing like that, I promise.'

'Anything... er... I can help you with?' He seems genuinely keen to help, and that's part of his appeal. Hughie is a genuine, affable man. He's not particularly handsome or charismatic – not that he isn't attractive at all – but he is stable and decent. I've appreciated that in my life recently. He'd help a complete stranger if they asked him for something. It's rare to find that level of genuine human kindness these days. At least, it is in my experience. Maybe it's an island community thing. No one else is going to help, so we have to do it ourselves kind of mentality.

'No, I wish you could, but this is something I have to do by myself.'

The smile fades and he studies my face before nodding solemnly, his brow furrowing as he looks at me sternly. 'Okay, but if I could do anything, then you'd ask, right?'

I force a smile. 'Yes. I'd ask you ahead of anyone else.'

'That'll do for me then,' he says with an accompanying sigh. Glancing over his shoulder, he rocks his head from side to side. 'Look at me, letting all the warm air out. I'd best get off and let you get on with it.'

'Thanks, Hughie. I'll see you later.'

'Aye, how about tomorrow night?' he says optimistically. I exhale loudly and he winces. 'Maybe not, eh? I could stop by or,' – he looks nervous now – 'we could just play things by ear.'

I tilt my head to one side. 'Aye, let's play it by ear. Keep it casual. No promises. Sounds like a plan!'

He steps out into the gently falling snow, and I slowly start to close the door. He's walking backwards and nearly trips over a flowerpot, stumbling. 'I'll give you a phone, maybe?'

'See you, Hughie.'

I close the door, turn the lock, and lean my back against it and fear grips me.

The scraping sound again, only this time it is louder. I turn my eyes to the ceiling. The sound is coming from the loft. Something is there, moving above the ceiling.

NINE

My first thought is to run. To get out, run over to Hughie's and tell him what's going on. But I can't. Instead, I stand in my kitchen, staring at the ceiling.

Whatever is in the loft is moving away from me. I tentatively take a step forward. Is someone in the crawl space above me? You can barely stand up in there. Moving to the living room, I trace the movement above as if I can see through the ceiling. Could something have found its way in from outside? A bird, perhaps? Whatever is making that noise, more regular now, is far too large to be a bird or even a cat.

It's passed over the living room now and is over the bedrooms. There's only one way into the loft space, through the hatch in the ceiling in Lauren's bedroom. My eyes dart to the fireplace and instinctively I reach for the brass poker, lifting it as quietly as I can from the stand. Grasping the handle, I make my way out into the hall and towards my daughter's bedroom.

Someone grunts. It's a man. There's someone in my house and he's making more noise now as I come to stand outside my daughter's bedroom. I'm terrified. Realising I'm holding my breath, I draw in a ragged gasp and brace myself as footsteps on the wooden floor approach me on the far side of the door. I heft the poker in my hands, taking a double-handed grip like I am holding a baseball bat, and I wait.

The door wrenches open, and Donnie McInally screams, leaping backwards and falling over. I scream too.

'Donnie!'

'What are you doin', woman?' he yells at me, flat on his back, hands in the air before him.

'What am I doing? What are you doing in Lauren's bedroom?'

He has his hands in the air, palms facing me. 'I was checking the water pipes... like my dad told me to do!'

'What?'

'The water pipes running through the attic to the bathrooms,' Donnie says, wide-eyed. 'My dad said they are blocked.'

'The drains are backing up, Donnie! Not the damn water pipes.'

His expression softens and his cheeks flush. 'Aye, that'd make more sense, to be fair.'

'You were up in the loft?'

'Checking the pipes, aye,' he says, lowering his hands. I mirror his action and lower the poker. 'Is it... er... all right if I get up, Doctor Kelly?'

'Yes, of course it is, Donnie.' I offer him my hand to help but he ignores it, clambering up and making a concerted effort to keep his distance from the psychotic client brandishing a poker at him. He dusts himself off, having collected some strands of glass wool insulation on his journey through the roof space. 'Where's your dad?'

'Oh, he went back to the yard to put a few bits away,' Donnie says. 'Don't want the snow freezing on them, you know?'

'Yes, I know.'

'He'll be back to get me in a minute,' Donnie says, checking his watch. 'That's why I was finishing up, up there.' His eyes move to the ceiling hatch above the stepladder he used to get up there. 'Do you mind if I put the hatch back?'

'Well, I'd rather you didn't leave it open.' I can feel the draught coming through from above, and I'm annoyed about the strands of insulation and the dark, unidentifiable clumps of organic matter that are strewn over Lauren's bed now. She'll be upset to see that when she gets home. And she will come home. Donnie sees me looking at the mess as he slides the loft hatch back into place with a scrape and a thud.

'Sorry about the mess. I can clean it up if you like?'

'No, I'll sort it. Don't worry.'

'If you're sure?' Donnie says, getting down from the stepladder and closing it up.

'Yes,' I say absently.

A horn blasts from outside and Donnie glances towards the window.

'That'll be my dad, eh?'

I smile weakly. 'You get yourself off home, Donnie. I'll get this right.'

'Aye, thanks, Doctor Kelly.'

He hefts the stepladder and walks to the door.

'Donnie?'

'Aye?'

'I guess you'll not be heading to the bothy tonight?'

'Ah this storm will pass over by this evening. It'll be grand.'

'You'll still be going?'

He shrugs. 'There's nothing else for us to do around here, is there?'

'True,' I say forlornly.

'Is... everything all right, Doctor Kelly?'

I draw a deep breath. 'Yes, it is. Thanks, Donnie.' I don't look at him; I'm now lost in thought.

'Right, well I'll see you tomorrow then, aye?'

'Oh, Donnie,' I call and he stops again, setting the ladder down that was under his arm. I look up at the hatch. 'When you were up in the loft, did you see or hear anything odd?'

'Odd? Like what?'

I shrug. 'Anything out of the ordinary.'

He shoots me a confused look. 'No, I can't say I did. Why, are you expecting something?'

I shake my head. 'It doesn't matter, Donnie. Thanks. I'll see you in the morning.'

'Okay. Right you are.'

Donnie gathers up the few tools he has with him, hoisting the stepladder up under his arm again, and goes out into the hall. 'Goodnight, Doctor Kelly.'

'Donnie?'

He stops at the door, failing to mask his irritation at me stopping him again. The horn outside blasts again, and Donnie frowns. 'Aye?'

'Where is the bothy?'

'Out on Corran Sands, towards the far end, not far from the Old Lodge. It's not really a bothy, just an old ruin but some people used to use it for shelter, and so it gets called the bothy. You know where the lodge is?'

I nod. 'I do, yes. Thanks, Donnie.'

'You're welcome,' he says, setting off but at a much brisker pace this time.

I don't know how long I spend sitting there in Lauren's room. It's so overcast outside that the passage of day into night is barely visible. The days get dark here early afternoon at this time of the year anyway.

There's no greater pain a mother can experience than when her child is suffering. It's a deep, emotional and yet physical pain. But right now, I feel numb. Am I in shock? Is this my body's way of protecting me, stopping me from feeling anymore because it's too painful?

Lauren has been keeping secrets from me, that much is clear. But she can keep all the secrets she likes as long as she comes home safely. Staying in touch with Cameron Stewart, arranging to meet Niall and hanging out at the bothy are all things she kept from me. And somewhere among these secrets is the answer to whatever has led her to this.

The bothy. Corran Sands.

I'm going to find answers there, I just know it. I'm starting to think there are people on this island who know my daughter much better than I do. Someone will be able to tell me where she is.

If not, then I'll just have to make them.

TEN

Corran Sands is arguably the best beach to be found on the entire island. Beginning just beyond Craighouse, the pristine, white sands stretch along the sheltered bay on the east coast of Jura, separated by the Corran River.

I remember standing here with Lauren, the first time we visited the island – so much hope and optimism for a fresh start – with the backdrop of the mountains in the west behind us, in mid-winter, the sun setting between two of the three conical mountains, the mighty Paps, watching the tide gently lapping at the sand.

It was from here that hundreds, if not thousands, of islanders departed in search of a better life on the mainland, or the distant shores of North America and Australia. Many did so under protest, others in desperation.

Now, I can imagine how they must have felt, with life as they knew it under threat. I'm at the mercy of another too, just as they were. And nothing will ever be the same again.

Donnie was right. The storm front passed swiftly, and now I can see an amazing canopy of stars overhead. As if I could feel any more insignificant than I do already, the night sky reminds me how small I am. Not much of the recent snow has stuck, certainly not in Craighouse itself. Here on the beach though, there is a layering of white glittering atop the sand, reflecting the glow from the moon.

Usually, all I would be able to see at this time are the whites of the breakers, hearing nothing but the wind as it rattles across the machair, alongside the roar of the sea coming ashore. Tonight though, everything is clearer.

Looking along the beach towards the Old Lodge, standing in darkness set back from the water's edge and closed up for the winter, I see the flickering of a campfire. The fire is not large; the shadows of people passing in front of the flames emphasise the flickering and dancing orange and yellow light in the distance.

Will these people know my daughter as well as I hope? Has she made enemies in our short time on the island? Most importantly, I suppose, is whether there is a code of silence amongst the youth of Jura, similar to what exists in Edinburgh?

Music is playing, and when the wind drops I can hear it clearly, along with raised voices and laughter, before the next gust carries it out into the bay. There are fewer people here than I thought there would be, perhaps nine or ten. I thought – hoped – for more. There's no chance I can blend in casually.

They don't hear me. The glow of the fire and the sound of the waves probably masking my approach. I'm almost upon the group, sitting or standing before the fire, when eyes drift up to me. Conversation dies as those with their backs to me follow their friends' gaze and glance around at me.

I recognise a couple of people, one dark-haired girl in her late teens and a boy of a similar age. I think her name might be Tina, but I've not treated either of them, so maybe I've met them with their parents at some point. There's no sign of Donnie McInally.

'Hello.'

Several of the assembled group smile and one girl, the dark-haired teenager, smiles and reciprocates. There is mistrust in their expressions. One lad throws what I thought was a cigarette into the flames but a waft of something potent carries across me. That smell, one I know as well as anyone who's lived in a city, and the fact he won't meet my eye tells me what I need to know.

'Is everyone having a good time?' I'm trying to be casual, friendly, but I have no place here. And everyone else knows that too.

'Yes, thank you, Doctor Kelly,' the girl says. At least someone is speaking to me. 'How are you?'

I smile. It's artificial and everyone recognises it as such, I'm sure. 'I was wondering... if any of you are friendly with my daughter, Lauren?' Most of those who aren't looking my way already lower their gaze. One lad – I say lad, but he must be twenty-something – sniffs and shakes his head almost impercep-tibly. Damn. I only want to have a conversation but you would think I was PC McLean by their reaction to my presence. More eyes dip as I look around, making eye contact where possible, and no one seems keen to talk.

A flaming branch in the fire cracks, spitting embers out towards those sitting nearby and they recoil. 'Whoa!' one boy says and a couple of his friends laugh at him for flinching. The laughter fades though, as I look their way.

'Have any of you seen Lauren recently?' I ask, but no one answers. 'Listen, I know she comes here, a-and it's fine. I don't mind. I'm not here to cause any of you any trouble.' I look at the boy who threw the joint into the fire. 'Honestly! I don't care what you get up to out here... not that you're getting up to anything,' – I silently curse myself for living up to the parental stereotype – 'I just mean... Have you seen her?'

'Not for a while, no,' the dark-haired girl says.

'Oh, right. Tina, isn't it?' She nods and smiles, but it's fleet-ing. 'How are your folks?' I ask.

'They're good thanks.'

The exchange appears to break the ice and several people strike up their own conversations, lowering their voices.

'Tina, can I... speak with you, about Lauren?' She seems reticent, glancing nervously to a boy sitting opposite her. I follow her gaze, and I'm sure he knows I'm looking at him, but he keeps his eyes on Tina. Only when he looks away from her, lifting a bottle of beer to his lips, and engages with the boy sitting beside him, does she nod and get up from the collapsible chair she's sitting on.

Tina comes away from the fire, almost encouraging me to follow her lead and I fall into step alongside her. Looking back, I see the boy's eyes trail us. The conversations are already louder as we walk away, my feet sinking into the soft sand the further we move from the shore.

'So, what is it you want to know about Lauren?' Tina asks me, turning to face me and sweeping the windswept hair away from her face, trying in vain to tuck it behind her ear. She looks very young, much younger than my daughter but maybe Edinburgh makes you grow up faster.

'Are you friends with her?'

Tina shrugs. 'I guess.'

'Is she... is Lauren popular?'

'Aye. She's all right.' Tina is reticent and I implore her with a hopeful look. 'She is. People like her, but it took a bit of time.' She shrugs. 'It's like that on the island, you know. Sometimes, people come in from the outside and it takes a while before you get to know them.'

'I think that's the same everywhere.'

'Probably. Are you looking for her?'

'Why would you ask that?'

Tina frowns, glancing back towards her peers. No one is looking at us as far as I can see anyway. 'Why else would you be here?'

'Has Lauren had any issue with anyone?' I'm deliberately ignoring her question. 'Anyone here or on the island, perhaps?'

Tina's eye flick towards the campfire and I see a couple of people watching us. She shrugs. 'No, not really.'

'Not really?'

'Lauren is popular.'

'Yes, you said that—'

'In many ways,' Tina says, lowering her voice. 'She's attractive.'

'She is, yes. What are you saying?' Tina looks uncomfortable with the question. 'It's okay, I won't be angry or anything.'

'It's just the boys stumble over themselves around her, you know? Boys will be boys and all that.'

'Jealousy?'

Tina wrinkles her nose. 'Among the boys and the girls. Your daughter – Lauren – turns heads. It ruffles a few feathers, you know?'

'Did she fall out with anyone?'

Tina furtively glances towards her friends and one person in particular is paying us attention. The lad with the steely look who, unless I'm mistaken, seems to have some kind of power or influence over this conversation. She shakes her head, and the boy turns away again. 'No, nothing like that.'

'Who is he?'

'Who?'

'That young man who is trying to see what we're talking about. He's not half as subtle as he thinks he is.'

Away from the warmth of the fire now, Tina hugs herself, rubbing her upper arms to generate heat. 'That's Billy.'

'Billy?'

'Billy Jackson. He doesn't mean anything by it. He's harmless. It's just the way he is.'

'Strange that.'

'Strange how?' Tina asks.

'That you reach for that description, to say he's harmless.'

She shrugs. 'Well, he is.'

'Harmless is a mouse or a pigeon. To me, he looks like he has an edge to him.'

'Ah, he's all right, most of the time.'

'Does he like Lauren?'

Tina scoffs. 'Who doesn't?'

'Did Lauren like Billy's attention?'

Tina is growing more uncomfortable. 'I think I should get back to—'

'Tina, I wouldn't ask unless it was important.'

'Is Lauren in some kind of trouble or something?'

'No! Not at all,' I say, trying to sound sincere but she's unconvinced. 'I just want to know, that's all.'

'I'm going to go back to my pals now, if you don't mind?'

'Yes, of course.'

'Tell Lauren I said hi, will you?'

I nod and Tina smiles forlornly, and makes her way back to the campfire. I watch her go, internally berating myself for making a hash of that whole conversation.

There's more to this, there has to be. Envy and jealousy, especially with competing boys and girls, can be brutal, sure. But to do something like this? Why set up this whole façade? Why instruct me to kill one of my patients? What kind of twisted mind would do that?

No sooner has Tina rejoined the group and taken her seat by the fire, than Billy is up and across to join her, shooing the girl who had been next to Tina away and sitting down beside her. I can't make out what he's saying but Tina is unhappy or, at the very least, doesn't appreciate his attention, shying away from him as she is.

Off to my left, another figure is lurching across the sand towards the group, and his silhouette is very familiar to me. He has an odd way of walking, Donnie McInally. So, he decided to come along after all. Standing away from the group, keeping to the shadows, I watch Donnie as he's greeted. Big smiles and fist bumps all round. He's a popular member of the group too.

Lauren has not mentioned Donnie to me; if they're friends then it's news to me. Billy gets up and the two of them embrace briefly, before something is said and Donnie turns, following his friend's curt nod in my direction. Donnie's smile fades and he looks away as soon as we make eye contact.

They pay me no further attention, larking around as youngsters do, sharing drinks out and probably something more. They will as soon as I'm out of the way, I suppose. Feeling the cold, I also long for the comfort of the fire.

Is Lauren cold, wherever she is?

As I turn, I catch Tina looking in my direction from the corner of my eye. I look back and smile, but she pretends not to see me and strikes up a conversation with her friend.

Then my phone beeps and I take it out. It's another message from Lauren's phone.

> *You're looking tired, Kelly. What are you doing all the way out here? Have you lost focus again? Perhaps I should do something about that...*

I spin around, staring back towards the group. They are the only ones who can see me here. I'm searching the group and there's one boy, perhaps he's in his early twenties, but from this distance it's hard to tell. He has his mobile phone in his hand and he's staring at the screen. *Is it him?*

I type out a reply. *I want to hear from my daughter.*

The green text shows someone is typing a reply and my eyes sweep back to the camp. That boy is typing, but so is Billy. Was he on his mobile a moment ago when I looked? I don't remember. My mobile beeps again.

That's not in the rules, Kelly. I thought you understood the rules.

I try to quell the rising anger in my reply. *To hell with your rules! Let me speak to her.* As soon as I tap send, I regret it. I stare at the screen, my eyes hurting from the brightness of the glare. He isn't replying. Why won't he reply? Thankfully, the text flickers green a moment later.

It's your choice, Kelly.

What does this mean; he will let me speak to her or have I made a massive mistake? I'm still looking at the mobile in my hands but the screen blacks out as it goes into hibernation through inactivity. I'm willing it to flash back into life, but nothing happens. I look at the group beside the comfort and safety of the fire. Neither Billy or that other guy have their phones in their hands anymore.

To hell with them! I'll have it out with them, all of them, right now.

My phone clutched in my hand, I stalk towards the fire. Tina sees me and looks ashen as our eyes meet. Her expression is almost frozen, her eyes locked on mine. Billy sees her and glances my way, then does a double take and stares at me striding across the sand towards him.

My mobile rings, stopping me not twenty feet from the group. I forget them and accept the call from Lauren's phone. 'Darling! It's me, it's Mum—'

I know this is my daughter on the line.

I have had her with me every day since she was born, on good days and bad ones.

I would know her scream anywhere.

ELEVEN

I can't breathe. I didn't realise whilst running flat out across the sand back to my car and slamming the door that I couldn't breathe at all. Gasping for air now, I start coughing, and I can't stop. Wracking coughs, feeling bile rising in the back of my throat. I think I'm going to be sick on myself.

My daughter. My beautiful baby.

I can't do this. I just can't do any of this anymore. Who did I think I was, acting like some kind of vigilante superhero or private detective, trying to get the better of him? He has my baby girl and there's not a damn thing I can do about it.

The coughing subsides and I'm able to breathe, albeit with a sharp pain stabbing in my chest and echoing throughout my ribcage with every intake. Leaning back against the headrest I clamp my eyes shut, but that doesn't stop the images flashing to mind. I can still hear her; it won't stop. The pain, the sheer terror she felt while that monster did God knows what to her.

And it's my fault. I should have done what I was told to do. I should have just focused on the rules.

I shouldn't have tried to figure it out, to dare to think I could get to her first.

A bang on the glass next to me snaps me forward. A torch is shining in through the window and I cannot see beyond the light. I'm holding my breath again, feeling the tightness of the skin in my cheeks as the tears have already dried in the bitter wind.

Slowly turning my head, the beam of light blinds me momentarily before it's moved away. He's there.

A large man standing in the darkness.

He stoops low and I see the heavily lined but kindly face of Ian McLean, the solitary policeman on the island. Blinking furiously to clear the dancing lights from my vision, I press the switch to drop the window but the ignition is off. Hastily searching for the key, I fumble with it in my hands and drop the fob into the footwell.

Ian is standing beside the car, patiently waiting for me to sort myself out. I blindly rummage at my feet before my fingers curl around my keys and I can insert the car key into the ignition.

Catching a glimpse of myself in the rear-view mirror, I look an absolute state. My makeup around my eyes has run and smudged as I've tried to hide myself from the world and my eyes are swollen and bloodshot.

Eventually, I manage to open the window. A bitter breeze drifts over me and I shiver involuntarily.

'Evening, Doctor Kelly,' PC Ian McLean says, stooping lower so we can see one another. 'I didn't expect to see you out here.'

I sniff loudly, my nose running having ugly-wailed since the man who has my daughter hung up on me. 'I was just going to say the same thing to you, Ian.'

'Ah,' he says, standing upright and looking down towards the beach. 'The kids. Lighting fires and larking about again.'

'They're just having fun,' I argue. The last thing I want is the police crawling around that group. Whoever has Lauren saw me there tonight. What would happen to Lauren if Ian starts sniffing around?

'I saw you coming back from the beach. I never had you pegged as one for weekend campfires with smelly teenagers.'

'Come on, we were young once, too.'

'Aye, I know,' Ian says, straightening his back and puffing out his chest. 'Usually, I'd turn a blind eye but when someone makes a complaint, I have to show willing. You know how it is.'

'Who complained?' I ask, wiping my face with a tissue that I found in the pocket of the door. Anything to make myself more presentable.

'Oh, I shouldn't really say, lass. It'd be poor form.'

'Of course. I'd say let them be, though. There's very little to do on the island at this time of the year. They're just blowing off steam.'

Ian McLean looks down at me with a curious look. Leaning over, he rests his forearm on the roof of the car, fixing me with a stare. 'You never did say.'

'Say what?'

'Whit are you doing out here, lass?'

'I just fancied some air.' I glance up at him and away again. I'm a terrible liar at the best of times, only managing to be successful when it really, really counts. My better bet is to stare out at the sea. 'Lauren is... away, and the house seems empty without her there.'

Ian sighs. 'I hear you. When mine finally left home, almost three years to the day since my Ailsa passed away, it was tough. I'm not sure I'll ever get used to how quiet the house is now.'

'Thanks, Ian.'

He chuckles, embarrassed. 'Sorry, Doctor Kelly. I know Lauren is away for her university interview, isn't she?' He sighs again, and I silently wish she was safely at St Andrews. 'Oh well, she'll be back during the holidays, so you still have a few years of her getting under your feet. Don't worry.'

'I suppose so.'

'No *suppose* about it, dear,' he says, tapping his palm on the roof of the car a couple of times. 'You'll have time to adapt to it. In the meantime, it'll free you up to see more of your fancy-man.'

I look at him. 'My—'

'Aye, you and Hughie. I hear there's quite the budding romance going on there.'

'Do you? That's great, but I think the gossips are getting a little carried away. We're... friends—'

'I'm so sorry. I didn't realise,' Ian says, grimacing. 'I thought you were a couple these days.'

'No... well, yes, sort of.'

'Well, as long as you're sure, lass. That's the main thing.'

I snort a laugh, and laughing is the last thing I feel like doing just now. 'That's okay, honestly.' Ian's face splits into a broad smile and he winks at me.

'Is everything all right, Doctor Kelly?'

'Y-Yes, why do you ask?'

'You seem distracted, is all.'

'I had a rough day. Some of my patients... leave a lot to be desired sometimes.'

'I don't doubt it, lass. You should see some of the things I have to deal with in these parts.'

'Sorry, Ian. I didn't mean to sound like I have it really bad—'

'Think nothing of it,' Ian says, waving away my apology. 'This island, we all know each other's business, aye?'

'True enough.'

'Well, when I see the likes of Thomas Baird, and others, going about their day without a care in the world,' he says begrudgingly, 'it makes my blood boil, if you know what I mean.'

'I know the feeling,' I say, knowing exactly what men like Thomas get up to behind closed doors.

'Everyone knows the type, and no one will say anything about it. I have to pretend they're normal folk, same as everyone else.'

'You and me both, Ian.'

'Aye, that's a good point, Doctor Kelly. How do you feel about treating the likes of him?'

'I can't treat them any differently than I do anyone else, Ian. You know that.'

'Aye,' he says softly, looking around as if worried someone else might overhear him. 'And maybe that's where we're all going about things the wrong way, lass.'

'I think I should go home, and maybe get something to eat,' I say, starting the car. The engine turns over, but it takes a second attempt to start the car.

'Right,' Ian says, stepping away and turning his attention to the beach. His patrol car is parked behind mine. 'So you think the wee ones are okay down there?' he asks, tilting his head towards the party in the distance.

'They're not doing any harm.'

'Aye, you're probably right.' Ian tucks his torch into his utility belt. 'I'll write it up as a casual word then. Let them have their fun. Fair enough, you reckon?' he asks, looking into the car. I nod.

'I would say so, yes.' I glance up at him. 'You're a good man, Ian.'

'A soft touch, some might say. You have a safe drive home, Doctor Kelly.'

'I will, don't worry.'

'After all, if you come off the road, who do I get to come and save your life, eh?'

He winks at me, and the comment piques something in my mind. I feel like I could cry at any moment again. Hastily putting the car into gear, I set off, make a U-turn and head back towards Craighouse.

I can see PC McLean standing by the side of his patrol car in his high-vis jacket, watching me driving away. I don't see him move and when I round the bend and head into the village, he disappears from view.

Pulling into the driveway of my house, the interior is in darkness. Switching off the engine, the wind gently buffeting the car is the only sound I can hear. There is a light on in Hughie's house, but I know it is the one he leaves on when he goes out to make it look like someone is home. Up until this morning I would have said he was insane because there's no crime here on Jura. But that was this morning. My world has changed since then.

Entering the house through the back door into the kitchen, I don't hesitate, going to the cupboard and fetching a glass tumbler. The next stop is the little cupboard above the fridge freezer which I need to stand on a chair to access. Reaching into the back, I feel the cold touch of the glass neck and withdraw my hand holding the bottle of gin.

Stepping down, I reverse the chair and sit down with the bottle and tumbler on the kitchen table. Staring at the bottle, I know it's the last thing I should do but, in this moment, it is the only way I can cope. Breaking the seal, I pour myself a large measure and put the cap down on the surface of the table, rather than back on the bottle.

I knew this day would come, even if I always denied it to myself. Why would I keep the bottle if I never thought I'd drink again?

Taking a deep breath, my fingers curl around the glass and I sit there staring at it.

'Is this it, Kelly? Is this really going to be you?'

Lifting the glass to just beneath my nose, I can smell the potency of the alcohol. In that moment, it is all I want to feel, knowing that it might stop me feeling anything else. It won't though. I've been here before. What it will do is take the edge off the pain, at least for a time.

Catching a reflection of myself in the polished surface of the oven door, I stare at myself, staring at the gin. I look wrung out, drained of almost all energy. The aroma of the alcohol is almost daring me to drink it.

'Lauren deserves better,' I say, meeting my own eye. Pushing back the chair, my action sees the legs scrape on the tiled floor and I hurry to the sink, tipping the contents of the glass into the basin. Screwing the cap back onto the bottle, I put that on the counter and shove it away from me. The bottle slides away stopping when it bumps the splashback. 'Not tonight, Kelly. Keep it together.'

My mobile vibrates with a notification. I stare at it and slowly crossing the kitchen I pick it up, my breathing increasing. I open the message.

Get some sleep. You have a house call to make tomorrow, Kelly. And it's important. Focus. Lauren is depending on you.

Closing my eyes, I try to stay calm. Tomorrow I am scheduled to see Alistair Aitken. Now, why would that be significant to Lauren's kidnapper?

I know my approach has to change. I must remain conciliatory. I can't afford to anger him. And I have to stick to the rules. So, I reply. *I am sorry about earlier. Please don't hurt my daughter.*

The cursor flashes and I wait, in hope more than expectation. There is no response. Deflated, I sink down onto the chair, all thoughts of alcohol forgotten.

Alastair Aitken is a retiree who passes his days volunteering as a church warden. Why mention him?

Using my phone, I type his name into a search engine and return pages of links to Alistair Aitkens across the world of social media. Something tells me the Isle of Jura entry will be some way down the list, if he appears at all.

My mobile flickers and a message drops down from the top of the screen.

You now have fewer than sixty hours. Tick-tock, Kelly. Tick. Tock.

In sixty hours, someone will lose their life because of me. Again.

TWELVE

DAY TWO

Waking to the caw of gulls wheeling overhead, near the house, I feel a sharp pain in my neck. My back is stiff and I don't recall falling asleep. It is still dark outside; the birds must have been drawn inland by adverse weather over the water.

The clock on the oven says it is a little after six in the morning. The last I remember it was almost three o'clock. The rest of my body is also stiff, but that's what you get for sleeping on a kitchen chair. My mouth is dry; my tongue feels enlarged and sticks to the roof of my mouth with the texture of sandpaper.

Crossing to the sink I run the cold water and drink directly from it, then cup a handful and wipe my face with my palm. Blinking the grit from my eyes, I stifle a yawn and run a hand through my hair. I didn't think I would manage any sleep last night, but mental exhaustion will overcome anything physical. Did Lauren sleep last night? Taking a glass from the drainer, I fill it with water and down that in two takes. Is Lauren getting water, or food for that matter? Does he care how she is feeling? The thought that he doesn't makes me feel nauseous.

Catching my reflection in the kitchen window behind the sink, I look a proper state. A shower and a change will help me to at least 'look' normal and go under the radar as per the wishes of Lauren's kidnapper.

I keep the flow of water cool in the shower. I need to wake up, be mentally on point. Leaning my head against the tiled cubicle wall, I know I can't have another day like yesterday where I blundered around like some amateur detective. I don't know what he did to Lauren, but her screams will stay with me forever.

And it was my fault. Yes, he abducted her and not me, but all I have done since then is make her situation worse. I wasted time thinking I could figure out who is behind this and save her and now I have less than forty-eight hours remaining to save my daughter's life. To decide who I am going to kill in order to get her back. I never thought I'd have to contemplate such a scenario but, then again, only an insane person would believe it likely to happen.

Suddenly Billy Jackson comes to mind. I didn't like the way he looked at me last night when I approached the group out at the bothy. I think the feeling was mutual too. Is he behind this?

Glancing down, I see the soap and water is approaching the lip of the shower tray. I wish I had my old life back, the one where I cared about things like the water backing up in my drain. Shutting off the flow of water, I lift the drain cover up with my toe and push it aside to allow the water an easier passage.

Stepping out of the shower, I take the towel from the rail and hold it against my body, feeling the cold on my damp skin. Is Lauren cold? I remember how she would shiver when I picked her up out of the bath as a child, wrapping her in a towel and holding her to me while I dried her.

Pushing the thought aside, I have to focus on getting her out of this situation. Wallowing in self-pity won't fix this. There's only one way I can see to get her out of it right now. My entire career has been about saving lives and not taking them. But wouldn't any mother, any parent, do the unspeakable to save their child's life?

Despite showering in cool water, the mirror hanging behind the basin has still steamed up. I draw my palm across it several times. My face is drawn, my eyes sunken and hollow. I'm pale too, paler than one might expect even for a someone living in Scotland.

I'm looking in the face of someone who is about to become a killer.

I just don't yet know who I must kill, and they have no idea they have so little time left to live.

I remember these hypothetical conversations had over a lunch break or across a table with my friends in the pub. Extreme circumstances. *What would you do if...* None of us ever thought we would be faced with such a dilemma in real life. This is the work of twisted fiction, an urban legend, film and television. And yet, here we are, living out the plot of a Hollywood thriller with me as the central protagonist.

Dressed and presenting myself as best I can – I've hidden my lack of sleep with makeup, brushed my hair and put on a trouser suit – I'm examining myself again in the mirror. I've not eaten since breakfast yesterday, and I'm not hungry at all. Has Lauren eaten anything since he took her?

'Ready for part two, Doctor Kelly?' I ask myself. On the surface I look like I do every day. No one here knows me well enough to see through the façade. At least, I hope not.

Gathering my bag, I leave the house and get into my car. It's only a short drive out of Craighouse to Keils, a small hamlet sitting astride a ridge overlooking the larger island capital. There are fewer than twenty houses here, and Alistair Aitken lives in an old croft house nestled within trees as you approach the hamlet.

The church warden's home is painted white, as are most of the traditional houses in these parts. The roof would once have been thatched but that has been replaced with corrugated metal sheeting; in this case it is lime green. It's not unusual to see red, black or stainless steel used or slate, quarried on the neighbouring mainland.

It's still dark when I arrive, and the two tiny, forward facing windows of the single storey property are also dark. Alistair is expecting me; Ava confirmed the home visit at the beginning of the week. The gravel crunches beneath my feet as I walk to the front door. The breeze is coming from the west and here, on the sheltered east coast of the island, it doesn't feel as raw as it has done in previous days.

Knocking on the front door doesn't lead to a response. Peering through the nearest window, thankfully with no covering to shroud the interior, I can see the bed is made up and unslept in. He could be an early riser, but he's been unwell recently, hence the home visit. Crossing to the other window, into the kitchen with a small sitting room beyond it, I can see a figure in an armchair.

I rap my knuckles on the window and I'm thankful to see him stir. He narrows his eyes, straining to see me without his glasses. I wave and he returns it, gesturing to the front door. I find it unlocked and let myself in. The air is stuffy. I doubt he's been outside, and I can't blame him for keeping the doors and windows closed to keep the heat in. They breed folks hardy among the islands. You had to be, otherwise you wouldn't survive.

'Hello, Alistair!' I say with a warm smile. 'May I put some lights on?'

'If you want to, Doctor Kelly, but not too many. Electricity is expensive these days,' he says, sitting forward and resting his hands on top of one another on the handle of his ever-present walking stick. 'It's lovely of you to stop by, I must say.'

'More than happy to come and see my favourite patient. And I'd do so even if I didn't have to give you a check-up, Alistair.' I place my hand on top of his and give it an affectionate squeeze.

'You're very kind.'

'How have you been?' I ask him, pulling up a chair from the collapsible dining table against the rear wall of the small sitting room and setting it down beside the old man.

'Oh well, all right, I suppose,' he says, sounding as frail as he is looking. Alistair is well into his eighties now, and despite nature's best efforts to slow him down, he's still something of a force around the local community. He's been the warden of our parish church for years, well before I came to the island. He's a fixture in the community as much as the Paps themselves. He grins at me, revealing several missing teeth and receding gums. 'Nothing some fresh cranachan wouldn't take care of. I don't suppose you brought something with you, did you?'

'No, Alistair. Whisky and cream are not the things I usually prescribe.'

'Shame,' he says, exhaling. 'At this point I don't have much else left to look forward to.'

'Nonsense. You'll be around for years yet,' I say as I slip a cuff over his hand and lift it to his upper arm. 'I'm just going to check your blood pressure, okay?'

'Aye. No problem,' he says, sitting back and sighing.

'Any dizziness, nausea or new aches and pains recently?' I ask, busying myself with the basic checks I had planned.

'Nothing more than usual.'

'And what is usual?'

'My maker is calling me, lassie. I'll no' be here for much longer, mark my words.' I read his figures, make a note and then slowly deflate the cuff. 'What do you say, Doctor Kelly? Do I get to live a little longer on this blessed isle?'

'Your blood pressure is higher than I would have hoped, that's true.'

'That's just the result of having a pretty young lady taking care of me.'

'You old charmer, you,' I tell him, smiling.

'I still have the gift, obviously.'

'You never married though,' I say, unpacking a kit to draw a blood sample.

'I was married once,' he says, taking on a faraway look. 'A long time ago.' He sounds sad and I study him for a moment until he looks at me, shrugging it off. 'Long time ago.'

'What happened?'

'She... left.'

'Sounds ominous. Couldn't she handle your raw, naked charisma?' I ask, donning a pair of gloves before taking the blood sample. 'You'll just feel a little prick in the skin—'

'I'll not, you know. My body is halfway to the afterlife already, and I feel very little these days.'

Tapping his arm, a suitable vein comes to the surface and I begin drawing blood. 'So, what happened?'

'To what?'

'Your wife.'

'Oh.'

He seems reluctant to talk about it. 'You don't have to say, forget I asked. It's none of my business.'

'No, you're all right, lass.' Alistair wipes his free hand across his mouth. 'It's just not something I choose to speak about, that's all.'

'You surprise me. You're the most garrulous man in the parish.'

'Ah,' he says, shrugging off the melancholy and grinning. 'In His house, I am always welcome though.'

I finish taking the sample, withdraw the needle and place a small swab over the contact point. 'Hold this for me, would you, please?' Alistair dutifully places two fingers over the gauze, holding it in place while I mark the label on the tube and put it away in my bag. 'We've certainly missed you at the church.'

'And I've missed attending services,' Alistair says glumly. 'And all of you too, of course.'

'Of course,' I say, patting his arm gently. 'And for the record, you will always be welcome in my house.'

'That's very kind, Doctor Kelly.' He winces as he bends his arm at the elbow. I try to assist and he shakes his head. 'It's fine, don't worry.'

'How is your health generally would you say? Better? Worse?'

'No less than I deserve.'

'I beg your pardon?'

He shakes his head dismissively. 'I'm all right. Honestly, things have got better. It's almost like He isn't too keen for me to join Him.'

I can't help but smile but when I look at him; there is something in his expression. Is it sadness? Bitterness, perhaps? 'Is everything okay, Alistair? Do you need anything? Are people taking care of you?'

'I have everything I need, Doctor Kelly. No more. No less.'

'That's not what I asked you though, is it?' I say sternly and he grimaces, releasing his arm so that I can attach a small sticking plaster to where I'd drawn blood. 'What with everything you do for the community, I would hope people are looking out for you.'

'They are. More so than I would like.'

'You say that like you're annoyed or that it's a bad thing that people care about you.'

He tilts his head to one side. 'Maybe they shouldn't.'

'Of course they should. What a thing to say?'

'You're a new believer, aren't you?'

I'm surprised by the question. He's right. I stopped attending church as soon as my parents stopped forcing me to go. 'I took a different path for a while, that's true. But I found my way back.'

Alistair nods. 'It took you some time to find the path back though, didn't it?'

I'm pensive. I don't really want to have this conversation. Especially bearing in mind what I've been contemplating this past day. 'Yes, I have had my faith tested, it's true.'

'And, in your opinion, would you say decades of sacrifice, of service to others, makes up for anything you may have done in the past?'

I feel out of place now. It's almost as if Alistair has pulled back the veil on my life, and is looking at everything I've done well and, more importantly, the mistakes I've made. 'Why do you ask?' I say, making a show of rearranging my equipment in my bag before putting anything else away. I can't look into his face or he'll know. I don't know how, but he'll see through me.

'Why won't you say?' he asks and I look into his eyes. They are gleaming in the artificial light of the lamp beside his chair, one of two I switched on. I take pause, considering my reply, and I see his eyes narrow as he studies me. 'What is it, Doctor Kelly?'

'N-nothing.'

He inclines his head, looking more like my grandfather than I care to say. He cared for me, my grandfather, looked out for me when others wanted to wash their hands of me. He's probably the reason I made it all the way to medical school. And his face is what I see when I look at Alistair now. 'Does it?' he asks again.

'I... I suppose it depends—'

'On what?'

'On what it was that you did in the past, as to whether you can make up for it with good works.'

'Ah, can the paedophile redeem himself with a life of good works? Or is he eternally damned for his sins?'

'That is' – I don't know what to make of that question – 'quite a question. I know there are psychologists who argue that such a person is unable to switch that side of their desires off and will always be a danger. Others argue therapy works. I don't know, it's beyond my knowledge—'

'But that is a scientific debate, Doctor Kelly. I'm asking you for a debate on the soul.'

'Which will be decided when he leaves the mortal world—'

'Depending on which version of the Bible you interpret, yes.'

'Are you trying to tell me—'

'No, certainly not,' Alistair says indignantly. 'It is simply a philosophical debate, that's all.'

'So, what's your answer?'

He snorts. 'What do I think?'

'Yes, you asked the question, so you must have an opinion.'

He draws a deep breath. 'I think there are actions that one can make that are so terrible to be irredeemable in life. But that doesn't mean that one should not make the effort.' He smacks his lips. It is as if he is relating something to his own life, but I don't know what. 'Is it enough? Well, that's not for you or me to judge. A power far greater than us will make that decision.'

'Kicking the can down the road—'

'And into the afterlife, aye,' Alistair says, nodding sagely.

That conversation took an unexpected turn, I must say. Looking around, I can see the house is in a bit of a mess. The kitchen also has a lot of items needing to be washed up and put away.

'Is there anything I can do for you while I'm here?'

He smiles. 'No thank you. Your time is precious.'

'It's no trouble.'

'I'll manage, Doctor Kelly, but I appreciate the gesture.'

I stand up having packed away my things, and then I return the dining chair to where I found it, beside the table. 'Would you like me to have someone collect you for this coming Sunday service? We haven't seen you for a while.'

'Not you then?'

'No. I have... something on.'

'More important than celebrating the glory of God?'

I incline my head towards him, thinking of my daughter. 'Even more so, yes. Something important to me.'

'You're what they call a fair-weather parishioner, Doctor Kelly. If there is something important that will keep you away from church, then you *need* to attend church not avoid it.'

'I'll bear that in mind, Alistair.' I gently place a hand on the back of his, but I'm keen to leave now. The sooner the better. 'I'll be in touch soon with your updated results.'

'With His leave, I'll still be here.'

At the door, I look back. 'What was her name?'

'Whose?' Alistair asks, offering me a forlorn look, disappointed at my departure, maybe.

'Your wife's?'

'Isobel.'

I smile warmly. 'That's a beautiful name.'

'Yes,' he says, nodding slowly. 'She was a beautiful woman.'

I hurry out of the house with Alistair Aitken's moral dilemma still reverberating in my mind, and my moral compass spinning out of control.

THIRTEEN

TWO YEARS PREVIOUSLY

The sound of excited voices carry through the French doors to me. Glancing around the kitchen, I'm confident everything is all but ready. We need to start taking things out soon now that everyone is here. Glancing at the clock on the wall, it's almost one and I told Niall to have the hot food ready by then.

Where's he got to?

Peering through the open window overlooking the pool, I can see Lauren with her friends around the bar. 'Darling!' I call, but almost on cue, someone raises the volume of the music to a cheer from the assembled teenagers. Arms fly into the air, shouting and laughter follows and someone is hefted into the air and heaved into the water. A massive cheer erupts. It's like being on an eighteen to thirty holiday back in the day, or I imagine so. I was never allowed to go.

'Lauren!' I shout through the window, and I can see her sipping at her cocktail, moving the little yellow umbrella aside to avoid losing an eye. Seeing one of her friends who I know better than most others, I wave at her, managing to get her attention. 'Cassie! Can you get Lauren for me, please?'

Cassie gives me a thumbs up and weaves her way through

the crowd, disappearing. There's still no sign of Niall. I swear there is smoke coming from the closed lid of the barbecue and I'm not sure there should be.

'Hey, Mum. What do you need?' Lauren asks, bounding into the kitchen in her bathing suit. Thankfully, for her modesty, she has a sarong wrapped around her waist although this generation seem less concerned about that sort of thing. I'm still undecided on whether that's a good thing.

'Have you seen your father?'

'No, why?'

'He's gone off somewhere again.' I let out an exasperated sigh, looking around at the various salads, vegetarian, vegan, three bean, to name but a few. Along with those there are various dips, finger food and cheeses for Lauren and her friends to get stuck into. The bread rolls are here too. Everything is ready, everything barring the meat. I've already had to hunt him down once today. 'We need your father to finish with the meat, and then people can start helping themselves.'

Lauren looks out of the window at some of her friends behind the bar. 'I think we have that taken care of.'

I follow her gaze and roll my eyes. 'I promised your friends' parents that this wouldn't get out of control.'

'Mum...'

'And you promised me your friends would be sensible—'

'Oh, leave them be, Kelly,' Niall says, entering the kitchen behind me. He's changed into a linen shirt and shorts now, finished off with the suede loafers I bought him for his birthday. Taking off his sunglasses, Persol branded, obviously, he throws his arms open and Lauren hugs him. He squeezes her tightly. 'Your friends, they'll be grand, won't they, love?' he says to Lauren, who leans back from him, eyeing his upper body.

'You smell good, Dad.'

'I always smell good,' Niall says. 'And you are proving to be quite the host.'

'True,' Lauren replies. 'Everyone is having a great time.'

'Thankfully,' I say. 'No thanks to your father for sloping off again, this time to get changed.'

'It's getting hot around the barbecue,' he says. 'I had to change.'

'Well, I'll tell you what you don't smell of,' I say, and they both look at me, interrupting their mutual appreciation. 'You don't smell of salmon, sausages or burgers.'

'I'm on it,' Niall says, detaching himself from his daughter and making for the pool house where we have a purpose-built outdoor food prep area.

'It had better not be ruined!' I call after him. He waves a hand in the air without looking back, scooping up a bottle of beer from an ice bucket just outside the door.

'It's all under control!' he says commandingly, navigating the crowd and fist bumping several individuals en route to where he should have been already.

'Honestly, your father is such a child at times.'

Lauren shrugs. 'From what I hear this party is tame in comparison to when he celebrated his Highers with his pals.'

'And remind me to encourage your father not to set unrealistic expectations with those tall stories of his.'

Lauren rolls her eyes. 'Do you want me to help you get all of this out onto the tables?' she asks, her eyes sweeping the assembled food, wrapped in cling film to keep the flies away.

'If it's not too much trouble?' I ask and she misses the sarcasm or chooses to ignore it.

'No bother at all.' Lauren pokes her head outside, puts two fingers in her mouth and splits the party atmosphere with a shrill whistle. 'Yous lot, come and get the food!'

The partygoers immediately set down their drinks, or neck them, and hustle into the kitchen picking up plates, bowls and the jars of cutlery I've already set out for them. Like a plague of locusts, they've picked the kitchen clean in a matter of minutes and transferred everything outside.

Lauren has one hand on her hip; the other is holding her large glass with an orange cocktail inside. I notice she didn't have to help with the transfer. She winks at me. 'All under control!' Before I can reply, two of Lauren's friends bound into the kitchen and grab my daughter, hauling her back outside just as the sound of another body hitting the water draws a cheer.

Niall gets my attention as he's making his way to the tables with the foil-wrapped side of salmon in his oven-gloved hand. I pick up the mats for the hot pans and beat him to the table, where he sets the tray down and opens the foil. Steam escapes but the fish is cooked to perfection. He shoots me his best smile and I know he's pleased with himself.

'Sausages and burgers are done, I've just got to bring them over.'

'I'll help!' Bonnie says, seemingly appearing from nowhere. Niall smiles at her, nodding for her to accompany him back to the grill. I dislike that girl. She's older than Lauren by a year, and much older still in experience. Lauren comes to stand beside me; Freya – her longest-serving school friend – is with her.

'Hey!' Lauren says, nudging me.

'What?'

'Stop staring.'

I look away from Bonnie. 'I wasn't staring.'

'She's all right, Mum. You're...'

'What am I? Choose your words carefully if you want an increase in your allowance,' I say, arching my eyebrows and Lauren knows not to finish that sentence.

'A great mum,' she says, leaning in and kissing me on the cheek as I turn my face side on to her. At the same time, I can see Bonnie across the pool, flicking her hair to ensure she gets maximum attention from those around her. As if the outfit she's wearing, what little there is of it, isn't already having that effect.

'It's true, Doctor Murray,' Freya says as Niall returns a moment later, with Bonnie in tow but she breaks off from him having not helped carry anything and leaves Niall to bear the plates of cooked meats alone.

'What's that, Freya?'

'You're great,' she says, beaming. 'This is great, letting us have a party at your place like this.' She's genuinely appreciating the effort I've made. I'm not surprised though. Freya has always been a stable influence on our daughter. Her parents raised a kind-hearted, smart, delightful child.

'I am not a slut!' Bonnie screams, to shrieks of accompanying laughter from the three boys closest to her. Bonnie then nudges one with her backside and he overbalances, toppling into the pool fully clothed, beer and all. Everyone laughs. Everyone except me.

'Unclench, will you,' Niall whispers into my ear, and no one else hears him.

'I don't know what you mean.'

'They're just blowing off steam,' he says, peering at me over the rim of his sunglasses. The glare of the summer sun reflecting off the surface water in the pool has me squinting as I look around.

'Is that what you call it?' I say, lowering my voice to a conspiratorial whisper, matching his.

'Come on, you were young once!' Niall says, stepping away and joining in the clapping as more of the teenagers are encouraged into the pool, whether by their own volition or not. And the music gets louder.

We were all so happy and free at that time or, at least, I thought so. But that was the moment before our lives changed forever.

FOURTEEN

PRESENT DAY

The rain is falling steadily now, activating the wipers, and they drag across the windscreen as I sit outside Alistair's house.

Everything I've done in the last eighteen months was to make a fresh start. Not just for me but for all of us, Niall included. Now it looks like it was all in vain. I'm cursed, leading my family into pain and chaos.

I should never have brought my daughter to this place. It was supposed to be a haven, a sanctuary for us to regroup and yet all I've managed to do is introduce her to some nutcase. Niall warned me this was a mistake, and I wouldn't listen. Not that it mattered what he said at the time. I was done. We were done.

Glancing at my mobile I have no new messages. I've less than forty-eight hours to save my daughter's life.

When I have killed someone, whoever it is supposed to be, how will I ensure I get away with it? I would go to jail for Lauren, of course I would, but the kidnapper was clear about that third rule – I must not get caught.

I am able to sign death certificates, and if it looks natural then a simple post-mortem will be all that takes place. Ten minutes for me to do the deed. A further twenty minutes for a cursory post-mortem examination.

All of this could come down to roughly half an hour. Thirty minutes that will define the fate of my daughter. Although, as Alistair made clear, I will have to live with my sins for the remainder of my life.

I have to wait for the windscreen to clear, thinking about Alistair and why the kidnapper directed me to him.

Our conversation was odd, even for a man who spends so much time alone. Presumably his wife was the love of his life. She left him, but he still loves her. I read that in his eyes and you cannot fake that. You can try but it always comes across as insincere unless you win Academy Awards.

Alistair Aitken was sincere. And yet there are no photos of Isobel in the house. No wedding picture. No holiday snaps. Nothing. I open a search box on my phone and type in the name *Isobel Aitken, Scotland.*

The mobile signal is stronger in Craighouse but I see the search results are coming through. The first five hits are links to newspaper articles. *Wife and Mother Perish in Blaze* is the first one. I open it, and the page goes white as a narrow blue bar edges its way across the screen.

'Come on!' I hiss at the screen as it changes.

The page cannot be loaded. Please refresh and try again.

'Damn.'

My phone rings and I answer it.

'Good morning, Doctor Kelly,' Ava says cheerfully.

'Good morning, Ava.'

'How are you feeling, dear?'

'Much better, thanks,' I say, heaving a sigh, my mind focused on Isobel. Alistair didn't mention a child. Did she leave him and take his child too, and then they died in a fire?

Does this have something to do with why the kidnapper highlighted him?

'That's good. I assume you managed to get out to Keil and see Alistair?'

'I did, yes. I'm just leaving there now, heading over to the Allens' house to check in on Mhari.'

'That's why I was calling, dear. Amelia has just given me a phone and says they don't wish to trouble you—'

'She was insistent yesterday that something was wrong, so I need to see her. Morgan is off the island and so me going to them is the only way this is going to happen.'

'I'll not disagree,' Ava says, 'but I'm just telling you what she said.'

'Let's see what she says when I knock on the door.'

'Please yourself,' Ava says and I detect a touch of mirth in her response. She likes a bit of mischief does Ava. In fact, I'd say she is one to seek it out on occasion. 'How was Alistair?'

'Good. I think he's looking rather frail.'

'He is eighty-four,' Ava says. 'I know he's been sprightly, but it catches up with us all in the end.'

'Ava, how well do you know him?'

'Alistair? Reasonably well, I suppose. Why?'

'What about his past?'

'He was on the island before I arrived, but I don't think he's always lived here. What do you want to know?'

'Did you know he was married?'

'That doesn't surprise me as he can be a bit of smooth operator when he turns it on. I dare say he was quite a ladies' man back in the day.'

'Has he ever mentioned Isobel to you?'

'No, I can't say I've heard anything about her at all. Why?'

I take a deep breath. My windscreen is clear now. I can see into the bay but the mainland is still shrouded by the passing front. 'I was just curious. He mentioned her, is all.'

'I can ask around a bit, if you like?'

'Um... no, no, don't do that. I don't want to be caught gossiping about one of my patients.'

'I can be very discreet, dear.'

I laugh. 'I'm sure you can, but no. Don't do that. There's no need. I'll see you in an hour or so, after I've finished at the Allens'.'

I hang up and open the browser again. The page is still trying to load. I will have to wait to learn the fate of Isobel and her child. I put the car in gear and pull away. In the rear-view mirror I can see the stationary figure of Alistair Aitken watching me from his kitchen window. There's something about that kindly, selfless man. I'm having to look at people in a different way now. You never know what could be hidden in their past.

After all, when people look at me, they see a loving single mother and the island's dedicated family doctor, caring for her patients from birth to death.

They have no idea what everyone accused me of doing, before we came here.

FIFTEEN

The small hamlet of Cabrach lies almost three miles southwest of Craighouse. Mhari Allen's property is accessed from the main island road by a short track running adjacent to the old stone wall boundary of what was once a croft. My car tyres lose grip on the wet surface. What had been frozen mud has been softened by the rainfall. The old stone cottage is sheltered from the elements by a copse to one side and the incline of the hill to the rear. I park in front of the house.

To the rear is another house, converted from a byre into a residence for Mhari's son, Morgan, to live in. Amelia shares the primary house with her mother, taking care of her day-to-day needs. Keen to get out of the rain I hurry up to the front door and knock firmly. Holding my bag close to me, keeping my shoulders tight, hunkering down against the wind which appears to be getting stronger I knock again.

The door cracks open and Amelia peers out at me, wide-eyed. She looks like she hasn't slept well in days, dark rings around her eyes and a pale complexion.

'Hello, Amelia.'

'Doctor Kelly,' Amelia says, opening the door further and looking out past me to both the left and right. 'You're here.'

'I said I would stop by.'

'Yes, yes of course.' She opens the door fully and reluctantly, in my view, beckons me inside, closing the door after I pass by.

Everyone's home has its own characteristic scent to it, and the Allen house is no different. I can't describe it exactly, but it has a distinct smell of age about it. The house is well lived in. The carpet in the hall has furrows worn into the well-trodden passage through to the back of the house, and is threadbare in places.

The sitting room has wooden floors, with a large rug centred within it, and the exposed planks are pitted with gaps in between some, where rotten timbers have been replaced by ill-fitting planks of different widths. The windows are still single glazed, and I can feel a draught coming through them.

A crackling fire is burning in the hearth and Mhari is sitting before it with a tartan blanket across her knees, a thick, woollen cardigan wrapped around her upper body. Amelia closes the door to the hallway behind us, the hinges shrieking with the effort.

'Hello, Mhari,' I say, coming around to stand to her left. Her eyes slowly drift from the fire up to me and I smile at her. She doesn't acknowledge my presence, but our eyes do meet. Bending over, I lean closer. 'How are you today, Mhari?'

Now she seems to recognise me, and her lips turn up at the corners and she speaks in barely a whisper. 'Doctor Howlett.' Mhari Allen is one of the few who uses my full title and insists on doing so. 'How nice of you to come and see me.'

'It's my pleasure, Mhari. How have you been?'

'Getting old, Doctor. That's all,' she says, demonstrating her apathetic tone that I've become used to.

'Amelia thinks there might be a bit more to it than that.' I look at her daughter and Amelia's cheeks flush, and she looks away.

'She worries,' Mhari says. 'She always has.'

'Still, maybe I should take a look at you, hey?'

Mhari nods, but her reticence is clear. I have to say, Mhari Allen is ninety-three years old and as tough a patient as I have ever known. And it may sound odd, but she's looked better. When she last came out of hospital, I saw her go from strength to strength, revitalised by a period of convalescence after her undiagnosed complaint. Now though, she's looking haggard. Her eyes are hollow, and it might be the firelight but her complexion seems jaundiced.

She looks tired. Although that shouldn't be unusual for a woman her age, I am a bit shocked. 'How are you feeling in yourself?' I ask, having measured her blood pressure and taken a temperature check. Putting my index and forefinger on her wrist, I check her pulse again. It feels erratic which isn't a good sign.

'Old.'

I smile affectionately. 'Aside from feeling old, how are you?'

'I've been better.'

'Mum, tell Doctor Kelly about your stomach pains—'

'Oh, they're nothing to concern the young lady with.'

'Why not let me be the judge of that, Mhari,' I say lightly. I glance at Amelia. 'Stomach pains?'

'I say stomach, but I mean her abdomen,' Amelia says. 'Like before, you remember?'

'I do, yes. Do you mind if I undo your cardigan for a moment?' Mhari has no objections, and once the knitwear is out of the way I can explore her lower abdomen, gently pressing in places around her stomach. 'Let me know if any of this hurts, won't you?' It doesn't take long before Mhari is flinching with my application of pressure in various places. She winces several times. 'I'm sorry, love,' I say calmly. Taking my hands away, I'm puzzled. There are no lumps or abnormal tissue that I can detect.

'You're feeling the cold as well, aren't you, Mum?' Amelia says. Mhari is cold to the touch despite the blaze in the hearth and her clothing, which I would deem sufficient.

'Any other symptoms that are a change to the norm?'

'She's very weak, Doctor Kelly. Some days, she can hardly get out of bed. I had to carry her to the fire this morning.'

I sit back on my haunches, feeling uncomfortable with the heat behind me now. 'And how long has this been the case?'

'A while now, but it's been getting steadily worse.'

'The pains or the weakness?' I ask.

'All of it,' Amelia says, disheartened. I glance at her standing behind her mother and it's almost like I can read her mind. I've seen this look so many times before in the offspring of an ageing parent. Amelia fears she's losing her mother, and she feels powerless to stop it.

'Are you drinking enough fluids, Mhari?'

'I'm always thirsty,' she says. I pass her the glass of water from the table beside her chair and she sips from it.

'Any nausea or vomiting?'

'I do feel sick, seeing as you mention it,' Mhari says, passing the glass back to me.

'But no vomiting?' I ask and she shakes her head.

'And I can barely feel this glass in my fingers,' Mhari says, glancing at the glass as I set it down beside her.

'Your fingers are numb?' I ask and she nods. 'What about your feet?'

'It is the same with my toes.'

I frown. That's something new that didn't manifest last time.

'What do you think it is, Doctor Kelly?' I look at Amelia, and then towards the kitchen and she takes the hint. 'Would you like a cup of tea?'

'I'd love one,' I say. 'Let me help you.'

I help Mhari with the buttons of her cardigan and then join Amelia in the kitchen. She wears a concerned expression when I enter.

'It's the same thing as last time, isn't it?' she asks, lowering her voice so as not to be overheard. 'Only it's come back worse.'

I incline my head. 'It does seem to be progressing faster than last time.'

'What is it? They couldn't figure it out at the hospital.'

'I know. I fear they may have, simply, put it down to old age.'

Amelia scoffs. 'There has to be more to it than that. She gets ill, then recovers in hospital only to go downhill once she's back home again.' Amelia busies herself with arranging cups and making tea for us, but she's clumsy and obviously distracted. 'Maybe it's this place? What do you think?'

'Something in the house?' I ask and Amelia nods.

I look around. Some of these old properties take their water from age-old lock-ins further up the hillside, rather than from the mains. It gives the water a brown discolouration and is less filtered. It is possible that this has become contaminated, but that wouldn't explain why only Mhari is unwell.

The same could be said for the old water pipes, having been made of lead that could lead to poisoning, but the same rationale applies with that theory too. Why would Mhari be the only one affected? Amelia isn't in great health, but her symptoms are completely different.

'Has she been eating normally, regular intake of nutrients, fresh fruit and vegetables?'

'Of course,' Amelia says. 'The dietician at the hospital gave us a regimen to follow to build up her strength and I've stuck to it.' She seems on the verge of tears. 'I don't understand it.'

I can't sugar-coat this particular pill. It might just be that

Mhari is right, and she knows her own body. 'Amelia, your mum is ninety-three—'

'Ninety-four in three weeks,' Amelia says.

'And it might be that her body is breaking down. It happens.'

Amelia glares at me. 'So... you're going to do nothing?'

'I didn't say that. I'll take a blood sample today. I've another one to send over to the mainland as it is already today, and I'll put your mum's in the same package. We can try and see what is going on. It might be that we have to take her back to the hospital.'

Amelia looks horrified. 'She'll no' like that, Doctor Kelly. Not after the last time.'

'I'll not like what?' Mhari calls from behind us. I'm impressed she could hear us. 'What scheme are you two hatching that I'm sure I won't like?'

'Nothing, Mum. We're just... chatting.'

'I'll not be going back to the hospital. If I go in, then they'll be carrying me out in a box.'

Amelia moves to the door so she can see her mother. 'We'll have less of that talk, Mum. If you don't mind.' She glances at me. 'There are plenty more years in you yet. Right, Doctor Kelly?'

'There's no reason why not,' I say.

'See!' Amelia says to her mum. 'I don't know what I would do without you, so you can't be speaking about such things, let alone thinking them.'

'My thoughts are the one place left that are my own,' Mhari mutters. 'And no one can take them from me. Not even you or your brother.'

'Is Morgan back from the mainland yet?' I ask, looking out of the window towards his house. Nothing is moving over there and the car is not parked out front.

'No, but I'm expecting him back at any moment,' Amelia

says, lowering her voice again. Does she not want her mum to hear?

'The ferry is fixed then?'

'Aye, so I'm told,' Amelia says. I walk back into the sitting room.

'Mhari, I know how you feel about hospital, but I'd like to take a little bit of blood from you, send it away and try to see if we can make you a little better. Is that okay?'

'Don't take too much, Doctor Howlett. I don't have much in me.'

I place a reassuring hand on her forearm, patting it gently. 'I'll make sure I leave enough behind. Okay?' She places her right hand over mine.

'Thank you, Kelly. You're a good girl.'

I meet her eye, and she seems more lucid, the best I've seen her in a long time. And she's never used my given name before. Not that I can remember at least. She squeezes my hand but her grip is weak; the skin on the back of her hand is so thin and has a grey tone to it. I smile at her. 'We'll have you feeling better, Mhari, don't worry.'

'I'm not worried, dear. I've had my time in this life and for the most part it's been wonderful.'

I feel sad for her, but an ugly thought comes unbidden to mind. If Mhari Allen passed away today, who would raise an eyebrow let alone question it? Shocked by the darkness I never knew I possessed, I have to leave. Amelia comes into the sitting room carrying a tray of cups alongside a teapot.

'I... I have to go,' I mumble.

'What, now?' Amelia asks.

'Yes, I-I forgot an appointment.' Hastily gathering my things, I stand up.

'But what about the blood sample?' Amelia asks.

'I'll have to come back.' I hurry out of the sitting room. I don't dare to even look at Mhari or her daughter. What if they can see what I'm thinking somehow? What would they think of me, of what I'm becoming?

Slamming the front door behind me so no one could catch up to me before I reach the sanctuary of the car, I get in and rummage through my pockets for the keys. 'Come on, for crying out loud!' I chide myself, struggling to find them and ever more frantically looking. My hand gets caught in the lining of my coat pocket and pulling it free, I strike the steering wheel, hard. 'Damn it!' I shout and burst into tears. My fingers hurt, but that's not why I'm crying.

I don't know what to do. I don't know how to fix this.

SIXTEEN

Driving back to the surgery on autopilot, I don't recall the route I took or anything I saw on the way. Ava is at the reception desk, a phone clamped between her ear and shoulder whilst she types away at her keyboard. No sooner have I walked in, she says her goodbyes and hangs up.

I'm in no mood to talk and keep my head down, making for my consulting room.

'Kelly?' Ava calls just as I thought I was about to make it past her. I turn and walk back to where she is now standing behind her desk. 'I thought you said you were feeling better? You look dreadful.'

I heave a sigh. 'I won't take offence because I know you're right.'

'Have you been crying?' Ava asks, coming out from behind her desk with all her fussing energy. I raise a hand to try and head her off but she is a force of nature when she has a mind to be.

'I'm fine—'

'You most certainly are not, young lady.'

'I'm not much younger than you!'

'You don't look it just now,' Ava says, taking my hand and placing the back of her other hand to my cheek and then forehead. 'Well, you don't feel warm.'

'I'm okay,' I tell her. 'Honestly, it was just a hell of a morning.'

'Have you slept?'

Perhaps I should have Ava do my consultations. She's pretty good at reading people. 'No, not anywhere near enough, but,' I say pointedly, raising a finger, 'I'm okay.'

Ava narrows her eyes, sceptical. 'That's as may be, but I'll make you a cup of tea and then you can tell me all about it.'

I'm about to protest but she shoos me away towards my room and crosses to the entrance, locking the door and reversing the *Back in five* sign that we often employ. She doesn't need to tell me twice and I go through into my room, closing the door and putting my bag down. I slip off my coat and hang it up on the peg before sitting down.

Pushing my hands across my face, and running them through my hair, I feel a hundred years old. My head is pounding.

My eyes are drawn to the clock on the wall. Forty hours, possibly less because I don't know from when he started the countdown. Was it when he took my daughter or from when he contacted me? I can't risk it, anyway. I have to get her back with time to spare.

Alistair Aitken. The kidnapper wants me to explain why I've chosen the patient I kill. If it's Alistair, surely it's something to do with this fire? I turn to my computer screen, typing *Isobel Aitken* into the search box, but this time I add the word *blaze*.

The returns are almost identical to what came up previously, only far fewer in number, and this time they are all detailing a historic house fire that shook the population of a town called Crieff. I click on the most reputable source I can see, an article from the archives of *The Herald*.

Isobel Aitken died at the age of twenty-eight; her body was recovered from the burnt-out shell of the house she shared with her daughter, six-year-old Siobhan, whose body was also found in her bedroom. It was presumed the little girl passed away in her sleep due to smoke inhalation. The tragedy of the story hits an emotional chord, and I think of Lauren. How will I cope if I lose my daughter? I can't allow that to happen.

The door opens and I quickly change the screen to another page. Ava pauses as her eye is drawn to the screen, or to my reaction, probably. She is bearing a cup of steaming tea and she smiles as she brings it to me.

'Thanks, Ava.'

'Now,' she says, again looking at the screen, 'what's going on with you?'

I shrug. 'Don't worry. I'm just a bit worried about... Mhari. She is adamant she won't go back into hospital. She's scared that if she does she'll not come out again.'

Ava frowns. 'Are you sure that's the issue?'

'That's what she said. What else could it be?'

Ava grimaces and I encourage her with an open-handed gesture.

'Well, it's just that she has these bouts of feeling really unwell, doesn't she?'

'Yes, but she's elderly and frail. That is allowed, Ava.'

Ava waves away my comment. 'That's not what I meant. She has these illnesses, and we arrange a stay in hospital where no one can figure out what is wrong with her. She gets better, returns home only to—'

'You think she's faking it?' I ask, scoffing at the prospect.

'You say that,' Ava says, wagging a finger in the air, 'but old people get lonely, and they look for attention.'

'She lives with her daughter, and she has her son next door!'

'And neither of them can stand the woman,' Ava says. Before I can be offended by her blunt assessment, she continues, 'Don't be fooled by the dear old lady act—'

'Act?'

'I have it on rather good authority that her poor daughter—'

'Amelia.'

'Yes, Amelia, had the chance to leave the island with a dashing young man many years ago, and Mhari scuppered that plan, to keep her here at her beck and call.'

'That's... an awful thing to allege.'

Ava arches her eyebrows knowingly. 'Mark my words, there's an edge to that woman, and she's more than able to tie you up in knots to keep you going round.'

I sit back, lifting the mug of tea and blowing the steam away from the surface. 'I'm sure that can't be it.'

'Hmm. You think so? Did you find anything actually wrong with her?'

My brow furrows. 'Nothing specific. Her heart rate was a little erratic.'

'Which it would be when trying to pull the wool over someone's eyes.'

'You're too cynical,' I tell her.

Ava shakes her head. 'Every December, Mhari manages to fall ill just before Christmas. She gets a bed in a warm hospital ward surrounded by people, decorations and a lovely lunch.'

'Why would she do that when she can have the holidays at home with her children?'

Ava snorts. 'A good question. One that no one ever asks. Trust me, like clockwork. You'll see again this year, the same as last.' She turns towards the door, hearing the phone ringing in reception, and then pauses. 'That son of hers is a card as well.'

'Morgan? He seems okay.'

'As long as things are going his way, yes. I wouldn't want to be on the wrong side of him though.'

Ava leaves, dashing back to answer the call before the voice-mail kicks in. I turn to my screen and bring the newspaper article back up. Isobel Aitken, dead at twenty-eight along with her daughter.

The fire brigade initially suspected arson and... I stop reading. I can't quite believe it. As I scroll down, a photograph of Alistair is displayed on the screen.

Alistair Aitken, Isobel's estranged husband, was interviewed, and speculation persists this was in relation to a suspected arson attack. More details to follow.

Checking the foot of the page for the article's publication date, I find it is very old. There are links to related articles though. The most comprehensive cites the blaze as significant in a review of building regulation standards around fire safety. I recognise the charred remains of the building from the earlier report. No charges were ever brought by the Procurator Fiscal, and the case remains open in the deaths of both Isobel and her daughter Siobhan.

Maybe this has nothing to do with Lauren at all, and we're simply pawns in someone else's twisted revenge plan. Standing up, I close the browser window and gather my bag and my coat, leaving the mug of tea untouched. Seeing me walking across reception, Ava is surprised, and I cut her off before she can speak, taking Alistair Aitken's blood sample from my bag and putting it down in front of her.

'Can you arrange to have this sent across to the lab on the mainland for me? I'm just popping out. I'll be back in a little while.'

'Of course I can,' Ava says, picking up the bag containing

the test tube. She then looks out of the nearby window. 'Are you going anywhere nice? It looks like it could rain, or worse, at any moment.'

'I just need to get some fresh air. I have a headache.'

'Can I get you anything—'

'No, thank you. A walk will do me good.'

SEVENTEEN

The rain has stopped falling, not that I'm bothered either way. Sometimes the weather matches your mood perfectly, maybe even lifts it when the sun is shining. Today, the wind is coming from the south bringing milder air across the island.

There isn't a lot of traffic on the road through Craighouse and I wander along it towards the little harbour, hemmed in by the stone wall. Opposite the world-famous scotch distillery, I walk over to the solitary standing stone above the bay. I'll bet this was a marker to denote the safe harbour to ancient seafarers.

Thrusting my hands into my pockets, I'm looking out across the harbour where several small fishing boats are at anchor. The sea is surprisingly calm, bearing in mind the strength of the gusting wind gently buffeting me.

What would I give for a safe haven right now? My phone vibrates in my pocket and I take it out.

What do you think is an acceptable punishment for wasting someone's time?

He can't be angry with me. I still have more than a day left to do as he wants. I hastily begin typing out a reply but he beats me to it.

How is Mhari? A doctor's time is precious. Her daughter's is even more so.

'Hey, you!'

I turn towards the shout, belatedly hearing a car engine. They can't be talking to me, surely. But he is. Morgan Allen, with a face like thunder, pulls his car into the side of the road and gets out, marching towards me. I look at my screen but there is no sign of another message coming through.

My hair is blown across my face and I move it aside, out of my eyes, and watch him striding towards me. 'Morgan, I—'

'Where do yous get off' – he grabs the collar of my coat and hauls me towards him, and I feel his spittle strike my cheek as he growls at me – 'coming to my house and seeing my mother?'

'I-I... Amelia came to see me yesterday, and she said your mum—'

'You should nae be listening to her, should you?' he says, his lip curling into a sneer, pulling me even closer. He's taller than me, stronger, and I can't push him away despite trying. 'I'm my mother's point of contact and you should be going through me before seeing her.'

'What's the issue, Morgan?' I ask, managing to lever an arm between us and loosen his grip enough to slip out of his grasp. 'Your mum is my patient—'

He jabs a finger in the air in front of my face and instinctively I want to take another step back but the standing stone is hemmed in by a metal railing and I've nowhere to go. 'You've no business seeing my mother without me. Right!'

'If she's ill, surely you—'

'It's none of your damn business!'

'Okay... I was doing my job,' I argue, reassured that he's no longer trying to manhandle me. 'I am trying to help.'

'Just stay away from us unless I say otherwise, or—'

'What's going on here then?' We both look to the approaching PC McLean, and I'm grateful for his timely arrival. Morgan immediately takes a half-step backwards, putting a little space between us. 'Well?' the constable asks.

'Morgan is a bit upset,' I say, once again sweeping my hair away from my face. Both of my hands are out of my pockets now, just in case I need to protect myself. I don't remember doing it though.

'Is he now?' Ian asks, raising an eyebrow at Morgan. 'What about?'

I am conciliatory. 'I r-really don't know.'

'Aye, it's nothing right enough,' Morgan says, shifting his weight between his feet. He seems much less aggressive now there's a police presence, or is it the male presence? 'Just a difference of opinion.'

'No need to be all feisty then, is there?' Ian says with an air of authority. I'm not sure at what point in this altercation he arrived. Morgan is a few years younger than Ian McLean, who is approaching retirement, but Morgan is not inclined to argue. His eyes dart nervously towards me and away again.

'I guess not, no,' Morgan replies, backing up further. I don't have anything to add, and I'm relieved to see him walk back to his car and get in. It doesn't stop him glaring at me as he starts the car and drives away, the front wheels squealing momentarily as they spin on the damp tarmac under the acceleration.

'He's a character,' Ian says wistfully, watching the car make a U-turn and head back the way he must have come from, towards his home in Cabrach. 'Something of a hothead, you might say.'

'That's one description. I wonder what pushes his buttons?'

'I don't think he's all there, that man,' Ian says thoughtfully. 'Relatively harmless, though. All bluff and bluster.'

'Relatively is doing a lot of the heavy lifting in that statement.'

'Aye, but they've been a strange family as far back as I've known them.'

'The Allens?'

He nods. 'Old Mhari is an odd sort. She loves her wildlife, especially the birds,' he says solemnly. 'So much so that she's been known to leave surprises out for the neighbour's cats every once in a while.' He taps the side of his nose with his forefinger.

'And by surprises... you mean?'

'Poison pellets. Wrapped in slices of ham.'

'That's awful!'

He nods again. 'Isn't it? I could never catch her doing it, but everyone knows right enough. And' – he gestures with a pointed finger in the direction of Morgan's car almost out of sight now – 'you've already experienced your man there.'

'I always thought he really cared for his mum.'

'Hmm. I'm not so sure. Same goes for that daughter of hers, Amelia. There's not a lot of love lost there either.' He sighs. 'Although, to be fair, the old bird has lost some of her edge in recent times.'

'Since she got ill?'

'I would say so,' Ian says. 'Not that I think either sibling is going to miss her when she passes, as awful a thing as that is to say.'

Ian glances sideways at me with a half-smile, just as Morgan's car disappears around the bend. Suddenly, I feel self-conscious about talking to the island's only policeman, looking around to see if anyone is observing us.

EIGHTEEN

Inside the safety of my own home, I lock the kitchen door. My hands are shaking after the confrontation with Morgan Allen. He caught me so much off guard that it's only now that the shock is manifesting. Ian McLean can't have seen the worst of it otherwise he'd have intervened more forcefully. At least, I think he would. Mind you, Ian is close to retirement and I'm not sure how he'd have coped if Morgan had turned on him.

The last thing I need is a policeman taking a statement from me. Me talking to the police would be around the island like wildfire, and I can't risk that. My eyes lift to the cupboard above the fridge freezer. I shouldn't. I can't. I need to focus.

But I find myself staring at the cupboard, my mouth dry. *I shouldn't.* Two steps. That's all it took, two short steps and I'm on my tiptoes, my hand reaching for the bottle. Bringing down the bottle, I hastily pick up a glass from the drainer. I'm deliberately not thinking about what I'm doing, as if it's not a conscious decision. I'm in denial, but I don't care.

Pulling out a chair at the table, I sit down with the glass and the bottle of gin set down in front of me. Only now do I take pause, staring at the bottle. It looks like water, the gift of life, but of course it's not. The contents are the destroyer of lives. My phone beeps and at first I ignore it but then it beeps again. Without taking my eyes from the bottle, I reach into my pocket and take out my phone.

Have you broken the seal yet?

Damn him! I look over my shoulder towards the nearest window, but no one is there. The hillside stretches up from the back of the house and all I can see are the hardy grasses fluttering in the wind.

You are craving the warm embrace of an old friend, aren't you, Kelly? It calls to you like the unrequited desire for a past lover.

I furiously type out a reply. *What would you know about it?* I stare at the message box, waiting for the reply but there's no sign of one. *Where are you?!* I type. *I know you're watching me.* I wait but he still doesn't reply. Picking up the bottle, I unscrew the cap and pour a large measure of gin into the glass. My fingers curl around the glass and I lift it to my lips, but I hesitate, staring at the contents. My phone beeps again.

It won't take away your pain, Kelly. Only I can do that. I see everything.

I leap out of my chair, knocking it over behind me, and run to the sink throwing the contents of the glass into the drain and running the cold water at full bore. Turning off the tap, I spin round and hurl the glass at the far wall, smashing it and showering the kitchen in shards of crystal. I know he's right. Other than having my daughter home safely, there's nothing else I want more than to have a drink.

But it won't stop with one. It never did.

My eyes search the room now. He knows. How could he know? I'm looking for anything out of place. Any item that stands out. Something in here, in my home, that doesn't belong. Whatever it is, I didn't put it here and someone else did. I'm prowling my kitchen now, examining every container, every box, every shadow where something small can be hidden. It could be the tiniest of holes. I've seen the films and television. Spy cameras embedded in nanny cams, microphones inside everyday devices.

It must be here. It's the only way to explain all of this. I'm opening cupboards, checking everything on or behind other items on shelves, but there's nothing.

'It's here. It must be,' I whisper. My eyes move from the shadows to the light fittings and then the fixtures themselves, wall sockets, the curtain and blinds hanging across the windows. My gaze moves to the ceiling and the smoke alarm. There's one in the kitchen, sitting room and the hallway outside the bedrooms. Righting the chair I knocked over, I place it beneath the smoke alarm in the kitchen and step onto it.

Inspecting the unit, there doesn't appear to be anything untoward about it, but these things are covert for a reason. Stepping down and opening the utensil drawer beside the oven, I gather a rolling pin. Standing beneath the alarm I take a swing at it. It takes three goes before I connect properly and the unit detaches from the ceiling, hanging from the mains electricity cable and dangling above me. I strike it again and the cover breaks off.

Placing the rolling pin on the counter, I stand up on the chair again to examine the interior of the unit. There are no cameras and nothing unusual as far as I can see. My eyes drift to the extractor unit tied into the ventilation and heat recovery system Blair installed. There are vents in every room of the house, either extracting hot, moist air or circulating fresh air.

'I see everything.'

Using my fingertips, I try to prise off the cover to the vent but it's fixed in tightly. It takes some manoeuvring and teasing of the cover plate but it pops off. The silver tube inside disappears into the roof structure but it's too dark to see inside. Grasping the foil, I tug it towards me. There is resistance but I'm not giving in now. Stepping down, I use my bodyweight to pull the ducting down and plasterboard comes down with it, showering me in dust.

There is no camera, but I'm just getting started. Moving into the sitting room, I do exactly the same, smashing the smoke alarm off the ceiling and attacking the vents. There is an air intake in the floor in front of the wood burner, and I set about that too. It is stainless steel and well secured, but it will not beat me.

By the time I've passed through the hallway, mine and Lauren's bedroom, reaching the bathroom I'm in a frenzy and breathing hard.

'You see everything, do you?' I yell at the vents in the ceiling. I'm past doing this carefully and I lash out with no regard for accuracy, attacking the vents, punching holes in the ceiling with my makeshift tool of destruction, sending plastic shards from the vents in every direction. Nothing! There has to be something. In a fit of pique, I hurl the rolling pin away from me and it strikes the mirror hanging behind the basin. The ear-splitting sound is a relief rather than a wake-up call.

I'm standing in the bathroom, my chest heaving as I draw in breath in ragged intakes. I'm sweating. There is plaster and insulation scattered on the floor around me. A scene repeated in every room in the house now. Running a hand through my hair, hanging loose to my shoulders, I catch sight of my reflection in a shard of the broken mirror lying in the basin. My eyes are wild, focused.

What have I become?

A loud bang, followed by another. Someone is hammering

on the back door. Tentatively leaving the bathroom, I peer down the hall towards the kitchen. The inside of the house is much darker now, the sun going down in the early afternoon at this time of year. Edging along the wall, I make my way to the kitchen, hugging the shadows.

I can see the form of a man at the door. He cups his hands against the obscured glass, trying to peer into the interior. It's not Blair, or Donnie for that matter. I wonder if it's Morgan, returning for round two, to finish off what Ian McLean interrupted down at the harbour. The figure steps back and then knocks again.

'Kelly!'

I recognise that voice. I hurry across the kitchen to the door as the shape retreats from it. Unlocking the door, I yank it open. 'Niall!' He is surprised, turning on his heel and smiling. As soon as he takes in my appearance, the smile rapidly fades.

'Kelly?' my husband asks, slowly walking towards me. I surprise him further by throwing myself into his arms, knocking him off balance. An awkward moment follows before he encompasses me with those muscular arms of his, drawing me into him. Now I feel safe. At last, I feel safe.

NINETEEN

Niall sits me down at the kitchen table and fetches me a glass of water, setting it down on the table before me. His eyes go to the bottle of gin and he puts the cap back on, screws it tight and removes the bottle, placing it down on the counter. He turns his back to it, folding his arms across his chest and studies me. He looks older, tired. There's been a lot going on these past few years. I guess it's taken its toll.

'Since when have you started drinking again?' he asks. I don't want to meet his eye. I can feel his scorn, his judgement.

'I'm not.'

He snorts derisively. 'Looks like it.'

'Why did you come?'

Stepping away from the counter, Niall pulls out another chair at the table and sits down. Taking a deep breath, he rests his elbows on the table, balls his hands together and rests his chin on them. 'I had to come.'

'Why?'

'Because... of how you were on the phone. You didn't seem right somehow.' I slowly nod my head. That moment of security I found in his embrace has passed and now he is a threat. Not necessarily to me, but certainly to my daughter. 'What's going on with you?'

'Nothing,' I whisper. I still don't want to meet his gaze, but he remains as he was, stoically watching me. In the corner of my eye, I see him look around the room. The decimation is obvious. I've torn my home apart looking for hidden cameras, and I found nothing.

'How much have you had to drink?'

Now I glare at him. 'I told you. I haven't had a drink.' His eyes flick to the bottle on the counter and I acquiesce, inclining my head. 'Yet. I was about to and changed my mind.'

'I'm pleased to hear it.'

'I haven't had a drink in eighteen months.'

'And yet you keep a bottle here for what? Emergencies?'

'I was in the Guides back in the day. Preparation for every eventuality is key.' My tongue-in-cheek sarcasm is wasted on him, and Niall takes a deep breath.

Niall looks around the room, and I can see he's trying to understand how I've come to wreck my house so comprehensively. 'I love what you've done with the place.'

I force a rueful smile. 'Yes, it's not been achieved without a great deal of effort.'

'Kelly—'

My mobile, lying on the table, rings and I see it is Ava. Moving my forefinger to the screen, I decline the call with a gentle tap.

'Friend of yours?' Niall asks.

'Colleague.'

He exhales, his forehead creased. 'How is Lauren?'

'What?' I ask, my head snapping up, my focus zeroed in on him.

'How is she?' I cock my head. 'You said she was sick.'

'Right,' I say, shaking my head and wincing involuntarily. 'I did say that, didn't I. She's much better.'

'Is she here? Can I go and see her?' Niall makes to stand up.

'No, she's not here. She's out.'

'Where?'

'Out with friends.'

'When will she be back this evening?'

'I don't know,' I say, my mind whirring. 'I think she said something about staying out tonight.'

Niall sits back in his seat and lifts one foot up, resting it on the other knee. 'Wow, Kelly Murray allowing her daughter to stay out overnight. Things have changed.'

'Howlett.'

'What's that?'

I heave a sigh. 'I go by Howlett these days.'

'Is that right?' he asks, disappointed.

'I thought it would be easier,' I say glumly. 'You know, avoid confusion once things are finally settled.'

'Is that why you're keeping Lauren from me too, to avoid confusion?'

'I'm doing no such thing—'

'Oh really? It seems like it to me.'

'Oh, stop being such a child, Niall. You know where she is. You could have seen her at any time.'

'I gave you your space,' he counters, 'just as you asked me to. I didn't realise you were going to cut me out of your life like I never existed.'

'Please don't be so dramatic. I have other things going on. Things... you don't understand.'

'Try me!' he says, dropping his leg and sitting forward, elbows on knees, looking at me earnestly. I shake my head.

Someone arrives at the back door and knocks. Niall gets up and hastens over to open it, but only a little. 'Oh, hello.' Ava's voice carries to me. 'I was looking for Doctor Kelly.'

'I'm afraid Kelly isn't up to receiving visitors just now,' Niall says calmly.

'Oh. It's only that she has patients—'

'Probably best if you reschedule them,' Niall says.

'I see.' Ava is unconvinced. 'And, could I ask who—'

'I'm her husband, Niall.'

'Oh, right,' Ava says and her tone lifts as the reply lands. 'Oh! You're Niall.'

'That's right. And you are?'

'Ava. I work for Doctor Kelly, in reception.'

'Terrific,' Niall says in that jovial, incredibly artificial way that no one seems to pick up as inauthentic. 'You'll be able to take care of things then?'

'Ah, yes. I suppose I can.'

'Great. I'll let you get on then,' Niall says, smiling and leaning on the door frame. Ava's silhouette appears to be trying to see inside, but Niall is having none of it. I'm happy for him to fob her off, although I feel a little guilty about it.

'Okay, well do let Kelly know I called round, and she can always call me if she needs anything.'

'Right you are,' Niall says, waving her goodbye and closing the door.

Once I'm happy Ava will have gone, I get up from my chair and rush around the kitchen and sitting room, closing the curtains and lowering the blinds.

'What are you doing?' Niall asks, turning on the nearest lights to him. It might be the way the spotlights illuminate his face, but he looks drawn, dare I say haggard.

'I just...' I don't honestly know what to say. I don't want anyone to know he's here. There's no bug in the room though, I checked everywhere. Ava knows, but that's fine. I doubt she'll gossip about me. I sit back down, exhaling heavily after that little burst of exercise. Niall is perplexed.

'What's got into you?'

I ignore the question and fix him with a firm look. 'Listen, I'm pleased you care enough to come and see me, but I'm

clearly... um,' – I look around the room and the notion is prepos-
terous, but I have to go with it – 'doing okay. And, like I said,
Lauren won't be home tonight.'

'I'll see her tomorrow then.'

'Tomorrow? Right.'

'That's okay, isn't it?'

'Sure,' I say. After all, I can hardly say no. 'Where are you
staying?'

'That's a good point,' he says, scratching his head. 'Do you
have the number for a hotel?'

I laugh drily. 'Sure.' I pick up my mobile, open a web
browser and, seconds later, turn the screen towards him and
slide it across the table in his direction. He leans forward and
looks at it. His eyes lift to meet mine with a quizzical look.

'There's one hotel?'

I purse my lips and nod. 'One hotel, one pub and one road
in and out.'

He blows out his cheeks, tapping the phone number of the
hotel into his mobile. Standing up, he walks through into the
sitting room to make the call. I let out a deep sigh.

I get a dustpan and brush from under the sink and set about
sweeping up the shards of broken glass from where I hurled a
glass at the wall earlier. It's a start. I don't want Lauren to come
back home to this.

Niall's voice is muffled, and I poke my head around the
corner to make sure he hasn't gone off exploring the rest of the
house. He hasn't though. He's standing at the window overlooking the front of the house.

It isn't long before he's walking back into the kitchen, whilst
I'm tipping the broken glass into the bin. 'Not good.'

'What isn't?' I ask, turning to face him.

'There are no rooms at the inn.'

'Really? It's winter; they can't be that busy.'

Niall is glum. 'Decorating a number of rooms. They might have something for me tomorrow.'

'And what about tonight?' He seems apologetic, putting his hands into his pockets, his lips pursed. 'Hell no.'

'What?' he asks innocently.

I shake my head. 'Not here. You can't stay here.'

He splays his arms and hands wide. 'I didn't ask, but now you mention it—'

'No!'

'It's one night!' he says, frowning and looking around the room. 'And I could help you tidy up a bit.'

'No.'

'I'll make dinner. Come on,' he says earnestly. 'It's not like we haven't shared space before.' I close my eyes. What am I going to do, make him sleep in his car? Wouldn't that look even more suspicious to the kidnapper? Niall can see me waning, and he smiles, his eyes gleaming. 'Come on, one night. What could possibly happen?'

I exhale deeply. 'One night, but you stay out of my way—'

'I promise,' he says, grinning. 'I can sleep in Lauren's bed.'

'No, you get to sleep on the sofa.'

'Right. Sofa it is,' he says. 'Any special requests for dinner this evening? Depending on what you have in,' he says, opening the fridge and perusing the contents. 'Sheesh. I suppose there's not a lot of variety here in the outback.'

'It's not that bad.'

'Yes, I'm sure I can rustle up... something.'

I'm too exhausted to argue, but I know I'll have to think of something. Fast. Niall has to go. He shouldn't be here. This is putting Lauren's life at risk.

TWENTY

Niall is going through the kitchen gathering together ingredients and exploring what kit I have to aid him. One thing he always impressed me with was his ability to cook. I've dated men in the past who knew their way around a kitchen and had, perhaps, one or two more complicated recipes in their arsenal to roll out when the occasion suited.

Niall is different though. The complete modern man. Self-sufficient, impressive and yet he has that air of vulnerability but not in a cringe-making, pathetic way, but a man in touch with his emotions. In a world of alpha and beta males, Niall is a sigma. In my experience, they are rare.

'So, tell me about life on the island,' he says, concentrating on chopping his selection of vegetables.

'I'm going for a shower before dinner.'

'Take your time. You have half an hour.'

If he is disappointed at my departure, missing out on the opportunity to learn about my new life, then he doesn't show it. I know his interest is genuine. What I don't know is why he's still interested. Surely he doesn't still harbour ideas of reconciliation? I think we are beyond that.

In the bathroom, I lock the door behind me. The lock is stiff because we hardly ever use it. Lauren and I respect each other's privacy, and we don't need a barrier to maintain that. Although, thinking about what I found in her diary, perhaps I've given her too much space. Maybe I've relied on the relative sanctuary of the island, the perception of isolation being a good thing when it was simply a mirage.

I set the water temperature cooler than usual. I need to be refreshed, remain alert. But even once this is over, I'm not sure I'll ever be able to properly relax again. Leaning forward with my hands on the tiled wall, cold water running over my head and down my face, I close my eyes and try to regulate my breathing.

Opening my eyes, I see the water reaching the lip of the shower tray and I frantically turn the water off before it overflows. 'Damn it, Blair!' I say, levering the silver drain cover up with my toe and shifting it to the side. Then someone knocks on the bathroom door as I step out and wrap myself in a towel.

'Ten-minute warning!' Niall says.

'Okay, thanks.'

Hearing him move away from the door, I run my hand across the mirror behind the basin, studying my reflection again. Should I say something to Niall? Would he understand what I have to do and help me, or do something else? If he chose to take control of the situation, by definition I would lose it. I know he cares for Lauren, he loves her like a daughter, but would he kill for her?

Staring at myself, I believe I can't answer that question. Only he could. I know how I feel about it. Lauren is worth more to me than anyone else, even an innocent. I don't know if I can live with myself for doing something so awful, but I'll do it if it brings my daughter home safely. Then it will be my burden to carry.

Opening the bathroom door, I peer down the corridor and

dart across into my bedroom, my bath towel around my naked body. Pulling on a clean pair of jeans and a white T-shirt, I towel dry my hair and return to the kitchen. I can't quite believe what greets me when I walk in, though.

The small table, usually pushed against the back wall has been brought to the centre of the room, a clean tablecloth has been draped over it and there are two place settings. In the centre of the table is a candle, standing in a ramekin, the flame flickering gently.

'What is this?' I ask.

Niall glances over his shoulder, stirring something on the hob.

'Dinner,' he says, smiling. Seeing my expression, he removes the pan from the heat, sliding it across the hob and raising his hands to placate me. 'I wanted to thank you for letting me stay over—'

'On the sofa.'

'Yes, on the sofa,' he repeats, looking sheepish. He raises his eyebrows. 'Look, don't read anything into it, I just thought it might be nice, that's all.'

'If you say *for old times' sake*, I will brain you with that pan.' I point to the hot pan behind him. Something smells good, to be fair, and I haven't eaten all day. Even if I tell myself I have no appetite, my body says otherwise.

'Can we just eat?' Niall asks, looking around at the stir fry he's prepped. 'If we don't eat it soon, it'll be too dry.'

'Fine,' I say, pulling out a chair.

Niall grins. 'I found the candle in a plastic tub underneath the sink.'

'It's in case of blackouts.' I pick up the jug of water and pour myself a glass. Niall notices and looks towards the other glass and I pour him one as well.

Niall exhales. 'That happen often, the power outages?'

'This is the west coast, on the Atlantic,' I say. 'It happens until the linesmen can get out here and sort things out.'

'I can't remember the last power cut we had in Edinburgh,' he says, plating up.

'No, I think it's against the city council regulations.'

'Haha,' Niall says, placing a plate in front of me. It really does smell delicious, and my mouth is watering. An image of Lauren leaps into my mind as a gust of wind pummels the house. Niall glances at the window. 'Things are picking up out there again.'

I don't reply, picking up my fork and absently playing with the noodles and the vegetables on the plate, pushing them around. When did Lauren last eat? Will he be feeding her, and keeping her warm? I hope God is watching over her, if God is there. Toying with the crucifix I still wear on a chain around my neck, but like so many people these days, the conviction I hold in my faith is little more than a box I tick on a government form than a real belief. Niall sits down opposite me.

'Since when did you turn to the dark side?'

'What?' I ask, looking at him, puzzled. He nods at my pendant.

'When did I return to the church, is that what you are asking?'

'Aye,' he says, forking a mouthful of noodles from his plate. 'You never struck me as the type.'

'We married in church.'

'But only because my mother insisted,' Niall counters. He's right. I was never an avid churchgoer, at least not in adulthood.

'I'm not sure I ever left,' I say quietly. 'And after' – my eyes flick to meet his and away again – 'everything... I felt the need to go back. I'm glad I did.'

'Do a lot of people go to service in these parts? Is it like Stornoway and all the Wee Frees?'

I shake my head at the reference. The staunch views of

those inhabiting the Isles of Lewis and Harris are legendary. 'No, it's not like that. There is a real sense of community here.'

'We had that back home—'

'It's different. Here, no one else is coming to save you. The islanders can count on one another. We're all we've got. It's the way it has to be.'

'Very prophetic,' Niall says and I glare at him. I catch his eye and he looks awkward. 'No offence, but it sounds almost like a standalone—'

'Island,' I finish for him. 'That's exactly what it is. Everyone counts on the island and we manage things ourselves, together, otherwise it falls apart.'

'Kelly?'

I look up. Niall is watching me intently, slowly chewing a mouthful of food. 'What?'

'You drifted away there.'

'Sorry,' I say, lifting my fork and struggling to load food onto it. My hands are shaking and I drop both knife and fork. They clatter against the plate and the table surface.

'Are you all right?'

'Yes!' I hiss at him and Niall is taken aback, sitting open-mouthed. Putting a hand across my mouth I take a breath.

'Sorry I asked,' Niall says quietly. The back door opens and we both look around. Hughie stops when he sees Niall, his eyes darting to me. I can't get an accurate read on his expression: shock, horror, or a combination of both, maybe.

'Oh!' Hughie says. 'I-I didn't realise you... um...'

Niall sets his fork down and sits back in his seat, folding his arms across his chest. His expression is readable. Surprise. I get up from my seat, the legs scraping on the tiled floor. 'Hughie, this...' – I look at my husband, for now at least, watching me intently – 'is Niall.'

Hughie gathers himself and steps forward, offering Niall his hand. Niall rises and accepts. They shake, if a little stiffly.

'Niall, pleased to meet you. Hughie,' he says, forcing a polite greeting. He feels awkward, and so do I.

'My pleasure,' Niall says. 'You...'

'Oh, I live next door,' Hughie says, thumbing over his shoulder and avoiding eye contact with him. His eyes flick up briefly. 'And you?'

'I'm Kelly's husband.'

Hughie exhales and snorts in surprise. He looks directly at Niall now, and I think he's trying to ascertain if Niall is messing around. Clearly not. 'Husband? Right...'

'Soon to be ex-husband,' I say pointedly, but it doesn't seem to cut much ice with Hughie.

'I... should probably go,' Hughie says, looking at the table. His eyes move around the room, but he doesn't want to look at me either. 'Let you guys finish dinner.'

I follow his gaze to where it's lingering on the candle. I lean over and blow it out, much to Niall's amusement. 'Hughie, this isn't what it looks like.'

'Aye... okay,' he says, frowning. 'I think it looks like dinner.' His brow furrows deeper still. 'Husband and wife dinner, I guess.'

I reach for Hughie's arm, but he draws it away from me. 'I wasn't expecting him.' I look at Niall. 'He came over to see Lauren—'

'But Lauren is on the mainland,' Hughie says. Niall can't help himself and he chuckles, apparently quite pleased that his presence has disconcerted Hughie. He soon falls silent after drawing a glare from me and an embarrassed look from Hughie. 'I should go.'

'No, wait—'

'No, I really have to go,' Hughie says and he turns, making for the door and a swift exit. I follow him but he's outside and off into the darkness before I can catch him.

Closing the door, I shut my eyes, silently cursing. Niall

clears his throat and I slowly turn to look at him, quelling my anger especially when I see his amused expression. 'Don't say—'

'I won't say a word,' Niall replies, a darkness descending over his face. 'At least now I know what you meant by *moving on.*'

'We're friends.'

'You might want to mention that to farmer Fred next door. Nice boots he had on, by the way.'

'He's a decent man,' I snap.

'And I'm not, is that what you're saying?'

'*You ruined* the life we had.'

Niall looks away, wincing at the comment. I fold my arms across my chest, leaning against the door. I don't want to sit down again. Niall takes a deep breath, exhaling slowly. 'I don't think we should go over old ground. It'll do neither of us any good.'

'On that, we can agree,' I tell him quietly.

'But let's not forget *we both* played our part in what happened.'

'So much for not going over old ground, huh?' I say, striding past him. 'Enjoy the rest of your meal. You'll find fresh linen in the hallway cupboard.'

'Kelly...' Niall says as I pass, but I'm through with him for one night. I don't have the energy anymore.

TWENTY-ONE
TWO YEARS PREVIOUSLY

'They're still there,' Niall says. 'Scum.' I glance towards him and away again, but I don't comment. What am I supposed to say? Everyone is speaking for me lately.

'They're just doing their jobs.'

Niall scoffs. 'You're defending them?'

'No, far from it, but we all have to make a living.'

My husband turns his gaze back through the slats, looking down on the throng lining the pavement. 'They've been there for two days now. I thought the rain might drive them away, but they're still there.'

'Yes, they're not leaving without their pound of flesh.'

Niall glances over at me before raising the tilt rod on the plantation shutters and closing them. I lift my knees up onto the sofa before me, hugging them tightly.

'You aren't looking so great,' he says, walking across the sitting room to the other window where he glances down into the street before closing those shutters as well. The room is made darker, although he quickly switches on a couple of lamps which complement the glow from the fireplace.

'Thanks,' I say, staring straight ahead at some random point on the wall. Of course they're still there. There's no greater draw than the hint of scandal to bring them all to your door. Unless the news cycle moves on – perhaps the result of a royal birth or a celebrity death – they won't be going anywhere anytime soon.

'I'm sorry,' Niall says, glancing at the space on the sofa beside me. He doesn't come to sit with me though. He won't extend his compassion to showing me physical support or affection. 'I just meant—'

'I know what you meant.'

I look a sight. I'm well aware. My scalp is itching and my hair feels greasy. I haven't showered in days and I'm wearing the same clothes I was wearing yesterday, possibly before that too. I've lost track. I haven't felt sunlight on my face or the freedom of breathing fresh air outdoors since Monday when I caught the photographer using my neighbour's house to get a picture of me.

It's reassuring to see how people will sell out someone's privacy for a few pounds.

The front door opens and raised voices carry from the media scrum on the pavement outside. The door slams, echoing through the marble-lined atrium of our townhouse and both Niall and I look to the doorway. Lauren comes into view, walking into the room with full-on negative energy. I can't tell if she's angry or upset, possibly both. Niall crosses the room towards her, but she raises a hand to stop him coming closer.

'I'm sorry, love,' I tell her.

'Is there anything we can do?' Niall asks. She looks between us dispassionately.

'I think the two of you have done enough already!'

'Hey! That's not on,' Niall says after her as our daughter turns and stalks from the room.

'Leave it,' I say but he doesn't. It's not in his nature to allow anyone, let alone our teenage daughter, to speak to him that way. He follows her into the atrium. 'Lauren! Come back here this instant!'

'Go to hell!' she screams, before running upstairs. I close my eyes, trying to shut out the images of what I know is outside on the pavement, waiting for anyone who comes to or leaves the house, and the pain my family is going through. Niall walks back into the room, gesticulating over his shoulder towards the door.

'Can you believe that?'

'She's feeling the strain.'

'We're all feeling the strain,' he says, crossing to the sideboard and overturning a crystal tumbler before taking the stopper from the decanter.

'It's a little early,' I say.

Niall snorts and pours himself a two-finger measure.

'That's rich.' He's right. I've been on it a bit too much lately, but can anyone blame me? I'm a prisoner in my own home. We all are. The stabbing pains behind my eyes are back, and applying pressure to my closed eyelids doesn't release the tension anymore. The phone rings and Niall looks to me, but I don't move. There's no way I'm answering it. 'I'll answer it then, shall I?'

I nod, ignoring his blatant sarcasm and he leaves the room. His voice is muffled but I can tell by the tone he's not happy with the caller. I don't wish to hear another request for comment or to be interviewed. The call goes on too long though; Niall would have hung up by now.

Moments later, he is at the doorway, the phone in his hand but the mouthpiece is covered.

'It's a representative from the MPS—'

'Who?'

'The Medical Protection Soc—'

'I'm not interested.'

'But they only want—' I get up from the sofa and walk out of the room, pushing past a frustrated Niall.

'I told you, I don't want to speak to anyone.' I climb the stairs and increase my speed, feeling his eyes upon my back. He returns to the caller making some mumbled excuse as to why I can't come to the phone.

Once on the landing, I approach Lauren's bedroom door. Knocking gently, I don't get a response from inside. With my face close to the door, I knock again.

'Lauren, honey. Please can I speak to you?' I listen, but she still doesn't reply and I can't hear anything from inside. I crack the door open and peer through the gap. She's lying on her bed with her headphones on. I push the door open and smile forlornly at her. She looks at me with an impassive expression.

I close the door and walk over to her, perching myself on the edge of the bed beside her, placing a hand on her thigh. She presses pause on her mobile phone streaming service and removes the headphones, folding her arms across her chest. She is less defiant than when she first arrived home. Just as I've always said, she's mostly all show.

'It won't always be like this, you know?' She nods and she's looking at me through glassy eyes. 'It will get better. I promise.'

'I just want things to go back to how they were,' she says, tears falling.

'I know you do, darling. Me too.'

I open my arms and draw her into me. She puts her head on my shoulder and it's like she's a little girl again.

She is my little girl though, and always will be.

I'm so relieved she's letting me hold her like this because since it happened, she's been avoiding me and she's had this look in her eyes. I've caught it a few times, before she glances away.

Like I'm a monster.

Like she believes them.

TWENTY-TWO

DAY THREE | PRESENT DAY

I find Niall in the kitchen, standing over the hob once again. The aroma of frying bacon is in the air and bagels pop up from the toaster as I enter. Niall smiles at me, stirring the scrambled eggs to stop them from sticking to the pan. How would he behave if he knew what was going on, what was really at stake here? Not this casual or pleased with himself, I'll bet. What is this anyway, some attempt at teenage seduction? He has to leave.

'Good morning, sleepyhead,' he says. I did sleep, it's true, but the last thing I remember was thinking about Lauren. I didn't think I was ever going to sleep again but I should know, better than most, that the body manages to circumvent trauma even if the mind has no intention of doing so.

'Good morning.'

'Come on, you can make more of an effort than that,' Niall says lightly. I purse my lips, and he inclines his head. 'I guess not. Take a seat; breakfast is ready.'

I sit down at the table. He must have cleaned up last night after I stormed out because the kitchen – and I glance through into the sitting room – and the entire downstairs, it seems, is immaculate. Niall always has been an obsessive. At least, when it comes to presentation.

He puts a plate in front of me. Scrambled eggs and crispy bacon on top of a cinnamon bagel, and all I can think is that Lauren would love this.

When she gets back home, I'm going to make this.

'Hey, I tried calling Lauren—'

'You did what?' I ask sharply. He puts a pan into the bowl in the sink, already filled with soapy water, and looks at me.

'I called Lauren.'

'I told you she was at a friend's place.'

'Overnight,' he counters, 'but it's morning. I wanted to let her know I was on the island.'

'Right.' He is staring at me with a peculiar look on his face. 'Right,' I say again, slowly. 'What... um... did she say?' I ask.

'I didn't get an answer, but I left a message and told her I was at the house and if she—'

'You said what?' I ask, coughing up the egg that I'd just swallowed.

'That I was here, at the house.' He seems puzzled.

'Why? W-Why would you say that?'

His eyebrows knit together. '*Because* I'm here... at the house!'

I nod, pinching the bridge of my nose between thumb and forefinger. 'You... er... need to leave, Niall.'

'I will,' he says, 'as soon as I see Lauren—'

'No, you need to go. Now.'

'What?'

'I can't explain, but you just do. Can you take my word for it?' He looks at me, incredulous, but I'm not backing down. 'I mean it, you have to leave.'

Niall seems ready to argue but I stare at him, unflinching.

'Fine!' he says, drying his hands on a tea towel and tossing it onto the counter. 'I'll do just that. Boyfriend coming round again, is he?'

I want to explain, to make him see I have no choice but I can't.

There's a knock on the back door and I get up, opening the door to find Blair with a bleary-eyed Donnie standing behind him. He smiles apologetically. 'Sorry about yesterday, Doctor Kelly.'

'Yesterday?'

'Aye, not showing up as expected in the afternoon,' Blair says, looking past me and obviously seeing Niall. 'Something came up, and I had to be someplace else.'

'It doesn't matter. You're here now.'

'So, you don't mind us being here?'

'Why would I?'

He frowns. 'It being the weekend and all. Some people like a break from the noise when they're not working.'

'It's Saturday,' I say and Blair nods, glancing back at his son.

'And I had to make enough noise to raise the dead to get this one out of his pit this morning!' Donnie shifts his weight, uncomfortable in the background.

'Mind? No... I guess not.'

'Unless you have plans?' Blair asks, nodding a greeting to Niall, who has returned to the kitchen, a gym bag slung over one shoulder.

'Oh, don't mind me,' Niall says. 'I'm just her husband.'

I could swing for him for saying that. Blair is surprised, but he tries his best to conceal it. 'Ah, right you are. I'm here to work on the house.' It's as if they are talking through me.

'You don't need to explain anything to Niall; he's just leaving.'

'That's right,' Niall says. 'No explanations necessary. Ever!' I roll my eyes and glare at him. 'Any chance you can fix the plumbing? The shower is proper backing up, and I couldn't loosen the blockage with the plunger I found in the cleaning cupboard—'

'Blair is quite capable, Niall.'

Blair nods. 'Aye, first order of business.'

'Good, thanks. I'll not keep you then,' I say, closing the door.

'Right, we'll be away to fetch our tools...' Blair says, angling his head towards the ever-decreasing gap between door and frame. Once it's closed, I turn to Niall.

'Look, I'm sorry. You just showing up... has thrown me, that's all. I wasn't expecting it.'

'That's my fault,' he says softly. 'I'm sorry.'

Taking a deep breath, he placates me with a conciliatory look. 'Can I just use your bathroom before I go?' I nod and he walks out.

Running a hand through my hair, the day ahead is clear. This is my final day to do as I've been instructed. To kill someone, the 'right' person, and to get my daughter back. My mobile phone beeps and I scoop it up.

You have company, Kelly. I hope you remember the rules?

'What is it?' Niall says returning to the kitchen and reading my expression.

'Nothing.'

'You look like you've seen a ghost.'

'It's nothing!'

He's irritated by my response, and now I see the folded newspaper in his hand. He holds it aloft.

'Seeing as you are being the way you are with me, I shouldn't be surprised that you came across to Edinburgh and didn't let me know you were in town last month.'

My eyes narrow. 'What?'

'This paper, it's a month old, and I'm pretty sure you got it in the Edinburgh area, seeing as I doubt they distribute all the way across to Jura.'

'What's your point?'

'This,' he says, unfolding it and slamming it down on the table. I can see the headline, the story that the paper is folded to. *Search for Missing Leith Teenager Intensifies*. 'I thought you came here to move on, Kelly? And yet, here she is, still front and centre: Freya McLaren.'

My phone beeps again and I glance at it, firmly gripped in my hand. Niall follows my eye. 'Is that going to be something more important?'

'I-I don't know.'

He exhales deeply, picking up his bag and making for the door. 'Please let Lauren know I'm here. I'll be at the hotel in town. If they haven't got a room for me, I'll sleep in my car in the car park.'

'Niall...'

He passes me and wrenches open the back door, leaving without another word. I don't have time to deal with this. Lauren is all I can focus on now. I open the message.

I think you need to be reminded of how serious this is...

No, I don't! I'm well aware. I abandon the typing and call Lauren's number instead, willing him to pick up. The call rings but directs to voicemail just as it had when Niall called her earlier. I leave a message. 'I've not said anything to anyone. I want my daughter back, so you don't need to punish her. I'll do what you ask!' I hang up, waiting anxiously for a reply, but nothing comes through.

The worst images my subconscious can imagine spring to mind, my daughter suffering at the hands of a monster. I'm startled when my mobile rings, a call from within the messaging app.

Tentatively, I answer in both relief and trepidation. 'Hello.'

A distorted, somehow disembodied voice speaks to me slowly. 'You are short on time, Kelly. Lauren is short on time. It's time for you to decide who deserves to die. Because you've done it once before, haven't you, dear...'

'W-What did you say?'

'You've made that choice once before, haven't you, Kelly?'

TWENTY-THREE
TWO YEARS PREVIOUSLY

'Come on, Freya, stay with me!' I say to myself more than to the girl lying prostrate before me. 'Give me something to work with, love!'

'She's breathing!' I hear someone say behind me. It might be Niall but I don't look round.

'Come on!' I repeat, willing her to come back to me. Leaning forward, I pinch her nostrils and blow a short breath in through her mouth. 'Quiet!' I yell to no one in particular. Most people are silent anyway, watching in abject horror as I try to resuscitate their friend. My ear is almost against Freya's mouth, but no sound or air escapes.

She's still not breathing. Hurriedly locating the end of her breastbone, where the ribs come together, I put two fingers at the edge of it and then place the heel of my free hand above my fingers. Stacking my other hand on top, interlocking the fingers, I begin chest compressions, trying to restart her heart. 'Don't do this to me, Freya,' I whisper, feeling sweat soaking my blouse now with all the effort.

The sun is beating down. It's a fine Edinburgh day in early summer. I can still smell the aroma of barbecued meat, smell the chlorine from the water on the clothes of those kneeling around me.

'Mum... you've got to bring her back.' Lauren is in tears, sitting on her heels, both hands across her mouth as if in prayer.

'Bonnie's stopped breathing,' Niall says, but I ignore him. 'Kelly!' He grabs my arm, tugging on it and pulling me off balance. 'Kelly, she's not breathing!'

I yank my arm away from him and continue working on Freya.

'Ambulance is on the way!' someone shouts. It's one of Lauren's friends but I don't know which.

'Kelly!' Niall shouts at me now, trying to grasp my arm again to get my attention. I shrug him off, but he persists, pulling me away from Freya.

'Get off me!' I scream at him, throwing myself back to Freya and blowing air into her lungs one more time.

'What do I do?' Niall exclaims and now I look at him, my face side on to Freya's mouth as I listen for any sign of exhalation. I ignore my husband, even as he stares at me. 'Kelly, what do I do?'

Resuming my work on Freya's chest, Lauren is almost hysterical now and, in my peripheral vision, I can see those gathered around us consoling one another, crying, or staring like people do when they pass a car crash on the motorway, watching on with morbid fascination, frozen in both time and space.

Freya is dripping wet, a pool of water forming around her body, and I can see Lauren has a gash on her forearm. Presumably she received that whilst they were all dragging and lifting Freya from the pool.

The music is still playing, 'Celebration' by Kool and the Gang. Irony. No one has thought to turn it off yet, and the upbeat melodic tune and lyrics blare out from the bar on the far side of the pool.

The celebration is over. The euphoria of graduation tempered by a harsh reality. Their friends are dying.

'Kelly!' Niall hisses at me and I glare at him. He is wet through, having been one of the first to throw himself into the water to play the hero. It is what he would do, a selfless act to save another. My rock. My hero. My husband.

But I hate him.

Our eyes meet and he reads my expression, and I swear that only at this very moment, he understands.

One moment that will change everything, almost in the blink of an eye. Our life together. Our marriage. Our family. What did he think was going to happen? That we would continue on with this sham? That we could go on just as before, pretending that nothing had happened? Who would that benefit? Other than Niall, of course.

'Kelly, please!'

Freya gasps, her back arching as she tries to draw breath into drowning lungs, desperate for life. Between Lauren and me, we roll her onto her side. Freya gags, convulses and then vomits water from her insides. Gasping for breath, Lauren moves wet hair aside from Freya's face, whispering soothing, reassuring words to calm her childhood friend.

I look sideways at Niall, and he implores me. Shuffling in my position, I now examine Bonnie. Her skin is pale; her lips have taken on a blue tinge. Feeling for a pulse, there's nothing. Niall's right. She isn't breathing.

'Do something, Kelly, for God's sake!' he says. It will take something of a miracle to bring her back now. But I couldn't have saved them both. Could I?

TWENTY-FOUR
PRESENT DAY

Dropping my mobile, I hear it clatter on the floor. Without thinking, I run for the door, hauling it open and sprint outside, almost colliding with Donnie, who leaps out of my way, startled. Niall is reversing his car back down the drive and his headlights blind me, but I continue on, waving my arms frantically in the air.

The revs drop and the car stops, the windscreen wipers clear the glass and I see him, Niall, leaning forward over the steering wheel, staring at me as I throw myself against the front of the car, slamming my palms down just to emphasise how much I don't want him to leave.

I'm breathing heavily, and I barely notice – nor do I care – that it's raining. The rainfall masks my tears. Niall doesn't switch off the engine, but he releases his seat belt and opens the door. With one hand on the door frame, the other resting on the roof of the car, I can see the concern in his face as he looks at me.

I know now. I understand. We've not been caught up in some crazy drifter's psychotic fantasy. We're not collateral damage in someone else's drama. This isn't even about Lauren, her life or her friends. It isn't about my patients and which of them deserves to die. This is about me.

'Kelly?' Niall asks. I suspect he thinks I'm having some sort of breakdown. Maybe I am, or that will follow.

'I-I... need you,' I say and for a moment we stare at one another. Then he reaches into the car and switches the engine off. The headlights go off leaving only the parking lights on, and we are alone in the darkness. He closes the door and walks around to where I am standing at the front of the car. He opens his arms and I fall into his embrace. 'I need you,' I whisper and he tightens his hold.

'I'm here,' he replies, kissing the top of my head. 'I'm here.'

Blair and Donnie are standing off to the side of Blair's truck, watching us make our way back up the driveway. Niall has an arm around me, and I feel like I've forgotten how to walk or something. My legs are numb. Maybe it's the cold, I'm wet through now, or maybe I'm overwhelmed by the realisation that this is all about the decisions I made, and the consequences of them.

'Maybe you could take the weekend off, after all,' Niall says as we pass. I don't want to look at them. I don't want them to see me for what I really am. These past eighteen months since I came to the island, I've been trying to mould myself into someone who counts, who makes a difference to people's lives.

But it is a charade. A weak pastiche stripped away by a ghost from my past.

'Is... er... everything all right?' Blair asks. I hear the concern in his voice as well as something else. What is it, surprise? No, I think it's fear.

'She'll be fine, don't worry,' Niall says, guiding me past them. Blair doesn't argue, and I hear rather than see the two of them moving across the gravel, followed by the squeak of the door hinges as they get into Blair's truck.

At the back door now, I'm pleased to be back inside, out of

the rain but with support. Niall was everything to me at one time, someone who supported my career and I wouldn't have made it to where I did without him. Now though, he'll have to pick me up again. Steering me to a chair, he pulls it out and I sink into it, staring straight ahead.

Niall notices my mobile on the floor and picks it up, turning it over in his hand, presumably to check if the screen smashed, and finding it in one piece, he puts it in front of me. I'm numb. Completely numb to everything. It's not the cold or the rain. I'm just rinsed out by all of this.

'Are you...' Niall hesitates, dropping to his haunches in front of me and placing his hands gently on my knees. 'Are you going to tell me what's going on, or what?' I don't know what to say, where to begin. My eyes move ever so slightly to the newspaper Niall threw down onto the table. He follows my gaze. 'Freya? She runs away from home and you're back to obsessing about all of that again? We can't be responsible for the girl for the rest of her life. If she runs away, it's none of our concern. Is this about her?'

'I-I don't really know.' My voice is a whisper, but Niall is patient. His brow furrows.

'Then tell me what you do know.'

I look at him, forcing my eyes to focus on his face. He looks tired, worn out himself. He was always so athletic, a mainstay of the gym, with a stunning physique and an angular jaw that could cut paper. I don't think he's working out anywhere near as much now. His hair is greying, and his face is lined, the skin starting to sag. That jawline of his has jowls to it now. He'd have been mortified with that previously. These past two years have been hard on him too.

'Lauren. Someone has Lauren.'

The furrowing of his forehead deepens, his eyes narrowing. 'What?'

'He took her.'

'Who took her?' Niall says, and I can see his mind turning. He's wondering if I've lost the plot completely, come off the rails again like I did before. He didn't catch me last time when I stumbled. If the truth be known, I fell onto him because he was already at rock bottom. We made quite a pair, falling apart while our daughter watched on unable to cope, unable to process what was happening as her safety disappeared in the space of six months.

'I don't know.' I feel his grip tighten on my legs; the penny has dropped. I'm not delusional. I'm not seeking attention. My daughter has been abducted, and I don't know what to do. 'You're hurting me,' I whisper and he releases my legs from his grasp.

'Sorry,' he says quietly, sitting down on the floor, stunned into silence.

'I can get her back,' I whisper, my eyes darting to his face but I think he's been stunned into silence. He's in denial; I can see it in his face.

'Lauren has been abducted?' he asks, and I nod. 'You're joking, right?'

'No—'

'That's ridiculous! Who would do that all the way out here on Jura? It makes no sense. Someone is pulling your leg—'

'For crying out loud, Niall!' I want to slap him. Does he think I'm an idiot and can't tell the difference between what's real and what's not? 'You don't think I've already considered that? She's missing, Niall. Someone's taken her. I'm trying to get her back!'

Reality seems to have hit home, and Niall is about to do what I feared he would and try to take control.

'When?'

'Two days ago.' A flash of anger crosses his face and he glares at me.

'And you're only telling me now?'

'Yes, I had no choice,' I argue. 'If I tell anyone he says he'll kill her!' Niall clambers to his feet, reaching for his mobile phone.

'We need to call the police—'

'No!' I say, in a moment of clarity, leaping up from my chair. I try to grab his phone but he eases me aside without difficulty, keeping the phone out of my reach.

'Kelly, don't be stupid,' he admonishes me, turning his back and dialling.

'I said no!' I yell and reach past him, but again he manages to keep his phone out of reach. 'Damn it, Niall, listen to me.' He lifts his phone to his ear, turning to face me and I take the opportunity, extending my left hand and he flinches the other way, bringing him in reach of my right and I make a grab for it. The next few seconds see us wrestling for control of the device.

'Kelly... let go!'

'Hang up the call!' I counter and we stumble against the counter. I manage to take the phone from his grasp, hurrying away from him and staring at the screen. He hadn't managed to dial 999 and I clear the screen.

'What the hell are you doing?' he asks.

'You can't call the police,' I say pointedly. 'Or tell anyone else. He'll hurt her—'

'Don't be ridiculous!' He shakes his head. 'If what you're saying is true—'

'If?'

He winces, holding up a hand apologetically. 'Then we need help.'

'We have each other!'

Niall scoffs, laughing. 'What do you think I am, a superhero or something? I left my bloody costume back at the house in Morningside.'

I stand firm, my fingers wrapped tightly around his mobile. I'll smash it into pieces if I have to. 'No police!' I say firmly. Our eyes meet and I know he's contemplating what to say. We may be estranged but we've been married for years. I know him as well as he knows himself, warts and all. I see the glimmer of recognition in his expression, and he relents.

'No police,' he repeats. 'As God is my witness.' I pass his mobile back to him and he slowly takes it, slipping it into his pocket. We are still eyeing each other warily. He's likely considering my state of mind and I'm gauging how much trust he has in me. 'So. Someone has abducted Lauren.'

'Yes, and that's not all. If I am to get her back unharmed then I have to do something.'

'Then do it!' Niall says. 'Whatever it is, just do it and then we can call the police. Is it money? How much do you need?'

I draw breath. I'm not supposed to tell anyone. I'm supposed to be alone with this, and he's been a step ahead of me the entire time. I scan the room, the corners, the shadows as I did before but without success. If the house has hidden cameras or microphones, I would have found them. Niall sees me looking and he does the same, although he can't know what I'm looking for. He reads my mind though.

'Is this why you tore your house apart?'

'Yes. He knows what I do, where I go and who I speak to.'

'How?'

I snort. 'If I knew how, I wouldn't be so scared, would I?'

'Well, you'd have found it if you were bugged, right?' Niall asks. Then he shakes his head. 'This is crazy!'

'I'm not crazy,' I say firmly. 'But he is. I have no doubt. Niall, I saw her and heard her...'

'You heard her what?'

'Scream,' I whisper. Niall becomes agitated, pacing the room, unable to settle. 'Niall, please, I need you to stay with me. Please don't freak out—'

He stops, his expression shifting to incredulity. 'Please

don't...' He shakes his head, but at least he's stopped pacing. 'And what is it he wants you to do?'

'I have to kill someone.'

He blinks, then holds up his hands. 'I'm sorry, I thought I heard you say you had to kill somebody.'

'I do.'

'Oh, thank God! For a moment there I thought this was an insane situation,' he says, grinning madly. 'Thank you for clarifying, and making it completely and utterly...' – he throws his hands wide, almost as wide as his eyes – 'absurdly ridiculous!'

'Niall—'

'No, please,' he says, gesturing for me to continue, 'do go on. Explain to me how you are going to kill someone to get our daughter back! I'm all ears.'

'I-I don't want to—'

He leans forward, laying his balled fists onto the table and he fixes me with a stern look. 'Well, I'm delighted to hear it! And, if I may be so bold as to ask, who is it you have to erase?'

'I don't know,' I say, looking down. 'I have to choose, decide who deserves to die. If I choose the wrong person then he will...' I can't say it. Niall purses his lips, studying me.

'So, there's a list of potential candidates?'

'Yes, it will be one of my patients, and I have to—'

He lifts a hand and slams it down against the table, startling me. 'Have you heard yourself? You are actually considering killing another human being. How do you know he'll give Lauren back if you do as he asks? Have you considered that?'

'Of course I have, but I-I don't know what to do,' I say, my speech getting faster as he looks to interrupt me. 'I only have twenty-four hours left,' I say, looking at the clock, 'to do it or we'll never see Lauren again.'

'We must go to the police,' Niall argues. 'They are trained for this—'

'No, they're not, and you know it. They are trained to arrest drunk drivers, break up bar fights or follow evidence to catch a criminal. They are bloody useless at catching killers until they've actually killed someone.'

Niall, open-mouthed, puts his hands in the air in desperation. 'And you are better qualified than they are to handle this? Really? Kelly Murray – Howlett – whatever, are better placed than law enforcement to get our daughter back?'

I sigh. 'I should never have told you.'

'But you did,' Niall says, 'and now I'm in this too. We have to go to the police!'

I step forward and jab a finger in the air before his face. I've never been more serious, more focused than I am right now. 'You will do as I say, and you will not go to the police, Niall Murray. And if you do, and my daughter suffers as a result, then I will haunt you until your dying day! Do you understand?'

Niall, taken aback, closes his eyes momentarily, then looks straight at me. His expression softens and he looks down at his feet, lowering his voice. 'Do you know what you're doing? I mean,' – he lifts his head, meeting my eye – 'really know what you're doing?'

'I have to behave normally,' I tell him. 'That means you can't stay here.'

'What?'

'You can't be here. We haven't been a couple for over two years and our divorce will come through any time now—'

'What's that got to do with—'

'It would be abnormal for you to stay here. He will guess that I've told you. Don't you see? But if you go to the hotel, as if you're expecting to see Lauren later on today, then...'

'Then, if he is watching, he'll think you're keeping it quiet?'

'That's right.' I take his hands in mine, squeezing them gently. 'Thank you for being here for me, but you can't be a part of this.'

'I can't just leave...'

'That's exactly what you have to do, for now.' I blink away tears, my vision blurring. 'And you know I'm right.'

Niall looks at the newspaper, a photograph of Freya McLaren, looking almost identical to the day when she came to the graduation party at our house.

After what happened, Lauren and Freya's friendship pretty much ended, so the girls haven't been in touch. I'm sure of that. Freya, and her parents, weren't too keen on all of the media attention. They moved out of the city soon afterwards. Lauren and her best friend forever lost touch very quickly.

'It's incredible, isn't it?' he says glumly. 'Freya died that day and you brought her back, only for her to disappear a couple of years later.'

'Do they have any idea where she went?' I ask. Niall shakes his head.

'Bonnie...' Niall winces. 'Freya didn't bring the pills that day, but she was the only one left to take the rap.'

'Not the only one,' I whisper. Niall looks down, clearly uncomfortable and emotions I'd long since buried – injustice, betrayal – come flooding back to me.

'Yes, well. It was what it was,' he says, taking a small step away from me. The barriers between us that had lifted descend as those memories that we share, painful memories, resurface. 'We'll find a way,' he tells me, and I believe his sincerity. 'We'll get Lauren back but promise me you won't do anything crazy until I've had a chance to come up with a plan.' He stares at me, refusing to let me break eye contact. '*Promise me.* I'll think of something. I will.'

I nod. 'Okay. I'll wait for you.'

'Good, thanks.'

'Look at you,' I say, impressed by his confidence.

'What?'

'You, going all Churchillian on me. You truly believe we can find our way out of this?'

Niall is pensive, thoughtful. 'I've always thought of Lauren as my own, you know that. I'd do anything for her.'

'Including killing someone?' I ask, and he looks away without speaking. Now he knows exactly how I'm feeling. 'You need to go.'

'I understand, and you're not wrong, but we need to talk about who might be behind this. Who would want you to suffer like this?'

'Someone with an axe to grind.'

'Have you considered Bonnie's family?'

I shake my head. 'She had been living in care, if you remember? I don't even think I saw pictures of them at her funeral. It's more likely to be one of the nutters who was sending me all that hate mail during the inquiry. The things some of those people wrote kept me up at night.'

Niall's eyebrows knit together. 'Cameron? He didn't like the way you stopped him from seeing Lauren, and he always thought you'd blamed him for bringing drugs to the house. Maybe he's trying to get even or something.'

'I thought of him, too, but would he be capable of organising something on this scale? Besides, I'm sure as hell not the only mother who disapproved of him dating her daughter.'

Niall sighs. 'No, probably not. Who else suffered because of all of that? Who would blame you, want to punish you by making you re-enact... involvement in someone's death?'

I survey him, deep in thought.

I can think of one other person who also paid a heavy price for what happened.

TWENTY-FIVE

TWO YEARS AGO

One Hour Before Bonnie Died

'Here's the stuff from the car,' Lauren says, hefting the carrier bags up and onto the kitchen island.

'Thanks, love.'

'Do you need me for anything else or can I...'

I smile at my daughter, giving her a wink. 'Go and entertain your friends. They're here to see you, not to swim in our pool.'

'Thanks, Mum,' Lauren says, heading for the French doors. 'And some of them definitely are here to swim in the pool.'

'Oh!' I say, starting to unpack the items from the bags that need transferring to the fridge, 'have you seen your father? I need to know when he's planning on lighting the barbecue.'

'Not seen him, sorry,' Lauren says, backing out of the kitchen and onto the patio. Freya dances towards her, passing her a bottle of beer. I know they are still underage, most of them, but I'd rather if they were going to have a binge celebration that they do it under my roof, under supervision, than hanging out in the meadows. They are a responsible bunch of kids, to be fair.

A few minutes pass and I've finished unpacking the bags. Food preparation is well in hand, and the meat is under wraps out by the grill, but my husband still hasn't put in an appearance. There's football on the television today, and I can see a handful of Lauren's friends gathered around the television we moved outside, watching the build-up to the big match.

The music is on, and growing louder, accompanied by the excited conversations teenagers have as they celebrate what they've achieved and talk over the next steps towards adulthood. It gets much harder from here, but they don't need me to tell them that. Not today anyway. *Where's Niall?* I can't see him among the guests.

Lauren's having a great time, and Freya seems more exuberant than normal. She's always been quite a shy girl. Perhaps she should slow down her alcohol consumption. Drinking and sunshine are lovely bedfellows but can easily lead to problems if you're not careful. I'll keep an eye on her. I step out onto the patio and wave towards Lauren, eventually getting her attention.

'Your father?' She shrugs, and I exhale. Typical of a man to go missing when you need him to do something. Fiona passes me, reaching into the bucket of ice with drinks wedged amongst the cubes to keep them cool. I smile at her.

'I think I saw Mr Murray on the back landing,' she says helpfully.

'When was this?' I ask, contemplating if it's worth me going up the rear staircase to look for him.

'A little while ago, twenty minutes or so,' she says. 'If you need help with anything—'

'No, that's okay. Thanks, Fiona.'

She breaks the seal on a can of cola and returns to her conversation with her friends. Filtering through the crowd, I make my way to the back of the three-storey townhouse we live in on Morningside and go in search of my husband.

The music volume is deadened by the stone walls, and that gives me hope that the neighbours won't be too annoyed by the party, but it is summertime and I'm sure they'll be all right with it. As long as we don't keep it going too late into the night.

At the top of the stairs, I stop on the first-floor landing. 'Niall?' But there's no answer and I don't hear anything. Leaning over the wrought-iron balustrade, at the foot of the twisty staircase, I look up the stairwell to the second floor, straining to hear signs of movement. 'Niall?' I call out again, but my shout yields no response. 'Honestly, men are hopeless.'

A door creaks open along the hall and I look around, expecting to see my husband at the end of the corridor but it's not.

Bonnie Campbell, one of the more recent additions to Lauren's peer group, steps into view and I don't know who is more startled as we almost collide. She's tucking the hem of her loose-fitting white shirt into the front of her cut-off jeans and didn't see me on the landing at the foot of the staircase.

'Oh! Sorry,' she says, through chewing her ever-present gum. Bonnie isn't someone I particularly approve of. Lauren has started hanging around with her at the same time as she's taken up with Cameron Stewart, as the two of them are close friends.

I don't know which of them I'm warier of. Bonnie is very glam, but in a – I don't know how to say this without sounding snobby – cheaper end of the spectrum. She likes bold lipsticks, striking shades of eye shadow, all on a substantial base of foundation, and a style of clothing that leaves little to the imagination. The girl is daring, I'll give her that, but she can't pass a polished surface without checking how she looks.

I hate to judge, but frankly I'd much rather Lauren spend her time with the likes of Freya and Fiona than with Bonnie. I know her type. I went to school with plenty of them myself, and it won't end well, of that I'm sure.

'That's okay, Bonnie.'

She looks past me and then over her shoulder. 'I was just using the bathroom. I hope that's okay, Doctor Murray?'

'Of course, it's fine,' I tell her. 'No problem.' She shoots me a confident smile and passes me, making her way downstairs, loosely tracing the line of the banister with her immaculately manicured, red-painted fingernails. I think she needs to take a bit more care with her presentation though, because she's smeared her lipstick. Bonnie glances up at me, catching me watching her, and I turn away as she notices me and I resume my search for Niall.

Walking along the corridor, I'm about to double back and go upstairs to his second floor, self-confessed man cave, when I hear sounds of movement in Lauren's bedroom. Curious. I'm sure Lauren's downstairs beside the pool. I throw open the door, ready to admonish my daughter for abandoning her guests, and Niall spins to face me in surprise.

'Geez, Kelly!' he says, putting a hand to his chest. 'You scared the daylights out of me.'

I laugh, one hand resting on the door frame, the other holding the handle. I look around the room. He's alone. 'What are you doing in here all by yourself?'

'Oh... it was so noisy down there,' he says, adjusting his belt and coming around from where he's standing at the entrance to Lauren's en-suite shower room. 'I was just looking for a moment of peace, you know how it is.'

'In here?' I ask, looking around.

'Sure,' he says quickly. 'No one will look for me in here.'

'Okay, whatever you need to get through the day,' I say, grinning. He comes over to me, looping an arm around my waist, encircling me, and pulling me into him. I let go of the door and put my arms around him, casually crossing my hands at the nape of his neck. I lean into him, and he kisses me. Drawing away from him, something has caught my attention. I look at him.

'What?' he asks. I narrow my eyes, studying him. I'm not sure, but something feels different, maybe even off somehow. 'What is it?' he asks again, smiling nervously, clearly self-conscious.

'You smell different.'

He looks at me, puzzled. Then his expression shifts. 'Oh... yes, I got one of those sample kits from Creed. It arrived in the post, this morning.' He gently removes my hands from his neck, and steps away. 'I'm not sure I like it.'

'No, it's a bit...' – I can't think of the right description – 'feminine.'

'Yeah, a bit of a mish-mash,' he says, wrinkling his nose, reaching back and pulling the door to the en suite closed. I look towards it and he smiles sheepishly. 'I'd not go in there for five minutes if I was you.'

'Well, I hope you opened a window or your daughter is going to kill you.'

'Of course,' he says, taking me by the elbow and gesturing for me to lead the way out. 'Come on, we have guests.'

'And you have to light the barbecue,' I tell him. 'Everyone will be getting hungry, and the drinks are flowing. They need to soak up some of that booze or this will degenerate into chaos.'

'I'm on it,' Niall says. I pull the door open and offer him an open hand to lead the way. Chivalry is not dead, but we are equal partners in this house. He goes ahead of me and as I close the door behind us, I look back into the room. Lauren has left her underwear on the floor of her bedroom beside her bed, but it's not the style I've seen in the laundry before. There are no black semi-transparent Brazilian briefs like those in her wardrobe that I can recall seeing.

'Hey!' I look round and Niall was already halfway along the corridor, talking to me, before realising I wasn't walking right behind him. 'Are you coming?'

'Yes,' I say, hurrying to catch up. 'Of course.' He throws an arm around my shoulder, steering me ahead of him as we reach the staircase and make our way back to the party.

I'm still thinking as he's talking, but I'm barely paying attention. The thoughts coming to mind are beyond unsettling and are beginning to form a narrative in my head. My husband is keeping something from me. I know it and, what's more, he knows I know it too.

TWENTY-SIX

Two Hours After Bonnie's Death

The room is small. I've been in these family rooms before, and they're all the same. A handful of chairs, a tiny window overlooking a brick wall that won't open. The air is stuffy, despite the air-conditioning unit mounted in the ceiling. Hospitals are warm. Uncomfortably so, but they have to be. Most people in them are confined to a bed and they can't move around to keep warm on the wards, but the rest of us feel it as a result.

Looking to my left, Lauren has been crying. Her mascara has run, and then smudged where she's tried to wipe it away. She shouldn't be here, but at the same time, she couldn't have stayed at the house by herself. The police are still there. I wonder if they'll be there when we get home, whatever time that is.

It feels very different when you are in the family room on this side of the fence. I've come in to speak to parents, siblings and spouses on countless occasions, giving both good and the worst possible news. This time, I don't know how it's going to go.

Opposite us, staring into space, are Freya's parents. Bethany and her husband, Alex. I don't really know Alex, having only spoken to him briefly in passing at school events, the Christmas service or similar. He's a nice man, Bethany's second husband. She has her hand in his, their fingers interlocked.

The door to the room opens and George hurries in. Alex stands up as George looks around the room, acknowledging all of us in a sweeping gesture, focusing on Bethany.

'I got here as fast as I could. How is she?' he asks. It's Alex who replies, offering George his hand. They shake.

'We're still waiting to hear,' he says, looking down at his wife, who has remained seated, but her eyes are no longer staring into space. She has them trained on me.

'What happened?' George asks, sitting down beside his ex-wife and following her gaze across to me. He's expecting me to answer. I blink, and Lauren squeezes my hand. I respond in kind.

'Freya fell into the pool,' I say quietly. George seems confused. 'She lost consciousness—'

'From the fall?' George asks. I shake my head.

'That was why she fell into the pool,' I say. 'Because she passed out.'

'Where?'

'Our house,' I say.

'She was drinking at your house,' Bethany says, and there is an undertone in her voice.

'Not too much,' I say. 'We were making sure—'

'No, you weren't!' Bethany almost spits as she speaks. 'If you were making sure, then my daughter wouldn't be here.' Alex, sitting beside his wife again, takes her hand supportively, but she dismisses him with a sharp stare and keeps her hands in her lap. I want to reassure her.

'We don't know what happened—'

The door opens just as Bethany is readying herself to spit

more bile towards me, and I'm grateful for the interruption. The doctor, one of my colleagues, Hamish Matheson, enters, glancing around the room. He acknowledges me with an almost imperceptible nod which I find odd, seeing as we've worked together in Accident and Emergency for almost seven years now. He looks over his shoulder and another man enters behind him.

'Doctor Murray?' he asks, and I nod. 'My name is Detective Sergeant Gordon.' He subtly brandishes his warrant card to me, in a little black leather wallet. 'Would you mind stepping out of the room for a moment?'

'Sure,' I say, standing up. Lauren makes to come with me and I wonder if she'd be better off waiting in here with Freya's parents. However, the scowl on Bethany's face is such that I gesture for Lauren to come with me.

Outside in the corridor, we are more or less alone with the policeman. There are some staff down at the nurses' station, and a porter is wheeling a lady off the communal ward but heading away from us in the other direction.

'Doctor Murray,' DS Gordon says, 'would you prefer if we spoke in private?' He means Lauren, and I shake my head. 'Very well. Our officers investigating the death of the young lady at your home have come across several substances that we would like to ask you about.'

'Substances?' I glance sideways at my daughter. 'What kind?'

'That is yet to be determined, but we are very confident that we are looking at controlled drugs, most likely Class A in nature.'

'Class A? That's...'

'Ecstasy tablets, known on the street more commonly these days as MDMA, along with another white powder,' Gordon says, 'which we believe to be cocaine.'

I snort in disbelief. 'That's crazy. There's no such thing

going on in our home,' I say, looking between the officer and my daughter. She is staring at the floor though, and she knows I'm looking at her, and won't look up. 'Where did you find them?'

'I should read you a caution, Doctor Murray, just to make sure everything is clean and above board when we—'

'A caution? You can't believe' – I lower my voice as a nurse passes. I know her and she smiles as she goes by, but doesn't speak to me – 'I would have anything to do with illegal drugs at my property? I'm a doctor, here at this hospital.'

The detective doesn't say anything directly, but his lips are pursed, and he does indeed read me a caution.

I can't believe it. 'Where were they found?'

'The amphetamine tablets were found in a plastic bag, hidden inside the cistern of the toilet in the downstairs cloakroom—'

'Plural? How many are we talking about?'

'At least fifteen,' DS Gordon says. 'More than enough to qualify for a charge of Intent to Supply. And then we found a substance that we believe to be cocaine, six grams of powder, split into three bags, in one of the upstairs bedrooms.'

'That has nothing to do with us!' I say and the detective remains unfazed, showing no indications of believing me or not. I look at my daughter.

'The downstairs cloakroom?' Lauren repeats, surprised.

'Lauren,' I ask her sternly, 'do you know anything about this?'

She shakes her head. 'No, of course I don't. Drugs aren't my thing.' My gaze lingers on her for a moment. I know my daughter well, and although I don't believe she would know-ingly bring such things into our house, I also know when she's holding back. I turn back to the officer.

'Do you... think that the drugs are related to...' I can't bear to say it. 'You think this has something to do with Bonnie's passing?'

'We believe that Freya McLaren suffered a drug overdose,' DS Gordon says flatly. 'Either that or she combined both substances or something inside the drug, an impurity that the amphetamine was cut with, led to the reaction that caused her body to shut down.' He inclines his head. 'You saved her life, of that I do not doubt, Doctor Murray. However, Miss Campbell – Bonnie – wasn't so lucky, and we suspect the pathologist will confirm she died from the same reaction.'

'That's awful.'

'Yes, it is,' DS Gordon says. 'And our investigation will seek to determine how these girls procured the drugs as well as who supplied them. I should tell you that I fully expect this case will be treated as a murder inquiry.'

'Murder,' I say, whispering the word. DS Gordon nods solemnly and in that moment I know Bonnie Campbell's death will see massive repercussions in our lives.

I always knew Bonnie was a bad influence to have around my daughter, and I thought it would end badly.

What I didn't know was that she would die in my home and on the same day I realised she was having sex with my husband.

TWENTY-SEVEN

Mercifully, the press is not waiting outside the house when the taxi pulls up outside. I hand the driver a twenty-pound note and get out, not waiting for the change. If I can get up the steps and inside before anyone leaps out of a bush or swings down from a tree with a camera in their hand, I'll be pleased.

There's movement on the other side of the shutters in the sitting room, but I pretend not to see Niall watching me mounting the steps, safe in the sanctuary of my bug-eye sunglasses. My suit is still immaculately presented, dry cleaned and pressed for the occasion. My hair, usually flowing freely to my shoulders when I'm off shift, is tied back in a neat ponytail. My makeup looks pristine as well, but that's only because I'm rocking waterproof mascara, and my glasses hide the streaking of the tears.

The front door swings open and I step inside, seeing one of my neighbours walking to her car on the far side of the road. She's seen me. I know she has, but I pretend I haven't seen her and she shows no interest in acknowledging me either. That's the way of things these days. I'm a leper, socially and professionally.

Thankful to have a barrier between me and the outside world, crafted from solid oak, I lean my back against it and take a deep breath. The performance is over. I'm safe. Well, to a degree anyway.

Niall steps out of the sitting room. He's dressed in a button-down Oxford shirt and tan chinos. He leans his shoulder against the door frame, hands in his pockets.

'How was it?'

'Oh, I got exactly what I expected,' I say, unbuttoning my jacket, removing it and hanging it on the rack beside the entrance door.

'As good as that, huh?'

'Yes.' I'm angry. No, not angry. Furious. Livid. Seething. All possible adjectives I could muster up but none of them alone, or combined for that matter, do my current mood justice. 'I need a drink.' As I walk past Niall, he takes a hand out of his pocket and almost reaches out to offer me a supportive touch, but I shy away from it and he changes his mind.

The decanter is on the sideboard, a quarter full which is a surprise. I'd expect Niall to have polished most of that off by now. After all, it is midday. I take a tumbler and pour myself a large measure, seeing it off in one swallow. Then I pour another.

'Are you going to hit that pretty hard today then?' Niall asks from behind me. I don't turn around but swirl the contents in the tumbler.

'Seeing as I have nowhere to go, and no job to do, I may as well have a drink,' I argue, turning to look at him. He can see my eyes now. His expression changes. I cried from the moment I stepped out of the hearing to the minute the cabbie pulled up outside. My eyes are bloodshot, my cheeks stained, and I have nothing to offer anyone, aside from the shareholders of any of Scotland's favoured exports.

'Was it that bad?'

'Oh, no,' I say, before taking a sip. 'It was much, much worse. I've been suspended pending the decision of the Procurator Fiscal's decision in relation to the criminal investigation.'

'Well, Ramsey told us to expect that.'

'Yes, he did, didn't he?' I say, mocking him with a sarcastic smile. 'But it still hurts to see my career officially go up in flames.'

'That's a little melodramatic, wouldn't you say?'

'Melodramatic? Really, you think so?'

'I didn't mean to sound flippant.'

'Then what did you mean?' I ask, raising my glass towards him. He shakes his head, stumbling over his words.

'I... I just meant—'

'I think what you meant to say is I'm sorry, Kelly, for allowing my genitalia to get in the way of our marriage.'

'Here we go,' Niall says, pinching the bridge of his nose.

'Yes, here we go,' I repeat, wrinkling my nose. 'Strap in, because I'm just getting started. Maybe you could apologise for keeping a Class A substance addiction from me or' – I lift my chin, cupping it philosophically with thumb and forefinger of my free hand – 'the fact you have a penchant for young girls—'

'She was eighteen!'

'And one of your daughter's high school friends,' I say, turning the corners of my mouth down in mock sorrow. 'But now she's dead.'

'You're out of line!' Niall says, stepping into the room and pointing an accusatory finger towards me.

'I'm out of line. Morality?' I ask, downing my second drink. 'From you? Really?'

'You want to question my commitment to our marriage?'

'Commitment?' I ask, turning back to the decanter and taking out the stopper. 'I can't believe you're bringing that up. I would argue you're on thin ice, but it's melted and you're drowning in a puddle.'

'How about you, working all hours, taking on shifts whenever they came about? And for what?'

I slam the glass down on the sideboard, scotch splashing out over the back of my hand and my blouse. 'To show willing. To make it to senior consultant before I turn forty. How about that?'

'We didn't need the money—'

'Well, the way things have gone in the last couple of months, I think the money would come in useful now, wouldn't it?' Niall looks away. He was sacked within a fortnight of his confession regarding the cocaine found in the house. You can't rightfully be the headmaster of the most prestigious independent school in Edinburgh if you have been charged with possession of a Class A drug, and that's before the world learned of his affair with a teenager.

'I screwed up!'

'I think we can both agree that that is an understatement, Niall,' I say, drinking the last of the scotch in my glass.

'If we're going to discuss personal failings,' he says indignantly, 'why don't we put Doctor Murray under the microscope, seeing as you're so damned perfect?'

I fold my arms defiantly across my chest, feeling the warmth of the alcohol spreading throughout my chest and the pleasant effect of intoxication beginning to manifest.

'Go on, then,' I dare him. 'I'm waiting.'

'You haven't been suspended because of what I did! And that's what you can't face. It's not my indiscretion—'

'Indiscretion?' I ask, incredulous. 'That's what you're calling it.'

'It wasn't me who let Bonnie die.'

I would have been less shocked if he'd hit me. I stare at him, open-mouthed. His anger subsides and he seems embarrassed. He's overstepped, and now he's feeling bad.

'What did you say?' I whisper.

'You let her die, and the guilt is eating you up inside.'

I scoff. I was wrong. He's not embarrassed. He's doubling down. This is what he's been holding onto these past few months. All of those times across the dinner table, those moments when he looked like he was trying to get something off his chest, just to dismiss it and move on. This is what he thinks. 'You think I let her die?'

'Are you telling me you didn't?'

I step forward and throw my hand across his face. 'How dare you!' Niall glares at me, but he doesn't flinch. He doesn't retaliate. He just glares at me, his eyes burning with thinly veiled fury.

'You let an eighteen-year-old girl die out of spite, because you were jealous of her.'

'*I did no such thing!*'

Niall laughs humourlessly, shaking his head. 'You couldn't handle the fact that I would find someone else attractive—'

'A teenage girl, Niall,' I counter, mocking him.

'That I would turn to someone half your age to find fulfil-ment because you couldn't satisfy me!' I make to throw another hand at his face, but he easily catches my wrist this time, pulling me towards him. My face is inches away from his and I can feel the warmth of his breath on my skin. 'You as good as killed her yourself!' he says, casting my arm aside. It would have hurt less if he'd punched me to the ground. Instead, he stares at me, his anger dissipating, and he leaves the room.

I sink down onto the floor, my body shaking as the adren-aline mixes with an emotional outburst, and soon I'm sobbing uncontrollably. I don't know how long I sit there in the centre of the room, but it gets dark outside and I'm vaguely aware of someone watching me in my peripheral vision. Looking to my right, I see Lauren at the threshold.

'Is it true?'

'Is-Is what true?' I ask.

'What Daddy said before. Did you let Bonnie die?' My breathing is coming in ragged gasps, and I can't believe my daughter thinks so little of me. Niall and I have massive problems, and deep down I know our marriage will not survive this, but Lauren, too? 'Did you?'

'No!' I say, but she's already gone. I can hear her footsteps on the marble floor, moving away. 'No, I would never do that!' I shout towards the atrium, but she doesn't return.

I'm alone.

TWENTY-EIGHT
PRESENT DAY

'What is it?'

Niall is watching me. He has a peculiar look on his face. 'Sorry, what?'

'You zoned out there for a minute,' he says. 'Are you thinking of something?'

'Just... um... thinking,' I mumble. I can't really go into detail, because I'm struggling to make sense of it all. There's a thought, something that might give me clarity on all of this, but it is slipping from my mind the more I try to tease it forward.

'Thinking? About what?'

I look at him. He shouldn't be here. Not only because I was told not to involve anyone else, but *Niall* shouldn't be here. I know it's wrong, but I don't know why. It's an abstract feeling, an instinct maybe, rather than anything tangible.

'You have to go.'

'I know. To the hotel,' he says. 'Keep up the pretence.'

'No, maybe you should go home, back to Edinburgh.'

He blinks, and twitches involuntarily. 'W-Why? You need—'

'You shouldn't be here.' Niall is about to mount an objection, but I won't allow him to. 'We've barely spoken in eighteen months. We communicate through our solicitors, and not even through our daughter.'

'Yes. What's your point?'

'Why did you come here?' He frowns at me, breaking eye contact. Is that guilt? Have I reached for something he didn't expect?

'I told you why—'

'Because I sounded odd on the phone.'

'Yes, and with good reason as it turns out, eh?'

'You didn't call,' I counter. 'You came all the way across the country and caught a ferry – two ferries – to see if I was all right. Really?'

Niall snorts. 'Well, forgive me for caring about you! What a terrible person I am, huh?'

'Did you care while you were taking your pants off for Bonnie?'

He sighs, his shoulders sagging. 'Are we going there again? You want to do this now, of all times, you choose now?'

'Well, you can *forgive me* for questioning your motives, Niall. Convenient timing, isn't it, you showing up here?'

'Oh, hell no!' He glares at me. 'You'd better not be saying what I think you're saying.'

'Someone has it in for me,' I argue, 'and life as you knew it was flushed down the toilet back then.'

'You must be joking!'

'Had I saved Bonnie's life that day, then none of what followed would have happened. You blame me for her death—'

'I was emotional!' Niall says sharply, throwing his arms wide. 'A lot of stuff went down. You weren't the only one who felt it, you know? I was there too, watching everything disintegrating around us.'

'And you blamed me.'

He looks down, and I see him take a deep breath, trying hard not to lose his temper. Niall has always had an even temperament, right up until he reached his breaking point, and then he had the propensity to unleash his inner demon. He lifts his eyes to mine, and he nods.

'I'm not going to lie to you. I did blame you.' I'm ready to announce my victory, but he raises both hands in prayer before him, touching his fingertips to his lips. 'But that was because I had to blame someone, and at that time I wasn't prepared to face myself in the mirror. What happened that day – the buildup to that day – was my fault. It wasn't yours. If I was feeling left out or marginalised in our marriage, then it should have been on me to raise it with you.' He exhales heavily. 'I didn't. I looked for the answer outside of the marriage – with Bonnie – and that was my mistake. We both have responsibility for the failure of our relationship, but it was still salvageable if I had done the right thing.'

'But you didn't.'

'No,' he says mournfully. 'I didn't, and that is for me to live with.'

'Except we are all living with it, aren't we?'

'Yes, and that fact burns me to this day,' he says quietly. 'And so it should. Look, I know what you're thinking and I'm not involved in this, Kelly. Lauren is my daughter—'

'But she isn't, is she.'

'She is as much my daughter as this hand is my own,' he says, holding his right hand in the air. 'And I will do everything in my power to bring her home safely. You can't' – he splays his hands wide in apology – 'please, don't send me away. Not now.'

I shake my head. I don't know what to do. To have someone here to share the burden offered me some relief, but now I fear it could do the opposite. I am putting my daughter at risk. 'You need to go, right now. It's too dangerous you being here.'

'Okay,' he says firmly. 'I'll leave, but I'm only going to the hotel in town. I'll not go back to Edinburgh until I see my daughter.'

'If you wish.'

He doesn't seem happy leaving like this, but he makes his way to the door, hesitating before opening it. A gust of cold air is drawn through the house and I can hear rain on the paving outside. Niall leaves without saying goodbye and I'm left with a sense of isolation again. The relief of having support dissipating, replaced by guilt.

Suddenly the back door is thrown open again, startling me. Niall steps through, fixing me with a determined look. 'Niall—'

'I know how to do it!' he says excitedly. 'I know how we can find her.'

'What? How?' He looks at his mobile phone in his hand, and he holds it aloft.

'Before, when all of this kicked off... and we weren't talking,' he says. 'You remember how disengaged Lauren was—'

'She hated both of us,' I say. 'For a long time.'

'And she spent more and more time away from us, shunning every approach either of us made to reconcile.'

I nod. It was a painful time for all of us and that was especially hard for Lauren. She had a ringside seat in her parents' collapsing marriage, and she had no one to turn to. No one aside from Cameron Stewart anyway. 'Yes, so what?'

'I...' Niall pauses, reticent.

'You what?'

'I tracked her.' I'm puzzled, thinking I must have misheard.

'You tracked her? How?'

'I put something on her mobile,' Niall says, and he strides towards me before I can comment. 'There's an app that tracks the phone's GPS signal, allowing you to locate the phone to within two metres...'

'You did that?'

'She was away with that loser Cameron, and getting up to God knows what. I wanted to be able to find her if... if anything went wrong.' He excitedly unlocks his phone now, struggling not to smile.

'I can't believe you would do such a thing—'

'Don't you get it? I can see where she is! We can go and get her.'

'Do it!'

He doesn't need to be asked twice, searching for an app on his screen.

'I tried to hide the icon,' he says, his eyes darting sideways to me. 'I... didn't want anyone to know because, well,' – he angles his head – 'you know?' He sighs.

'What is it?' I'm peering at his phone from the side, trying to get a better view.

'I need to enter a password.'

'So?'

He runs a hand through his hair, concentrating. 'I haven't used this for nigh on two years, Kelly. Give me a chance to think.'

'Niall, you'd better remember it or I swear it'll be the last thing you never do.'

'All right, all right,' he says, holding a hand up. 'I've got it. I think.' He types in a password, but it's rejected. He glances nervously towards me. If ever he shouldn't let me down, then this is it. On the second attempt, the app allows him in and he cheers. 'Yes! I'm in.'

He doesn't need me to push him further, and he goes through a couple of menus before the screen changes, revealing a satellite image of a land mass. I recognise Jura. Lauren is still on the island and the excitement flutters in my chest. Niall taps the screen and the map zooms in, getting larger and larger, until it stops.

My husband looks at me, and the smile fades.

'What is it?' His eyes meet mine, his lips parting slightly. 'Where is she, Niall? Where's my daughter?'

'It says she's... here. Right here.'

TWENTY-NINE

'What do you mean, she's here?' Niall slowly turns the screen to face me. There is a red pin on the map indicating the location of Lauren's mobile. 'That can't be right.'

Niall examines the location again. 'She's right here.' I'm about to ask him to check again, but he turns and walks to the back door, still staring at the screen. I follow and he leads us out into the back garden, half an acre of land to the side and rear of the house and medical centre.

'Where is—'

But Niall is walking away, head up, ignoring the rain driving down at us. It's heavy and it stings my face but I don't go back for a coat, and I set off after my husband. He walks about ten metres onto the grass and stops. I come alongside and he looks at me, crestfallen.

'She's here.'

'Where?' I ask, taking his lead and looking around us. The old stone byre is off to our right, fifteen metres away and the medical centre is to our left by a similar distance. 'There's nothing here!' I say, hearing the desperation in my voice. 'It makes no sense!' Niall looks at me, and takes another step to his right, and stops. 'What is it?' He lifts his foot and stamps. There's a hollow sound and I look down. He's standing on a metal cover.

'No,' I say, shaking my head. 'No, it can't be.' Niall drops to his knees beside the cover. It's heavy, secured in place and hasn't been moved for a while. It's the service hatch for the septic tank system for the house. Niall is struggling to free the hatch, and he passes me his mobile.

'Light this up, will you?' After fumbling with it for a few seconds, as he tries to manhandle the cover up, I find the torch function and illuminate him. 'Here,' – he points to the edges – 'so I can see why it won't move.'

The sun is up, but the winter days in the Inner Hebridean islands can be dark and gloomy, worse when there is a storm front passing through like this one. It may as well be night-time. The extra light from the mobile shows the cover has been moved recently, fresh scrapes visible at one corner. It appears as if the cover has warped over the years though and no longer sits well in the housing. However, Niall manages to work his fingers in and loosen it. Grimacing with the strain, he then prises it up at one corner and between us we can elevate it further, getting it to a tipping point where we can lever it up and aside.

The smell from the interior is rank, and we both recoil from it but the idea that Lauren is inside draws us back straightaway. 'Light!' Niall asks and I hand him the mobile. I can't bear to look. I can feel a darkness building, a sense of foreboding, as if evil is in the very air escaping the tank. Niall covers his mouth with his hand, peering down inside.

Lying flat on his stomach, he sets the mobile aside and reaches down into the tank, his arm disappearing up to his shoulder. His face turns to me, and I can see the horror in his expression. I can't see into the tank, and neither can he, but he doesn't pull back. The rain is driving down upon us, and we are staring at each other.

'What is it?' I ask him, but he doesn't answer. 'What's there?' I shout. He still doesn't answer, but I can see the rain on his face. Only, it's not rain. He's crying. 'What is it?' I scream, and Niall lifts himself up onto his knees. He is straining; the muscles in his neck are tense. He has a hold of something, and it's heavy. He's shaking his head now, leaning in through the drain hole with both hands, struggling with a weight. 'No.' I can't see it. 'No!' I shout as he tries to stand, off balance, his hands grasping an object wrapped in plastic and secured with gaffer tape.

Niall leans back, his knees bent, straining, as he tries in vain to lever whatever it is out of the tank. It's clear he has reached an impasse. 'I need your help,' he says without looking over. I tentatively approach. 'Quickly.'

I come to his side, and try to take a firm hold, but the plastic is tight, slippery and stinks to high heaven. All I can do is wrap my arms around it as tightly as I can, ignoring the filth transferring onto my clothing. I can't ignore the smell though and I retch repeatedly, the taste of vomit coming up into the back of my throat.

'Nearly there,' Niall whispers, grimacing from the strain as much as from disgust. We back away, dragging our haul out of the tank and onto the grass. We both sink to the ground, my hands in my lap as I sit on my haunches over our find. I know what it is without breaking the gaffer-taped seals.

A body.

Lauren's body, wrapped from head to toe in black plastic sheeting, bound with tape at the ankles, legs, arms and wrists. The sheeting is so tightly wound around the head, fixed with more tape, that even in this light I can make out facial features.

Neither of us speak, and Niall crawls towards her, tears streaming down his face. How could I have doubted him? You cannot fake the absolute despair in his expression.

'Don't,' I whisper, my voice cracking, but he doesn't hear me or ignores me, I don't know which. He pulls at the sheet around her face but it is thick material, much thicker than the material used in bin liners. When he manages to break through, he reveals another layer and it's not long before he's pulling and tearing at the plastic like a man possessed. I'm in tears, sobbing as he breaks open my daughter's makeshift funeral mask.

I failed her. I didn't protect her. She was here this whole time, and I still couldn't save her.

Niall tears through the final layer, the plastic stretching and finally giving way to reveal the face of innocence. I can't look; my eyes are clamped shut. This can't be how it ends for her. My baby girl. Not like this.

Niall hasn't spoken, but I can feel him beside me. He reaches out, his hand tracing up my body to the hands covering my face. Allowing him to take my hand in his, he pulls it down to his side and squeezes it firmly. I'm sobbing; my whole body is shaking. I think I'm going to throw up.

'Kelly,' he says quietly. I open my eyes and look at him, but I can't look down. I can't see her like this. Niall is staring down at her though, with a vacant expression. He doesn't realise I'm looking at him. 'Kelly... it's not Lauren.'

THIRTY

'Help me!' I look at my husband. He just spoke to me, but I've no idea what he said. 'Kelly, help me!'

I've no idea how long we've been sitting here in the damp grass, staring down at Freya McLaren's lifeless body.

She'd gone missing from her home in Leith, disappearing having left her parents' house early one morning. There was a report of a girl matching her description being seen standing on the dock at Leith, and her car was found abandoned a week later close to the old Rosyth shipyards.

Ever since that day when she overdosed at our house in Edinburgh, Freya had struggled with life. She never went on to university as planned, losing contact with her friends and becoming something of a recluse.

She was also struggling with her mental health, having lived with two years of illness. Then, she vanished. They scoured the hills surrounding the city, widening that to the coast and Leith where she was known to have a boyfriend. Despite the intensity of the search, there was but the one unconfirmed sighting. The discovery of her car did little to aid the investigation.

Freya McLaren was a runaway. Twenty years old. A grown

adult who left her life behind without a word. No one knew of her whereabouts. Until now.

'Kelly!' Niall grasps my blouse, roughly shaking me. 'I need you to focus.'

'Y-Yes,' I say, swallowing hard and blinking the rainwater from my eyes. 'What should I do?'

'Grab her legs,' he tells me and without question, I crawl around him to the foot of the body and stare at the wrapped legs. I have my hands above the body, but I don't know where to take a hold of her. 'Under the ankles,' he says. 'We're going to lift her up.' I look at him, uncomprehending, and he gestures towards the byre. 'We'll take her in there, to that stone building.'

I don't argue, and Niall levers her up, slipping his arms under her upper body and I grapple with her legs. Between us, we heft her into the air. She is surprisingly light. I thought she'd be much heavier based on the trouble we had getting her out of the septic tank. The grass is slippery, the ground uneven. I was never much of a keen gardener and out here, on the islands, the grass is far from the pristine, manicured lawns we keep in genteel Edinburgh.

I almost fall, losing my footing and Niall curses several times bearing the weightier part of the body, but between us we manage to get her across to the byre. It's unlocked. Despite using it for storage, including Blair keeping his tools here, we see no need for security on Jura. After all, there's no crime.

Once inside, out of the rain, Niall casts an eye around. There is racking against one side wall and pallets of materials, sheets of rigid foam insulation mainly, are stacked at the far end. 'Over there,' he says, nodding to the gap between these pallets and the rear wall. We shuffle through the byre, bumping into various bits of kit, and I curse. The space is cramped with everything stacked all around.

Setting Freya's body down with as much reverence as we can bearing in mind our situation, we both stop to catch our breath. Before, I couldn't look at her, but now I can't look at anything else. Freya's face, although recognisable, is discoloured. That happens after death when the blood ceases to flow and the organic cells begin breaking down.

'How long...' Niall asks, breathing hard, 'do you think she's been in there?' The plastic wrapping, restricting the exposure to oxygen and the chemicals of the tank, will have slowed the decomposition process, and it has been cold. I can't possibly make an accurate assessment.

'I don't know,' I say, still staring at her face. She looks like she's asleep, pale and with a blueish tinge to her skin, but sleeping, nonetheless. A thought comes to mind and Niall picks up on a micro-expression.

'What is it?' I don't answer, and he gets frustrated. 'Kelly! What is it?'

'Th-The shower... keeps backing up,' I say, forcing myself to take my eyes away from her. 'The water doesn't go down properly.'

'I think we found the root cause,' Niall says, looking at Lauren's childhood friend. I extend a hand towards her, as if I can somehow reassure her or let her know everything will be okay now. That she has gone to a better place. But she hasn't passed on properly. There have been no sober farewells from friends and family. No church service. No mourners to remember happier times. Instead, she has been disposed of in the cruellest and most disrespectful way, as if she was filth.

'What are we going to do?' I'm still staring at her. Niall doesn't answer my question, but he is also looking at the body.

'Where is my phone? Kelly!' he snaps, and I look at him. 'Where is my phone?' I glance around us and then remember.

'It's on the lawn, beside the tank entrance, I think.' Niall nods. I'm grateful he's here. I sent him away, but now I don't know what I'd do without him. Niall looks at me, his face a picture of concentration. He looks me up and down. 'Go back to the house. Shower and then throw those clothes away.'

'What?' I ask, but he inclines his head, indicating for me to leave. I had almost forgotten. From the moment we pulled Freya from the septic tank, I'd stopped thinking about the fact I was covered in a mixture of mud, chemicals and human excrement. Now, in the relatively confined space of the byre, I can smell it again. I gag but raise the back of my hand to my mouth. 'W-What will you do?'

'Freya will be okay here for now—'

'But what are we going to—'

'I'll get things squared away here.' Niall looks around the byre and, spying a folded-up sheet of tarpaulin on the racking, he pulls it down and starts opening it up. 'Go and shower. And then we'll talk,' Niall says dispassionately. I think about asking him again, but his mind is made up and I simply nod, offer Freya, that poor, sweet girl, another furtive glance and then I back away from them both, making my way back to the house.

Wiping the steam from the surface of the mirror, I stand there in silence, staring at my reflection. Absently picking up a brush, I pull it through my hair, down to my shoulders. I have a haunted look on my face. I'm living through the plot of a real-life horror film. Glancing into the shower tray, the backing up of the waste pipe is no longer a problem. Niall was right.

There's a knock on the door. I haven't bothered to lock it. What would be the point? I'll never feel safe in this house again. The door opens and, in the mirror, I see Niall's head poke around it. 'Can I shower too?' I nod, and he enters the bathroom. Without a word, I gather up the bin bag containing my filthy clothes and I walk past him, out into the corridor. I can smell him as I pass. He smells awful, but I'm past caring.

In the kitchen, I find a large resealable plastic zip-bag on the table. The exterior has smears of something disgusting on it. Inside is a mobile phone. It's Lauren's. I bought her the case. It's Day-Glo pink – an in-joke between us because she kept forgetting where she'd left it and I said it would be easier to find. I want to touch it, and I reach out, my hand hovering over the bag's seal. It's as if holding something of hers will bring me closer to my daughter. But it won't.

I don't know if I'll ever see my daughter again. An image of me hauling her lifeless body out of a septic tank leaps to my mind, and the horror of such an event brings me to tears. Hurrying out of the kitchen, I put the bin bag full of my clothes outside the back door. Should I put it in the general waste bin? Hours spent watching Hollywood films and television suggest I shouldn't do that. They'll be discovered, but I haven't done anything wrong. I should have nothing to fear.

Mind you, I said the same when I was brought before the General Medical Council, but they still suspended me, casting me as the guilty party in the eyes of many and torched my career.

Niall enters the kitchen, drying his hair with a towel. He tosses it aside and leans against the counter. He's changed into a clean set of clothes from his travel bag. Neither of us says anything for a while. We just look at one another. I am the one to break the silence.

'Where did you find Lauren's phone?'

'Taped to the cover of the access hatch to the septic tank. It is definitely hers then?'

I nod, dispassionately. 'Yes. I'm sure.'

'Do you want to call the police?' Niall asks. We can't. I know we can't.

'If we do then Lauren is as good as dead,' I say matter-of-factly. 'He's shown he's willing to kill with Freya. I don't think he'll care about one more death on his conscience. Do you?'

Niall shakes his head. 'How long has your shower been backing up?'

I have to think about that.

'A week or two, I think.'

'And Freya went missing six weeks ago, more or less.'

'He's been planning this for some time, then.'

'I think so too. Who do you think it is?' he asks. I look at him. 'Besides me, obviously.'

'I never thought it would be you,' I lie. 'Not really.'

'It doesn't matter, but who?'

I exhale sharply. 'Someone who latched onto the case, a vigilante. Or... Bonnie's family, perhaps?'

Niall folds his arms across his chest. 'I remember they weren't on the scene—'

'No, Bonnie had been in the system for years, bouncing around foster homes. When she turned eighteen, she... went out in the world alone. It's no wonder she always seemed older than her years. But I guess you know more about that.' Niall purses his lips, and I see I've hurt him. 'I'm sorry. That was... unnecessary and uncalled for.'

'Did you ever hear from her family members? A brother, long-lost parent, perhaps?'

I think hard, but I don't remember any mention of family. Not that I was thinking much about Bonnie in the aftermath as my life disintegrated, followed quickly by my mental health. It's hard to pay attention when you fall asleep with a bottle of gin every night.

'Whoever it is has been close to the house all this time,' says Niall. 'Close enough to dispose of Freya in your back garden and to return with Lauren's phone.'

'Why do that? Why bring her phone back?'

'For you to find it, perhaps?'

'Then... it follows that he expected me to find Freya, doesn't it?'

Niall nods. 'Yes, that follows.'

'I told you earlier, he's been watching me. He knows when I do things, places I go to. He's been one step ahead of me the whole time. Texting me from' – I look at her mobile phone in the bag before me – 'Lauren's phone whenever I've deviated from what he wants me to do.'

'Until now,' Niall says. I glance at him to explain. 'He doesn't know about me. That I know—'

'How can you be sure?'

'Because that would be breaking one of the rules,' Niall says. 'Remember? You told me what his rules are and he hasn't called to threaten you, has he? So, he can't know about me. Otherwise, he'd have been onto you by now, right?'

I take out my mobile, checking to see if Lauren's abductor has sent a message through that I missed, but Niall's right. He hasn't contacted me since last night.

'Y-Yes... I see. I still don't know who it is though.'

'The who isn't exactly relevant though, is it?' Niall says, and I offer him a quizzical look. 'If we are not going to the police, and we don't know who has done this...' He looks at the clock on the wall. I follow his gaze. 'How long do we have?'

'Twenty hours, a little less in fact.'

He stares at me and I've not seen him this focused since our world fell apart over two years ago.

'Who are we going to kill,' he says calmly, 'and how are we going to get away with it?'

THIRTY-ONE

Niall pulls out a chair at the table opposite me and sits down. 'You're sure it has to be one of your patients?'

'Yes,' I reply, but then doubt myself. 'I think so.'

'You think so? You have to be sure.'

'I think that's what he said.' Picking up my mobile phone, I open the app and scroll through the messages, back to the beginning. They're not there. I start to panic. 'They're not there!'

'What's not there?'

'The messages!' I'm scrolling back and forth, searching for them but there's nothing there prior to the last exchange the previous night. 'I... I don't understand!' Niall reaches across and I hand him the mobile. He also begins searching but soon stops, putting the phone down. 'What's happened to—'

'He's set them to automatically delete after a given time.'

'You can do that?'

'Yes,' Niall says, heaving a sigh, 'and I know this app is encrypted. Once those messages are gone, there's no way of bringing them back. Not even if you got access to the data carrier's server.'

'But what if I'm remembering wrong?' I'm really panicking now. 'What if it's not one of my patients—'

'We'll manage,' Niall says firmly. I'm breathing hard, staring at him. He is insistent.

'Okay,' I whisper, then Niall chuckles to himself. 'What's so funny?'

'Not funny,' he says, the humour dissipating. 'Here's us worrying about leaving a trail behind for the police to follow... and this guy's already thought of that too.'

My confidence is shattered. He's back to being a step ahead, even when he didn't realise he was behind. I suspect he has everything planned. Even if I do as he wants me to, suddenly I'm thinking it won't matter. He is going to destroy me, destroying my family and all our lives in the process. 'I can't do this, Niall.'

'Yes,' Niall says firmly, 'you can.'

'No, I really can't...'

'Kelly, this is exactly what you had to do that day beside our pool.'

I shake my head. 'No, it's not. That was completely different.'

'It's *exactly* the same, Kelly. You had to make a decision. There were two girls, both deceased, and you had to decide which one to bring back because *you knew* you couldn't save both!'

'How is this the same?' I ask.

'Someone has to die. It's Lauren or one of your patients. You chose who lived and who died back then.'

'That was a snap decision—'

'It was a choice, Kelly! You *chose* Freya. You will have to make the same choice again, only this time you will choose Lauren to survive. I will help you figure it out, but I can only do so much without being suspected of involvement. In the end it has to be you. The kidnapper wants you to do it, that much was clear.' I look across the table to see the thinly veiled anger in his expression. 'You know your patients. Which one of them deserves to die? Kelly... choose!'

THIRTY-TWO

I knock on the door and wait. I'm nervous. I can't quite believe why I've come here or what I'm planning to do. Glancing back at my car, I figure I could make it back there and drive away. It would only take seconds and I'll be gone.

Niall has gone to check in at the hotel in Craighouse. They called him and they've rearranged things to make a room for him. I have to check in with him later. I wish he was here with me. If he was, would I find it easier to go through with what I'm about to do? This is madness. I turn around but I've barely taken more than a few steps before the door opens and Amelia is standing in the doorway, surprised to see me.

'Doctor Kelly? W-What are you doing here?' she asks, looking to her left and towards the side of the house. She's checking to see if her brother, Morgan, is home or has seen me arrive, I think. His car isn't parked in front of his house. What will I do if he does show up? I'll just have to cope, but I plan to be away from here as soon as possible.

'I just wanted to take that blood sample from your mum.'

Amelia seems nervous, and she pulls the door to a little as she steps out to speak to me. It's raining and she doesn't have a coat or proper shoes on, sporting a jumper and slippers. 'I'm not sure that's such a good idea, Doctor Kelly.'

'Is your mum feeling better?'

'No... worse, if anything,' Amelia says, looking over my shoulder and down towards the road, and then back to me. 'She's had such terrible stomach cramps overnight. She's in agony, the poor thing.'

'Then I should look at her, shouldn't I?' Again, Amelia looks anxiously towards the road. 'Are you worried about Morgan coming home?' She looks at me, reluctant to say but she nods curtly. 'I'll be quick.'

'Okay, come in,' Amelia says, pushing the door open and beckoning me inside. The door closing behind me with a thump startles me, and I'm already thinking Amelia will see straight through me. I must look guilty. I feel it, as well as dirty. I know I'm about to do something wrong, the worst thing that anyone could do, let alone a member of my profession.

Forget such lofty ideals as an eye for an eye – the way some people can make murder appear to be a noble act of justice – this is nothing short of premeditated murder. I can rationalise killing Alistair Aitken, although I still have no evidence other than a decades old hunch by the investigating officer, that he did anything wrong.

Thomas Baird would be easier; he is an absolute horror of a human being.

I even momentarily considered Ashleigh and her hypochondria, because maybe that's what he wants to see, me taking the life of an innocent to ensure maximum suffering on my part.

But I don't believe that's the case. If this is tied to me, and my actions beside the pool that day two years ago, then I think Bonnie is the key and she certainly wasn't an innocent. She brought drugs into my home. She passed them to Freya, and would have passed them to others, too, I'm certain. She was also not averse to sleeping with another woman's husband. Mine.

Her moral character was dubious, and she was a criminal. Does any of this mean she deserved to die that day? No. Did she die? Yes. Now, Mhari Allen is an ageing pensioner with a complex medical history. She's demonstrated a lack of moral character in the way she has treated her children, and the innocent creatures who happen to pass near her. Does this mean she deserves to die? No.

Will I do this anyway? Yes, I will.

'She's through here, in front of the fire,' Amelia says, leading me into the sitting room. There are two lamps on, one in each corner of the room, and the glow of the open fire illuminates the old lady, sitting in her armchair, a blanket across her knees. 'I'll make us some tea,' Amelia says, excusing herself and going through into the kitchen.

I come around to the side of Mhari's chair, slowly lowering myself down as I look at her. Her eyes are closed and she seems paler than she was on my last visit. Her skin is grey, and she is strikingly gaunt. I touch her forearm gently. 'Hello, Mhari, it's Doctor Howlett.'

Mhari's eyes open and she turns her head slightly in my direction, but her eyes are glazed over and she doesn't appear to be able to focus on me. Her breathing is shallow and taking her pulse, I can feel it is irregular and weaker than one would like. I should be arranging for her to go into hospital.

'Please...' she whispers, and it's almost inaudible. 'Doctor Howlett... please help me.'

'That's why I'm here, Mhari,' I say, and saying the words makes me feel sick.

'Help me,' she says again. I smile weakly, feeling the tears forming in my eyes. She's looking at me, and I can't meet her gaze. If I do, then she'll know. Mhari will realise that I'm not here to care for her. I'm here to kill her.

Fumbling with my bag, I can't undo the clasp, my fingers

slipping off the metal. My hands are shaking, but I manage to open it.

I paid a short visit to the surgery before I drove out here, and I have what I need. I don a pair of medical gloves and unwrap the packaging of a fresh syringe. *This is no different to assisted suicides.* People travel to Switzerland for this, paying a lot of money to do so. The doctors there are not judged for their actions. The little voice in my head corrects me, ensuring I know full well what I'm doing. *But their patients have a choice, Kelly. You are playing God.*

'Am I a god,' I whisper, holding a small glass bottle in my left hand, the syringe in my right.

'What's that, dear?' Amelia asks, poking her head around the door to the kitchen, and I hide the bottle in my hand, enclosing it with my palm.

'Nothing,' I say. 'I was just thinking... your mum isn't looking well at all.'

'No,' Amelia says, entering the room with a concerned expression. I can hear the kettle heating water behind her. 'She was up most of the night with those cramps I mentioned. She was sick at two and again at four.' Amelia shakes her head. 'You've not been able to drink much either, have you, Mum?'

Mhari doesn't respond, but I see she is still watching me, her lips parted slightly. Her lips move but I can't hear or work out what she is trying to say. Amelia excuses herself as the kettle clicks off, leaving the room.

Opening my hand, I look at the bottle. Diamorphine. One syringe of this opioid will be enough to kill someone as weak as Mhari Allen. Often used to relieve chronic pain, it is widely used in palliative care. Prescribed correctly, it can relieve some of the most painful conditions, post surgeries, Caesarean section births and even in cases of childhood fractures and trauma.

When overused, though, it can easily lead to respiratory depression. Administered directly into a vein, particularly in someone as frail as Mhari Allen, death will certainly follow within the hour. Popping the cap off the needle, I hesitate with the syringe in my hand, before I slide it through the bottle stopper and into the liquid inside. I slowly start drawing the syringe back up, pausing part-way, staring at it in my hands.

I can hear Amelia in the kitchen assembling cups of tea, and she's speaking to me, but it is just like white noise at this point. If I'm going to do this, then it has to be now.

I'm surprised by a light touch on my arm, and I look down to see four bony fingers, the skin pale and almost translucent it is so thin. My eyes lift to meet Mhari's and she tries to speak. I lean into her, turning my ear to her mouth.

'... trying to kill me...' she whispers. I'm shocked and I withdraw from her, eyes wide. How can she know? Mhari's eyes look towards the kitchen and then come back to me, glassy and brimming with tears. I lean in towards her again. 'They... want to kill me,' she whispers, and the hand she had resting on my arm falls limply to her side.

Amelia shuffles into the room carrying a tray bearing cups and a teapot, setting it down on the coffee table beside the second armchair across from her mother's, beside the fireplace. 'Here we are, Doctor Kelly. A nice pot of tea.' I smile, carefully withdrawing the syringe from the bottle and secreting them back in my bag. 'How's the patient?'

'I'm... a little worried, to be honest, Amelia,' I say. She looks concerned as well, casting an eye over her mother, whose eyes have closed. She may have fallen asleep or simply succumbed to her weakness. 'She's fatigued and her pulse is still erratic and not very strong.'

'Yes, she gets tired quickly these days,' Amelia says, pouring out the tea. 'You don't take sugar, do you?'

'No, just milk for me, please. I wouldn't be surprised if she is anaemic as well, based on the colour of her skin.' I examine

Mhari more closely. 'You said she was suffering with abdominal cramping overnight?'

'Yes, the poor thing. It's like before, you know, when she went into hospital.'

'Which time?'

'Good question,' Amelia says thoughtfully. 'I think she's had these symptoms each time.'

I try to remember all of the symptoms from Mhari's file. Dizziness and nausea, abdominal pain, vomiting and shortness of breath. She's showing signs of extreme fatigue, which is not unusual in a woman of her age and in poor health, but putting them all together for a diagnosis that encompasses all of them is not easy. However, what she's just told me changes everything.

Had this been any other visit I was making, another trip into the hospital, and I don't think it would have occurred to me. I would pass it off as the delirious mumbling of a sick woman. Aware of my motivation for coming here though, I think I know what is making Mhari Allen so ill. Amelia places a cup and saucer down next to me and then places another in front of her mum. I look at that cup, and Amelia notices.

'She loves a nice cup of tea, don't you, Mum?' But Mhari doesn't answer. Her eyes flicker open, and they look right at me. I know what she wants to say; I can see it in those eyes.

'I'm going to call an ambulance for your mum, Amelia.'

'You can't!'

'I'm sorry?'

'I-I... I mean... Morgan isn't here. He will—'

'Be happy that your mother is receiving quality care, won't he?' Amelia looks terrified, staring at me, eyes wide and she doesn't speak. I take out my mobile phone and stand up. 'I'll make the call.'

Stepping out into the hallway, I dial 999 and request an ambulance. A moment later the dispatcher comes onto the line and I identify myself, requesting an emergency ambulance be sent to the house as quickly as possible. I see a set of headlights take the turn onto the driveway and approach the house. The car doesn't pass, coming to a stop beside mine. I hear a door open and then slam shut.

Putting my mobile away, I watch the front door open and Morgan Allen strides into the house. He stops as soon as he sees me in the relative darkness of the hallway.

'What are you doing here?'

'I came to see your mum, Morgan.' He tries to look past me into the sitting room, and at that point the door opens. Amelia looks past me towards her brother, anxiously smiling but she's not pleased to see him.

'I didn't invite her... she just turned up!' Amelia says, fear evident in her voice.

'You shouldn't have let her in,' Morgan growls, his eyes trained on me.

'An ambulance is on its way, Morgan. It will be here shortly—'

'She's not going into—'

'Yes, she is, Morgan. I'll see to it,' I say, stepping forward to stand directly in front of him. 'I know,' I hiss and he seems startled.

'Y-You know... what?' he asks, the anger replaced by fear. I can almost smell it on him, on both of them.

'I know what you are doing to your mother.'

'How dare you—'

'I've already conveyed my thoughts to the medical team. They'll take the blood samples at the hospital. It's too late for you to stop it. Even if your mother passes tonight, they will check in the post-mortem and we both know what they'll find.' Morgan glances at his sister, who looks ready to cry. 'How is the croft doing these days, Morgan? I hear you're using a lot of pesticides.'

'So?'

'There's a lot of heavy metals in pesticides, Morgan, but I think you're aware of that, aren't you?' He doesn't argue, and I can see in his expression that I've troubled him. 'And I dare say you're well aware of what happens to the human body when it is exposed to too many heavy metals, particularly if they are ingested.'

'I don't care for what I think you're suggesting, Doctor Kelly.'

'I couldn't care less what you think, Morgan.' I look between the siblings. 'One thing you probably don't know is that heavy metals can't be processed by the human body. Once they are in the system, they stay there, gathering in the blood. If exposure decreases then the person can recover, to some extent. Adding more toxins bring the symptoms back, right up until the point of death if the ingestion doesn't stop. Your problem,' I say to Morgan, and then look sideways at Amelia, 'is that your mum's body is the evidence for her murder.'

The siblings look at one another, but neither issues even a vague denial. They are shocked, but only that they've been caught. Multiple trips to hospital and no one clicked what was happening, making them believe they would get away with it. Walking back into the sitting room, I gather my bag, and gently place a reassuring hand on Mhari's arm.

'The ambulance is coming, Mhari.'

When I return to the hallway, Morgan and Amelia are standing together, and I wonder what they are thinking.

'The ambulance is on its way. If anything happens to your mum before they take her into hospital, I will ensure everyone knows what to look for in her body.' Morgan is standing in my path, blocking my route to the front door. I pull myself upright in front of him. 'Anything you're considering doing to me or to your mother won't help you, Morgan. I've already relayed my findings over the phone. The tests will prove whether I am right. If you're lucky, by some miracle of medical intervention by the Lord himself, those tests will prove your innocence. In the meantime, get out of my way.'

We stare at one another, and for a moment I don't think he's going to back down. Then he glances at his sister and whatever she does sees him change his mind. He steps to the side and I walk past him and out of the house, relieved to feel the rain on my face.

Hurrying to my car, I get in and lock the doors. Morgan is hot-tempered and I've no idea how he will react to being called a murderer, even one who is yet to succeed.

Little does he know his accuser had been moments away from being a murderer too. Taking out my mobile, I ring Niall.

It's not the call he will be expecting, but I can't do it. I just can't. It's not who I am.

I can't look my daughter in the eye knowing I killed someone to save her life. I know Lauren. She would rather die than be the cause of another's death. It would torture her forever.

There has to be another way.

The call rings out, transferring to voicemail. I check the reception and I have three bars of signal.

'Do you have something more important to do?' I mutter, hanging up without leaving a message and putting my mobile down in the central console. I start the car and the phone immediately rings. Gathering up the phone, I hear the windscreen wipers squeaking across the glass as I answer. 'I was wondering where you were—'

'Ah, sorry, Doctor Kelly,' Ian McLean says, speaking over me.

'Ian... sorry, I-I thought you were someone else.'

'Sorry to disappoint,' Ian says. 'I've had an emergency call come through. There's a car off the road just out past Achamore. It's a bit nasty apparently, flipped over and all sorts. I'm on my way out there the noo.'

'Of course,' I say, silently cursing. That's the opposite direction to Craighouse, and where I need to be, but here on Jura, the local GP is the first responder in these scenarios. 'Any more details for me?'

'No, as I say, I'm just on my way, too. I'm almost there. It's this side of Gatehouse apparently, near to the forest. You know—'

'I know it. I'm on my way.' It won't be hard to find. There's only one main road running around the island. It will be hard to miss even in these conditions.

'Thanks, Doctor Kelly. Sorry to mess with your Saturday!'

'No problem, Ian. I'll meet you there.' I check the time as I hang up.

I have less than seventeen hours to rescue my daughter.

THIRTY-THREE

The rain has intensified in the short time I've been driving north along the water's edge. The sun has set but at this time of the year, on an overcast day, it's almost a full day of night anyway. The wipers are on full speed but I'm still having to slow down. The A846 is the main road around the island but out this way it remains single track, linking the various hamlets and estates to the island capital, Craighouse, and the southern tip of Jura with the ferry harbour at Feolin.

I can see a flickering blue light ahead in the distance, distorted and obscured by the driving rain. There are no street-lights here, no houses or buildings to illuminate the surround-ings. The snow is still present on the higher ground but towards sea level as I am now, the snow has thawed, aided by the rain. Pulling up on the grass verge behind Ian's patrol car, I switch off the engine and get out.

I'm immediately buffeted by a strong wind whipping up from the south, funnelled between Jura and the mainland which has been swallowed up by the darkness. I can't see Ian though. The blue lights on the roof of his car cast dancing shadows across to the pine forest behind me and reflect off a metal surface lost amongst the brush in the machair below me.

Leaving the road, this is the route I take but the going is difficult. Despite it being midwinter, and vegetation hibernating until spring, the ferns, long grasses and the broom that make up this stretch of the island's coastline is still thick underfoot, coming up to above my knees in places. In the darkness, with only the police car's roof lights to offer guidance, I almost lose my footing as I navigate a path to the crash site.

I can see deep gouges in the soil where the car left the road, some feat when the ground has been frozen solid for weeks. There are shards of glass and bits of plastic trim and light covers on the way to the stricken vehicle. The driver will have been travelling at some speed to leave the road in this manner.

Approaching the vehicle, I find it's lying on its roof, detritus and vegetation are caught among the wheel arches on the driver's side, and the panels that I can see along one side have been pummelled by the impact. The rear window has shattered and glass litters the ground.

'Ian?'

'Around here,' his muffled reply comes, and I make my way around to the other side of the vehicle, where the damage is less but still severe. The roof has all but collapsed over the cabin's front seats but the rear appears to have survived intact.

PC Ian McLean backs out of the passenger door on his hands and knees; the door itself has been torn off, presumably by colliding with a passing tree or coming open as the car rolled. I can make out a blood smear on the A pillar. Ian, a man in his sixties and far from being an athlete, grunts as he stands up, grimacing at the effort. Looking past him, I don't see anyone inside the car.

'Where is the driver?' I ask.

'Damned if I know, Doctor Kelly,' Ian says, forcibly wiping

his hands together to clear something from his gloves. He looks around the crash site, turning on a torch and scanning the machair. 'I've had a quick look around, but not found anyone. I thought the passengers might have been thrown clear, seeing the door off and all the windows broken.'

'Stands to reason if they weren't wearing seat belts.'

'Aye, but there's no sign,' Ian says, sniffing and touching the end of his nose with the back of his hand. 'They could be thrown some distance, I suppose,' he says, casting the light of the torch back along the path the car must have taken when it left the road. 'But it'll take some searching to find them.'

'Who called in the accident?'

Ian shrugs. 'No idea. It was anonymous, but the mobile number was recorded, so I dare say we can find out tomorrow when the sun comes up if we need to.' Heaving a deep sigh, he wrinkles his nose, absently scanning the surrounding landscape with the beam of his torch. 'They didn't fancy stopping to help though. It's probably the owner.'

'Why do you say that?'

Ian looks around casually. 'He's probably had a few too many beers and chanced the drive home. You know what they're like here on the island. The same conventions don't really apply like they do on the mainland.'

'Laws are convention now, are they?' I counter.

'It's different on the islands, you know that.' He fixes me with a knowing look. 'It's the way it is. He probably made a mistake in the conditions, got the back wheels on the verge,' he says, turning back to trace the car's route again with the torch, 'lost control and rolled it.'

'That doesn't explain where he is.'

'Stumbling back to his digs, I suspect,' Ian says. 'He probably called in the accident himself, so he can claim his car was stolen when he wakes up tomorrow, apparently none the wiser.'

'You're a cynical man, PC McLean.'

'Aye, but you know what mainlanders are like. That kind of nonsense passes as acceptable for the city folk, but it doesn't wash out here. No one steals cars on Jura. I'm sorry to call you out for a wasted trip.' He shrugs. 'I guess whoever called it in got the wrong end of the stick.'

'What about the blood?' I ask. 'The driver might be blundering around in the dark, looking for help.'

Ian aims the torchlight back onto the car, and he inclines his head.

'That's possible, but they'd have seen the lights by now,' he says, glancing towards his patrol car. 'Even in these conditions, you'd know I was here. If they are very seriously injured then they wouldn't have made it far from the scene.' It is logic that's hard to counter. 'No, I reckon the poor sod has stumbled home and will probably wake up screaming with a broken arm in the morning, once the drink wears off.'

'Whose car is it anyway?'

'A tourist, I reckon. Someone visiting friends or family.' Ian frowns. 'The car's registered to some guy in Edinburgh, Niall... something or other.'

I can't describe the feeling that immediately hits me. It's like falling from height, but never hitting the ground. An out of body sensation like no other.

'Doctor Kelly, are you all right?'

'W-What?' I mumble, staring straight ahead. I think I'm going to be sick. Ian shines the torch onto me, placing a hand on my arm, and I think I'm going to throw up on him.

'You don't look well,' Ian says, and I blink at the brightness of the light.

'I need to sit down...'

Ian steers me to the car and I reach out, bracing myself against it, leaning forward. I retch but nothing comes up.

'You aren't well, lass,' Ian says. 'Just take a breather there, while I make another sweep of the area. Okay?' I nod, but I'm staring at the ground, my grip on what was the floor sill of the car being all that's keeping me upright. *Niall. What were you doing all the way out here?* He had no business coming this way. It's the opposite direction from the hotel in the centre of Craighouse.

My eyes move to where the passenger door has been torn away, focusing on the blood smear. I move slowly towards it, lowering myself onto my haunches and peering into the cabin. There are pieces of broken glass scattered around the interior, that which wasn't ejected during the accident anyway. There's not a lot else in here, some bits of rubbish, and the damage is extensive.

Scanning the interior, I'm relieved to see very little blood. If he'd been seriously injured, then there would be more. Much more. I've attended to many victims caught up in car accidents over the years, and the blood loss and damage to the human body is often catastrophic.

Standing up and backing away from the car, I turn and search the surrounding landscape. I can make out the water in the distance off to my right, and there isn't a lot of natural cover between the road and the water's edge. The solitary flash from the Skervuile lighthouse, keeping shipping safe in the Sound of Jura, blinks at me through the murky night air.

'Where are you, Niall?' I say quietly. The bouncing light of Ian's torch signals his return and he's breathing heavily from his efforts wading through the brush in the dark. He stops when he sees me, his eyes narrowing, and he turns to follow my gaze.

'Have you seen something?' he asks, training his light on the area I'm staring at. The lighthouse blinks at us again.

'I was just watching the beacon.'

'Ah, right you are,' Ian says, ambling towards me with large strides. He blows out his cheeks. 'Well, if there's anyone out there, they'll have to wait until morning when we can mount a proper search.'

'You won't call in the mountain rescue team from Islay?'

Ian shakes his head. 'They won't go out until first light tomorrow anyway, but I'll make the call and have them prepped and ready to come across on the first sailing.' He studies my expression. 'How are you feeling?'

I'm wondering whether I should say something, and I want to, but I can't. This isn't a coincidence. I just know it. I should never have involved Niall. Now he's missing and it's all my fault.

'Doctor Kelly? You look like you've seen a ghost!'

I force a smile. 'Something like that, yes.'

'You should get yourself off home,' Ian says, glancing back at the wrecked car. 'I'll have to get this site secured – although no one else will come this way, I'm sure – and then I'll head back into Craighouse.'

'Right,' I say, nodding. 'And if—'

'If I find anyone or someone calls in for help, then I'll be straight onto you. If you're up to it?'

'I'll have to be, Ian. There isn't anyone else, is there?'

Ian smiles at me. 'The joys of island life, Doctor Kelly. There's never a day off or a dull day on Jura.'

Leaving Ian to secure the scene, I make my way back to the road, hesitating when I reach my car. The thick forest of plantation pine on the other side of the road stretches up the hillside; the impenetrable wall of branches is foreboding in the darkness. I feel as if there are eyes upon me and I search the treeline but see nothing.

Is Niall hiding somewhere in those trees? He can't be, otherwise he would come to me, surely? Is he still running in the wilderness, cold and lost... hurt? The thought brings tears to my eyes but I push the thoughts aside and get into my car, instinctively locking the doors straightaway.

With my phone in my hand, I ring Niall's number but just as it did before, the call goes to voicemail, only this time it's immediate rather than ringing out. I still have signal, but maybe wherever he is, he doesn't. My phone beeps and a message pops up on the screen.

I thought you understood the rules, Kelly? Fifteen hours, and not a minute more.

THIRTY-FOUR

Hurriedly looking in the rear-view mirror, I can't see another car besides Ian's. I check around me, my eyes searching the shadows, but everywhere is in shadow just now. Is this guy here, watching me from the forest? What has he done to Niall? Mhari Allen comes to mind but I know I made the right choice. I'm not going to kill an innocent person to appease a psychopath.

How would I know if he'd keep his word anyway?

No, if I'm to get Lauren back and work out what has happened to Niall, then I'm going to have to do it myself. This is on me, and I'm the only one who can bring this to an end, and I'm not killing anyone. Unless it's Lauren's abductor. I'll quite happily swing for him if the opportunity arises.

'Who are you?' I ask, staring at the message. 'And what did Bonnie Campbell mean to you?'

A fist bangs on the window and I scream, dropping my mobile into my lap. Ian leans down, peering into the car. I crack my window.

'Sorry, I didn't mean to scare you.'

'Forget it. I was... miles away just then.'

'I'm done here for the night,' Ian says, looking back towards Niall's wrecked car. 'I just have to put out a couple of warning triangles on the road, just in case.' He sniffs. 'There's no one around to see them, but it's procedure.' He looks back at me, leaning on the car with one hand. 'Are you sure you're okay?'

'Yes, I'm sure. I just have to send a message.' I glance at him. 'You wouldn't want me texting whilst driving.'

'No, lass. I'd have to give you a fixed penalty for that, and' – he looks glumly at the car on its roof – 'you might end up like that one.'

'Don't worry, I'll be off in a minute.'

'Okay, take care,' Ian says, tapping the roof with his palm and walking around to his car, lifting the boot lid and rooting around in the equipment for the hazard warning triangles.

Picking up my mobile, I open the web browser, typing Bonnie's name into the search engine. A list of links returns, most of which lead to newspaper articles around her death with multiple links to me and Niall. I narrow down the search, adding the word 'relatives' after her name.

There was little known by us about Bonnie's background prior to her passing. None of her relatives were ever in attendance at any of my hearings, and I never received any correspondence in relation to them. I knew she was troubled, and her difficult background was a large part of why she was the way she was. Children from broken homes, with traumatic upbringings, have to grow up fast to galvanise themselves against their experiences. In abusive homes, they are often forced to.

All I can see are descriptions of the foster homes she bounced between, never managing to find a safe haven to give her the security to grow into adulthood as a well-rounded individual. Taken into care at the age of nine, Bonnie was older than most adoptive parents prefer. I've seen that a lot too.

Everyone wants to adopt a baby, but the older the child, the harder it becomes to find them a place. The more troubled they are, the harder still.

Bonnie was expelled from school twice, once at the age of seven – bringing her onto the radar of social services. Then again at twelve when she attended high school. Finding another background article, I skip through all of the parts about me and Niall, and our roles in this story, focusing on Bonnie and her background. This article is deeper than most of the ones I've scanned through. Abandoned by her drug-addicted mother at the age of four, Bonnie moved to live with her paternal grandmother, but when she passed with Bonnie aged seven, she was taken into the care system.

'Where was your father when all of this was going on, Bonnie?' I find a fleeting reference to him at the foot of the article.

Callum Campbell, a convicted drug smuggler, was sentenced to fifteen years in prison for the importation of Class B drugs from the Continent. He was caught attempting to offload a vessel at Leith Docks, 14th August...

I sigh, scratching the side of my head having read that. Then something else piques my curiosity.

Bonnie's older brother, Craig, who is currently labouring on an Edinburgh construction site...

'You had a brother working in construction,' I say quietly to the photograph of Bonnie in the article. 'Where are you then, Craig?' I try to search for images of Bonnie's family but the results returned are dominated by shots of Bonnie, and by association, me, Niall and Lauren. My gaze lingers on Lauren. A school photograph taken at her high school graduation ceremony. She looks so carefree. Her whole life was ahead of her, promising, and everything changed only a few short weeks later.

Ian is walking back to his car, and I don't wish to speak to him again. I'm welling up looking at the image of my daughter, and he's already asking questions. Putting my phone away, I start the car, acknowledge Ian with a wave, turn my car around and set off back to my house.

I keep an eye on my mirrors, watching to see if anyone is following me, but I don't see any headlights. I'm relieved to come back into the outer limits of Craighouse and turn into my driveway, keen to get back into the house and lock the door.

But there's a vehicle parked in front of my garage. The headlights are on and the engine is running. I can see fumes coming from the exhaust. It's a pickup truck, but I can't see anyone in the cabin; the lights are pointed straight at me. I bring my car to a stop at the base of the drive, switching off the engine and plunging me into darkness, my hands gripping the steering wheel tightly.

Someone walks out of the shadows and passes in front of the headlights, breaking the beam. One person, a man, I think. He's moving with purpose. Then I see where he's going. The byre. My chest flutters. Freya! The strip lights inside the old stone building flicker into life and I can see the man's shadow cast onto the driveway. He's not moving, and then he does, stepping out of the building and reaching into the rear of the pickup. I can see his side profile. It's Blair.

I'm not breathing, staring at the big entrance door that's wedged open. I don't know what Niall did with Freya's body. He was wrapping it with the tarpaulin he found, but if Blair is rooting around then he might stumble across her. What is he doing at my house at this time on the weekend? He was going to be working this morning but we sent him away. He's got no business here.

The article I read at the accident scene comes to mind and I hastily get my phone out, searching my history. I reopen the page and search for the reference to Bonnie's brother. I find it and read it again. He was older than Bonnie, and worked as a labourer on a construction site. Bonnie was eighteen when she died. *How old is Donnie, Blair's son?*

He's in his early twenties, and that fits with the age range of Bonnie and her sibling. But what about Blair? Bonnie's father was in prison, but I have no idea when he was sent to prison or when he might be released. Starting a new search, I type in *Bonnie Campbell, father*, and hit return. There are no references.

'Damn!'

There's movement from the byre and I squint, trying to see what he's doing but from this angle I can't make it out. He hasn't seen me yet. What else can I search for? I think of Blair's trading name and I quickly do a search for *BM Construction*. The filing at Companies House is near to the top of the list and I click it. The page turns white and loads very slowly. Finally, the page loads and I can see the detail.

There are no companies listed with that name. Instead, there is a list of multiple businesses with similar names. Sole traders may not need to be registered, but I swear Blair had a limited company number printed at the foot of his quote. 'Are you registered, Blair?' I ask, typing in his name. Again, there are no returns but people with similar names show up.

Resorting to social media, I put in his trading name and hit return. There is a social media page, but there are only four posts and all of them are at my property. There are no other photos, links to previous projects or any comments made or received. Opening the photographs, I see Donnie posing in my back garden with a large shovel resting on his shoulder. The date tells me it was uploaded two weeks ago. From the line of the stone wall running across the boundary at the back of him, and the position of two trees in the background, I know where he's standing.

He's standing directly over the cover for the septic tank. A flicker of movement in my peripheral vision catches my attention. I look up towards the end of the drive and I see Blair standing in front of his pickup. He's watching me.

I should have considered this already. I let this man, and his weird son into my property. I gave them free rein over my home, and access to my daughter. They've been coming and going as they pleased for two months now. They have access to everywhere in my home, and they know it better than I do. While we were in the caravan, they were in our home, running cables, pipes, accessing the crawl space of the loft, the garage and everywhere in between.

How could I be so stupid? Why didn't I check the references he offered to supply?

'Because you trusted him, you silly bitch!' I whisper. Blair is still standing there, stationary, watching me. If I drive away then he'll know. He'll know that I've figured it out. I have to play it cool, not let on, until I can work out what I'm going to do. I silently chastise myself and start the car. I should have figured it out right from the beginning. These two are not from the island. They're the only people Ava knows nothing about, and she knows *everyone*.

Putting the car into gear, I drive forward. Blair watches me, and as I come around to the rear of the house, he looks pensive but his eyes stay with me. I park in my usual space and reach for my bag on the passenger seat. The clasp isn't secure and the bag opens as I haul it across into my lap. I see the contents, the syringe still in place from where I left it in my aborted murder attempt at the Allens' house.

Blair is alongside the pickup now, but keeping his distance. If he's found Freya, then he might suspect I'm up to something. *Play it straight*, I think and crack the door open. Stepping out, the wind whipping in off the Sound strikes me, blowing my hair across my face. I brush it aside with one hand.

'Blair, what are you doing here at this time?'

He cocks his head, then nods towards the byre. 'I needed to pick up a couple of things for something I'm doing tomorrow.'

'Right,' I say, noticing he hasn't any tools loaded in the back of his pickup and he's not holding anything. 'Working tonight as well? You must have a lot of jobs on at the moment?' I ask, picturing the scant projects on his social media account.

'Aye, rushed off my feet, like!' he says, taking a step towards me. He pauses as he clocks my expression. I've let myself down, even though I can put on an act when I'm under pressure. I've done it before. 'Where have you been?' he asks me, his tone harsh. Why would he need to ask me that? And in such an accusatory way?

'I had a call out,' I say. It's true, from a certain point of view. He's still looking at me, warily, I think. Have I blown it? If I have, and he realises I can identify him, then Lauren's as good as dead. He's older than I'd expect a parent of an eighteen-year-old girl to be but, then again, Bonnie died two years ago and if he spent a significant time in prison then it would age him.

'Something on your mind?' Blair asks, taking another step. He's within my personal space now. He could attack me and it would be over in the blink of an eye. I stare at him, hardening my resolve. Niall's words from earlier come to mind. I have a decision to make, and I must choose. 'Kelly—'

But Blair doesn't get to finish whatever he was going to say as I step forward and thrust the syringe into his neck, depressing the plunger a fraction of a second later. Blair's eyes widen, his mouth falls open and he draws a sharp breath as the diamorphine floods his system.

He tries to reach for the syringe, his hand flailing in the air, but I've stabbed him well. Close enough to see his pupils dilate, his hands pretty much freeze as the effect of the opioid kicks in.

Blair's eyes glaze over and I have to rush to support him as his body first goes into spasm, and then shuts down. We both sink to the driveway, Blair in my arms, landing unceremoniously on the wet gravel.

I brush a shock of wet hair away from his face. His eyes are closed, and it looks like he's sleeping.

'Right. Now it's my turn, you son of a bitch!'

THIRTY-FIVE

Switching off the strip lights illuminating the byre, I'm closing the doors when I hear footsteps approaching. That sixth sense tingles, the fight or flight instinct surging in me. Has Donnie come looking for his father?

'Hey, Kelly,' Hughie says, and I breathe easily, lifting the latch into place on the door.

'Hughie, you startled me,' I say, hoping that will cover my anxiety which I'm certain is evident.

'I was just getting back from the jetty, making sure my boat's secure with this passing front.' Hughie has a small sailboat moored at a jetty just outside Craighouse. 'I saw Blair's pickup, and thought you might have a problem.'

'A problem?' My fingers tighten around Blair's car keys in my pocket, and I glance at his pickup.

'Aye. It's a bit late for him to be working, bearing in mind it's the weekend and all.' My eyes flit to the pickup again, and I'm thinking hard. 'Is something wrong?'

'No, not at all. Blair... the engine has a fault or something,' I lie. 'Blair was here to collect a couple of things for a job he wanted to do at home tomorrow. Donnie came by and collected him earlier.' I rock my head from side to side, sporting a suitably glum expression. 'You know, cars... you never win.'

Hughie exhales, nodding. 'That's true. Everything all right?' he asks, glancing first at the house and then surveying the drive.

'Yes, sure.'

'Has your... um...' He hesitates and doesn't want to look into my eye. 'Is Niall still here?'

'No, like I said, he only came across to see Lauren. He's checked into the hotel in town—'

'Right, yes,' Hughie says, much happier. 'You said he wasn't stopping with you.'

'No, like I said, we're no longer together.'

Hughie smiles, but changes his expression quickly, evidently keen not to seem pleased about it. 'So... any chance of a cup of tea or—'

'Another time, huh?' I ask. 'I had a call out earlier, and I really want to put my feet up and... not speak to anyone for a while.'

'Sure, yes, of course,' Hughie says, disappointed. 'Maybe tomorrow, if you've not got anything on?'

I draw breath. 'We'll see, all right? I'll pop over if I fancy it. Is that okay?'

'Great! I'll look forward to it,' Hughie says, beaming, and then lifts a hand in the air. 'Unless you're busy, and that's great too, you know. Whatever, let's keep things... casual.' I can't help but smile at his awkwardness. If ever there was a man unsuited to bachelor life and the dating game, it's Hughie. He backs away, smiles nervously and sets off home.

I walk across to the rear of my home, entering through the back door. Closing it, I lock the door and turn to face the room. It took quite an effort to achieve this, particularly when doing so on the fly. There's a reason shifting something heavy is referred to as a dead weight. But he's not dead. At least, not yet.

Blair McIntosh is slumped in a chair in the centre of the

kitchen, but his eyes are wide, his face a shade of crimson and it's not anger that's causing it. I gave him a shot of adrenaline to counteract the diamorphine I injected into his system. I don't have the luxury of time. Neither does he.

The adrenaline has his heart pumping blood around his body at such a pace that his eyes are almost bulging out of their sockets. He'll feel hot, as if he's burning up. The entire roll of gaffer tape I've used to bind him to the chair, as tightly as I could obviously, will also be restricting the blood flow, thereby making his heart work even harder.

He's drawing rapid intakes of air through his nose; his mouth is also taped up, and I think he might be bordering on panic levels of anxiety. Good. I don't say a word as I walk past him, and I know his eyes tracked me until he could no longer turn his head, seeing as that movement, too, is restricted by tape. He's immobilised. And that's just how I need him.

Returning with my medical bag, I set it down on the table beside him. Opening it, in clear view of his gaze, I remove a pair of medical gloves. Beside those, I set down a fresh syringe, both of the bottles of diamorphine and the adrenaline, and lastly, exacerbating Blair's fears, a surgical scalpel. His breathing increases further, and I collect another chair, placing it directly opposite my captive and I sit down.

His eyes track me and he wrestles against his restraints but it does him no good. He has very little leeway to move. I purse my lips, staring at him. He blinks furiously, beads of sweat dripping into his eyes now.

'I'll bet you didn't have this scenario in mind when you woke up this morning, did you, Blair?' I ask and he shakes his head, but due to the tightness of the tape the movement is almost imperceptible. 'Now, you and I are going to resolve this situation swiftly, and amicably,' I tell him. 'Otherwise, you are going to have rather a long night ahead of you.'

Blair mumbles behind the tape, trying in vain to speak, but I raise a finger to my lips to indicate silence and he quietens down.

'You know, a person never realises just what they are capable of until you push the right buttons. Do you know what I mean, Blair?' His eyes stare at me, but he can't answer. 'And, as it turns out, apparently I am capable of doing truly awful things. Things that I would never have believed possible only a short time ago. And now, tonight, I'm going to share them with you.'

Again, Blair struggles in vain against his restraints. I slowly put on the gloves, and then I pick up the scalpel, holding it aloft in front of Blair. He is on the verge of tears, absolute panic in his eyes.

'Your extremities, your fingers and your toes, are tingling and going numb, aren't they?' I ask and Blair stares at me. 'Aren't they?' I repeat sternly, and he nods. 'That's because you are breathing so fast that the oxygen entering your lungs cannot get into your bloodstream fast enough, and so they are going numb. Soon, you won't be able to feel them at all.' I angle the blade, catching the light from the pendant above our heads on the polished metal surface, and I smile. 'That should make things a little less painful for you.'

Blair begins his struggle again, but to no avail. This time though, he doesn't give up after a few seconds, desperation driving him on. It's no use, and he runs out of steam.

Once he settles again, I stare into his eyes. 'I'm going to remove the tape over your mouth now, Blair. I expect you to behave yourself.' I reach forward, taking one corner of the tape between thumb and forefinger. Looking at him again, I incline my head. 'Behave,' I say quietly, and then tear it away.

Blair yelps at the sharpness of the pain, immediately drawing huge gasps of air into his lungs, but he's terrified. So frightened that he does as instructed and remains silent.

'That's better,' I say, exhibiting my best bedside manner. 'Now we can talk properly.' He nods and I smile. 'Now...' I say, gently placing the scalpel back onto the table and putting my hands together in prayer before me, 'we are going to carry on with a new set of rules. Rule one is you'll not lie to me. If you do lie to me, or I suspect you are lying to me, I'll remove one of your digits,' I tell him, waggling my little finger in the air in front of his face. 'Every time you lie to me, I'll remove another digit right up until such time as you have none left. Then... we'll look elsewhere.' I look him up and down, and Blair clamps his eyes shut.

'I would move on to rule two,' I say casually, then frown, 'but there is no second rule. I think I'll get everything I need from rule one, to be honest.' I clap my hands together, Blair's eyes open and he stares at me. 'Let's get started, shall we?' I lean forward, resting my elbows on my knees. 'I am going to ask you some questions. You will answer them honestly, otherwise you and I are going to be in for a very long night. But at the end of all of this, you are going to have told me where my daughter is. Then, if you're good, I'll allow you to phone Donnie, and he will bring Lauren home to me. Do you understand the rules – the rule – as I've explained it, Blair?'

'I don't know what you're talking about—'

'Wrong answer!' I say, pressing the tape back over his mouth. Blair howls behind the tape, trying to move away so I can't apply it, but I do so with ease, firmly covering his mouth. I shake my head, and pick up the scalpel. Blair's eyes widen and his muffled screams intensify. I hold the blade up, but don't move it towards his hands, taped behind the chair. I stare into his eyes. 'Are you going to tell me what I want to know?' He nods furiously, and I pull the tape off again.

'P-Please...' he whimpers. 'I-I swear... I don't know where she is!'

'I thought you understood the rules, Blair?' I say, holding the scalpel before his face.

'No, please, Kelly! Please don't!'

A headlight beam passes through the front window, catching my eye as a vehicle turns into my drive. I get up and hasten through into the sitting room and peer out into the gloomy evening. I curse inwardly, glancing back towards Blair. It's Ian McLean. The police car makes its way up the driveway, slowing as it comes close to the house.

THIRTY-SIX

I run back into the kitchen, forcibly reapplying the gaffer tape across Blair's mouth.

'Stay quiet.' He tries to resist, moving his head to one side and then the other, but I quickly manage to mute his protests. I then switch off the interior lights, plunging us into darkness, and hastily drop the blinds over the kitchen window. Taking up a position to the side of the back door, I try to see through the obscured glass, but the outside is inky black.

I can see the broad outlines of the patrol car, Ian pulling up beside Blair's pickup. The sound of the engine ceases and the headlights go out. 'What are you doing here, Ian?' I whisper. Blair mumbles something and I glare at him. I don't think he could make enough noise to give away his position to Ian, but I'm not entirely sure. Not that there's anything I can do about it now anyway. Short of giving him an overdose, but I'm not going to do that.

The car door closes, and I strain to see, shifting my perspective to try and improve my view, but it's a waste of time. Listening intently, all I can hear for a moment is the wind outside, buffeting the house. Then footfalls on gravel, drawing nearer. Should I pretend to be out? Would Ian believe that? I was with him a little while ago and told him I was coming home.

A shape forms at the door. From the shape of the silhouette, and the colour of his high-vis coat, I know it's Ian. He knocks on the door. I'm holding my breath, and I shoot a nervous glance towards my captive. If I let Ian in, I could explain. But would Blair give up his son, tell us where Lauren is, or would he deny everything? I can't take the risk, and so I stay where I am, silent.

Ian's hands cup the window and his face comes close to the glass. Reflexively, I try to sink further into the shadows beside the door, pressing my back against the wall and trying to become one with it.

Blair mumbles as loudly as possible, and I'm tempted to clear the space between us and strike him into silence, but the movement would almost certainly reveal my presence to Ian. And so I wait, hoping he leaves.

Ian steps back from the door and knocks again, this time banging his fist onto the glass. 'Doctor Kelly! It's Ian McLean.' I exhale slowly, fearing my breathing will give me away. The seconds pass and I've never wanted anyone to leave more than I want Ian to. His form moves away from the door, and I breathe again.

My mobile phone buzzes, and I look down, seeing the glow of the screen through the material of my pocket. And then it starts ringing, loudly. I can't silence it quick enough, and Ian's shape reappears at the door. I swear beneath my breath, managing to take out my phone and silence the call but it's Ian phoning.

Stepping out into the room, I put my phone down on the table, peel off the gloves, casting them aside into the corner of the room, and ruffle my hair with both hands, making my appearance unkempt. Closing my eyes, I take a deep breath and steady myself. Then I walk to the back door, unlock it and crack it open. Ian turns to look at me, lowering his mobile from his ear. He smiles, tapping the screen to end the call.

'Hello, Doctor Kelly,' he says, looking past me and into the house but I've barely cracked the door. 'I was just calling you.'

'Yes, sorry,' I tell him, doing my best to appear disorientated. 'I must have fallen asleep on the sofa... you know, when I got back.'

'Ah... how are you feeling?' he asks, stony-faced.

'I'm okay. A little tired.' I frown at him. 'What can I do for you?'

His gaze lingers on me for a moment, and he absently scratches an itch on his neck. 'Sorry to bother you with this, but it's about that car.'

'What about it?'

'Well, the car—'

'I've never seen the car before—'

'Aye... but the driver,' Ian says thoughtfully. 'I did a bit of background research on him, just to see if I could work out where he might go to on the island. Known associates and the like.'

'I see.' I'm feeling jittery now; the butterflies are making themselves known. 'And...' I say, arching my eyebrows.

'You don't recognise the car then?'

I wince and shake my head. 'Cars have never been my thing, Ian.'

'It's registered to Niall Murray, and I believe you know him, right?'

'Niall?' I ask, feigning surprise. 'My ex, Niall?'

'Aye, but he's your husband, isn't he?'

I scoff, surprised. 'Yes, but we've been separated for almost two years now.' I shrug. 'He didn't have that car when we were together.' I crane my neck towards him. 'Are you sure it's Niall Murray?'

'Oh aye, quite sure,' Ian says, his forehead creased in concentration. 'You didn't know he was on the island?'

I shake my head forcefully. 'No, I didn't. What's he doing here?'

'Aye, that's what I was hoping you could tell me,' Ian says. 'Who does he know on Jura?'

I blow out my cheeks. 'Besides me and Lauren?' Ian nods. 'No one, as far as I know.'

'So you've no idea why he might be here?'

'No, I... really don't. I'm... as surprised – more surprised – than you are.'

'When was the last time you spoke with him?'

I make a show of thinking hard, pursing my lips. 'I'm really not sure. A while ago.' I tilt my head to one side, still holding the door close to my body, keeping it as closed as I dare without offering up any cause for suspicion. 'We tend to communicate through our solicitors these days.'

Ian nods knowingly. 'That's difficult.'

'It is, yes.'

'And Lauren?'

'W-What about her?'

'Does she see her father?' Ian asks.

'From time to time,' I say, thinking of their plans to meet in Edinburgh this weekend.

'But Lauren is away, of course.'

'That's right,' I say, nodding dumbly. 'So... I have no idea why Niall would be on the island.'

'Can you contact him?' Ian asks. I don't know what to say, and I must look surprised. I cock my head. 'Do you have his mobile phone number, for instance?'

'Ah... no, no, I don't. Like I say... it was a bad break-up, and we don't have a lot to say to one another these days.'

'Hmm... shame,' Ian says.

'Yes, but... we've both moved on,' I say and Ian nods sagely.

'Is there anything else? Only... I'm still not feeling myself and I'd really like to get my head down again.'

'Of course,' Ian says. 'I'm sorry to bother you.' But he doesn't bid me farewell or make to leave. We stand there in silence for a moment. Ian nods towards Blair's pickup, parked beside his patrol car. 'Blair about, is he?'

I shake my head. 'He's just left his pickup here. There's some kind of issue with it, couldn't get it started. He'll be back tomorrow... and I'm sure he'll get it started.'

Ian's gaze lingers on the pickup, his hands at his waist, his thumbs interlocking in his utility belt. 'Right!' he says jovially. 'I'll be off then.'

'If you... do find Niall, please could you let me know?' I ask. Ian looks at me. 'I'd like to know he's safe and well.'

'Of course.' Ian turns to leave, and glances back. 'Like I said, sorry to bother you, Doctor Kelly.'

'It's no bother at all, Ian.'

I watch him walk back to his car. He opens the door, looking back at me. I offer him a quick wave goodbye and he returns it with one of his own, removes his cap, and gets into the car. I retreat into the kitchen, close the door and lock it immediately. I heave a sigh; the relief is palpable.

I hear Ian's car start up and then the wheels crunching on gravel as he reverses, turns around and sets off again. I walk briskly through into the sitting room and watch his car potter down the driveway, indicating right when he reaches the main road. There are no oncoming cars and he pulls out, heading towards the centre of Craighouse.

Walking back into the kitchen, I switch on a light and Blair blinks furiously against the glare overhead as I stand over him. I tear away the tape from his mouth and he gasps.

'Okay... I saw the body in the byre,' he says, speaking so fast he almost trips over his words. He shakes his head, his eyes glazing over. 'I'm sorry, I didn't mean to see it, I just wanted my tools. P-Please let me go. I'll not say anything... I swear as God is my witness, I'll not tell a soul anything! Just let me go, please...' He starts whimpering; spittle is drooling from his mouth, and he starts crying. 'I beg you... please...'

He's convincing, I'll give him that. He's so convincing that I doubt myself. Have I made the right decision here? It has to be him. No one else has been close enough to me, to Lauren, to our house to pull this off. I glare at him.

'You nearly had me,' I say.

'Please, Kelly... I swear—'

'Where's my daughter?' I ask firmly. 'What did you do with Lauren?'

'I didn't do anything,' he says, wailing pathetically. 'I wouldn't hurt her. I wouldn't hurt anyone...'

'Where is she?' I yell at him, startling him into silence. He shakes his head as much as he can, staring up at me.

'I don't know,' he whispers. 'I really don't know.'

'Have you been planning this since you came out of prison?'

'I haven't—'

'Is this what drove you to get through your sentence, revenge? How's that working out for you?'

'I've never been to prison—'

'Liar!' I scream, snatching up the scalpel. Blair flinches and tries to move away, but he's so tightly bound that he can't make any significant moves. I brandish the scalpel at him. 'I'll make you wish you'd never come here!'

'Please,' he cries, eyes clamped shut and trying to turn away from me. 'I can't... I didn't do anything!' I can feel the rage building, all of the stress, the fear, the overwhelming need to save my daughter, and it's all coming to a head right now. I should do as I threatened. I should torture him into submission, have him give me exactly what I want.

But I know, even as I hold the blade close to his face, that I'm not going to do any such thing. I never was.

I step back from the blubbering, sweating mass that is Blair McInally. His body is shaking; wracking sobs emanate from the physical and psychological wreck that he is. And now, I doubt myself again.

Could a psychopath be as convincing as this?

THIRTY-SEVEN

I pick up what's left of the roll of gaffer tape, tearing off a new strip about four inches long. Blair looks fearfully at me as I come before him, clamping the tape over his mouth again. I walk to the back door, glance over my shoulder at him and then switch off the lights before going outside, slamming the door behind me.

The wind has dropped away, and the threat of more rain appears to have passed. The air feels heavy, murky, with mist sitting just above the machair now where a partial thawing has set in on the lower ground. I can no longer see the Sound of Jura, and even Hughie's house is barely visible now with only the outline perceivable. The lights are off and his house is in darkness. He's the only person who could observe me out here. Taking the keys to Blair's pickup, I unlock the cabin and climb up into the passenger seat.

The interior is a mess with discarded food packaging and odd receipts lying around. In the glovebox I find the vehicle's manual, a spare set of bulbs along with a small torch. Nothing that interests me. I don't really know what I'm looking for, perhaps anything that would indicate Lauren had been in the vehicle at some point. The problem is, I've no idea what that might be.

Leaning around the seat, I scan the rear of the cabin. There's a gym bag in the footwell behind the driver's seat and it's so tightly wedged in that I can't lift it out. I have to get out and go around to the other side and open the door. Heaving the bag up onto the seat, I unzip it, the interior illuminated only by the cabin lights overhead.

There's a towel and a set of clothes in the bag. I also find a wallet in one of the internal zip pockets, and inside that is Donnie's driving licence and a debit card along with twenty pounds in mixed notes. Upending the bag, I empty out the contents onto the back seat.

I hear an owl hoot, and it makes me turn my back to the pickup and look around me, paying attention to the shadows. Was the owl warning of someone's approach? Suddenly, I'm feeling vulnerable out here in the open, peering into the sea fog drifting in from the water. Gathering everything that came from the bag together, I stuff it back inside, and hurry back to the house.

When I throw open the door, Blair reacts to my return, an expression of terror in his eyes as I close the door. Placing the bag onto the table, I start examining it more closely in the better light on offer in the house. At the base of the bag, my fingers touch a small rectangular envelope and I take it out. Inside I find several photos and flicking through them sees my anger return.

'Is this Donnie's bag?' I ask, looking sideways at Blair. His eyes are trained on me, but he makes no sound. 'Is it?' I hiss, and he nods. 'He likes taking photographs, does he?' I turn one of the images towards him and Blair's eyes widen, and he begins struggling again. The image was taken at my house, from outside, looking through Lauren's bedroom window. 'How about this one?' I ask, flicking to the next photo. 'And this one?' I show Blair another, the image sickening me. My daughter, getting dressed one morning.

I throw the pictures into Blair's face and he flinches, screaming behind his gag. I reach into his pockets, taking his mobile phone. I pull away the gag and he pants, drawing breath.

'I had no idea! I swear, I had no idea he was doing anything like that!' I ignore his protestations.

'Give me your PIN code,' I say flatly.

'607... 706,' Blair says without hesitation. I unlock his mobile and scroll through his contacts, finding Donnie's mobile number. I call it. But he doesn't answer and the call cuts to voicemail.

'Donnie, I know what you've done. I know everything.' I look down at Blair, who's pleading with his eyes. I don't know what he expects from me. 'I want Lauren back, otherwise I'm going to start removing pieces of your dad. I'll readily send him back to you piece by piece, finger by finger... I will happily take him apart one bit at a time, every hour until I have my daughter home safely. Do you understand me?'

I hang up and toss the mobile onto the table where it bounces, clattering to a stop beside Blair. He's staring at me, shaking his head. 'I didn't know... I would never have condoned it.'

I cock my head. 'I guess we'll soon know just how much you mean to your son, won't we, Blair.' I sit down in the seat opposite him, settling in to wait.

Thirty minutes later, my mobile vibrates in my pocket and I take it out. It's a phone call from Lauren. He must have cloned her mobile phone somehow, because hers was taped to the cover of the access hatch for the septic tank. I know it's possible to do things like that, but where a moron like Donnie learned to do it, I have no idea. But that's the younger generation these days, I suppose. They can make technology work in the blink of an eye whereas I still struggle every time I buy a new phone.

'I see you have found your house guest,' a distorted voice says.

I laugh. 'You can drop the theatrics. The rules have changed,' I say firmly. 'Now you're going to listen to me. You will give me my daughter back, and you'll do so within the hour,' I say, fixing Blair with a piercing look, 'or I'll take Blair apart, just as I described.'

'No, please don't!' Blair says, but I glare at him and then stick the tape back across his mouth, waiting for a response, but Donnie says nothing. I know he's there, though, listening. The call is still connected.

'Do you hear me? I'll do it! This ends, tonight, my way and not yours. I want Lauren back, and I want my husband, unharmed, or I start cutting up your father. If you doubt me, I can give you a taster, just as you did for me.'

Standing, I first put the call on speaker and then place the phone on the table, picking up the scalpel. Blair struggles in his seat but to no avail. He's terrified. And he has good cause to be.

'What's it going to be?' I bark at the phone. 'My daughter and my husband in exchange for your father!' Am I bluffing? I'm not sure, but I'd better hear something positive soon, otherwise I'll have to set an example Donnie won't forget in a hurry. 'Well?' I shout. Blair is crying again now, but I have no sympathy. 'What's it going to be, you sick bastard?'

There's a moment of silence, where I can genuinely feel the tension in the highly charged atmosphere. I've heard the phrase before, but always saw it as hyperbolic. Only now, in the most extreme of circumstances, do I believe it to be real.

The line goes dead.

I glance at the phone. Blair's eyes dart to it as well, and neither of us knows what that means. Did I push him too far or not far enough? I look at Blair and he's looking up at me, silently pleading as he shakes his head. My phone beeps and a one-line message flashes up.

The Old Lodge. One hour. Come alone.

With smug satisfaction, I put the scalpel down beside the phone, taking a deep breath. Inclining my head towards Blair, I smile. 'Well, it looks like Donnie loves you after all. For a moment there,' I say, shaking my head, 'he had me wondering.'

I look up at the clock. One hour. A candid photograph of Lauren, taken on a wet and windy day down on Corran Sands, is pinned to the fridge. *I'm coming to get you, baby. I'm coming.*

THIRTY-EIGHT

The mist is so thick now that every sound is amplified but with a deadening effect. I know the Old Lodge. I've not been inside it before but I know the exterior and area around where the building sits. It's an imposing rectangular stone building previously owned by one of the large island estates, is seldom used now aside from for summer breaks by groups attending the island from June through to August.

The lodge is largely closed up for the remainder of the year, but it stands alone in the landscape. Blair and Donnie chose well. Not only do few people pass through the residence at this time of year, but the locals also pay it little attention. Donnie will also see me coming, even in this weather. There will be no element of surprise, and I suspect he'll be lying in wait for me.

The hour has given me an opportunity to come up with a surprise or two of my own.

'Damn!' Walking to the rear of the car to close the boot lid, I see one of the back tyres has deflated. It is down on the rim. Checking the time, I've only given myself ten minutes to make the five-minute drive out there. Even if I had the time to change the wheel, my car only comes with one of those useless cans of foam to seal punctures. That won't do. Glancing sideways at Blair's pickup, I figure I'll have to take that.

The approach road to the lodge is little more than a dirt track, and the pickup bounces and jostles me as I make a slow approach, pulling up around fifty feet from the entrance. There are no interior lights on, and the windows are either shuttered or they have nets hanging across the panes, shrouding the interior from prying eyes.

The engine is idling, but I switch off the headlights, leaving only the daytime running lights to offer any illumination. Peering through the patchy mist, swirling and parting on a gentle breeze, methodically scanning each window for any sign of movement, I see none. There are no other vehicles here, and a fleeting thought comes to me that this might all be a distraction to get me away from the house, allowing Donnie to rescue his father.

There's only one way to find out though. Putting the pickup into gear, I edge forward, slowly drawing the vehicle around to the left side of the property. In the gloom I narrowly avoid a coming together with two 47kg propane gas canisters rigged up on the external wall, presumably supplying heating and cooking fuel to the lodge. Reversing the pickup, I line up facing the way I drove in, just in case I need to make a quick escape. Taking a deep breath, I grab the kitchen knife I brought with me, still sheathed in its protective sleeve.

I have no idea what is about to happen, but I'll be damned if I'm going into the lion's den without some form of protection. Stepping down onto the side step, and onto the sandy surface beneath my feet, I tuck the knife into the back waistband of my trousers, and close the door.

I'm pretty sure I see movement in one of the upstairs windows, but as soon as I look all is still once more. It could be my mind playing tricks on me though. Walking to the rear of the pickup, I lift the edge of the tarpaulin cover Blair uses to protect his tools, and peer inside. Picking up a wrecking bar, roughly twenty inches long, I heft the weight, firmly gripping the base and dropping the hooked end into my palm.

'I shouldn't be too long. Try not to go anywhere, okay?' Blair can't see me. He has gaffer tape wrapped around his head, covering his eyes. His mouth is secured, with his ankles and wrists securely bound as well. He can barely move, which is the point. Pulling the tarpaulin sheet back into place, I loop the rope back onto the hook, holding it in place.

Wrecking bar in hand, I make my way to the front door. There is an old bell with a clapper mounted to the right of the door, but this isn't a social call. I tentatively try the handle, finding the door unlocked. The hinges are old but fairly well maintained and the massive wooden door moves aside with ease. A draught of air is pulled past me into the house, suggesting there are other doors or windows open elsewhere in the property.

Hesitating at the entrance, I peer into the dark interior. There are furnishings in situ, and I can see all the way through into a drawing room at the end of the corridor leading off the double height atrium, but everything is covered with dust sheets. The edges of several show flickers of movement, caused by me opening the door. I listen intently, but other than the sea breaking on the nearby shore, I can hear nothing.

Entering the lodge, I glance to the left and right. There are two rooms on the ground floor to either side of the entrance, but the dark-brown panelled doors are closed. Beyond the atrium, I can see the drawing room along with another closed door and an archway through to another corridor linking presumably with the rear of the property.

A staircase is to the left winding its way around the interior wall, via two half turns, and up to meet a galleried landing overlooking the atrium. I can see two further doors off the landing and a corridor disappearing into the shadows will have more I'm sure.

On the wall to my right is a lighting panel, a brass plate housing four old-fashioned Bakelite switches. They can't be original, surely. I try the first, but other than a loud click, no lights come on. The same results from trying the others and I have to rely on the pocket torch I brought with me from my emergency blackout stash.

Aiming the beam of light around the atrium, the dust particles in the air carry across the beam. Where's Donnie? Steeling myself, I walk forward towards the drawing room at the end of the hallway, pausing to try the first door on the right. It's locked, and I move on.

At the archway, I take a peek down the corridor, angling my torch in that direction. A barometer is mounted on the wall, the glass dome reflecting the light from my torch. At the far end of this corridor is the kitchen. The door is ajar, and I can see a massive Aga against the far wall with a black flue rising from it and into the chimney stack above.

Swinging the beam back towards the drawing room, I approach the open door, poking my head into the room. The shutters are closed and slim shafts of scant light penetrate at the slat edges, but not enough to illuminate the interior. The furniture is covered with white dust sheets, and I can see a grand piano on the far side of the room, positioned before a large bay window that must overlook the beach and the Sound of Jura beyond.

In the middle of the room, lying centrally atop a huge traditional Kashan rug, is an object. The light from my torch skips off it, but the form is instantly recognisable. Freya McLaren was wrapped in the same fashion prior to placement in our septic tank.

'Lauren!' I yell, running forward, all pretence of caution cast aside. Both the torch and the wrecking bar clatter to the floor, the sound echoing around the wood-panelled walls of the drawing room. As with Freya, the plastic is a heavy gauge and I struggle to tear it with my bare hands. The ends of my fingers are aching as I break through the first layer. Tape has been wrapped around her head, securing the plastic very close to her body. I find the same at the neck, wrapped around the torso and waist, clamping the arms to the sides of the body. The legs, too, are tightly wrapped, effectively mummifying the body.

'Come on, baby...' I say rapidly, pulling at the plastic, seeing it stretch but break slowly, and then I'm clawing at the tape, struggling to pull it clear. 'Not again. Not again,' I whisper, breathing heavily from the exertion. I finally manage to break through, revealing the face. I gasp, throwing a hand to my mouth. Closing my eyes, I have to look away. I don't want to see this. I'm breathing quickly, nausea threatening to overwhelm me, and I dry retch to one side, pushing the back of my hand against my mouth as my eyes drift back to the face.

'I'm so sorry, Niall,' I whisper, slowly reaching out with my left hand and lightly touching his cheek. His facial features have this odd shadow effect to them, the only light coming from the beam of the torch on the floor by his side. The skin on his neck is lukewarm, but I can't find a pulse. He has been dead for a little while, and there's nothing I can do for him now.

Sitting back onto my heels, my confidence has evaporated. Niall was left here for me. He may well have been alive when I made that call. This is probably my fault, too. I have Blair. Donnie has Lauren. He'll not hurt her while I still have something he wants. Two things, if I think about it. I have his father, and then there's his ultimate goal, me.

My eyes lingering on Niall for a moment longer, I stand up, picking the torch up at the same time and reach for the wrecking bar.

But it's not where I left it.

THIRTY-NINE

I scan the floor at my feet, sweeping the area with the torch but it's not here. It's not anywhere. On edge, I spin around, quickly sweeping every surface with the beam of light, reaching for the kitchen knife in my waistband at the same time.

Removing the sheath one-handed is tricky and made worse by circling the room at the same time, trying to be prepared for an assault that could come from any direction at any moment. I switch the torch to my left hand, brandishing the knife in my favoured right. There's another open door in the far corner leading in the direction of the kitchen. No one could have walked out there without me seeing them, and I back out of the room in that direction.

I put my back against the wall to one side of the door and chance a look through it, keeping my knife in front of me. There's a short corridor here. It is narrower than the one leading from the atrium to the drawing room, and a curtain rail is mounted just beyond the door. This must have been the route the staff took from the kitchen to the drawing room.

Halfway along there is another door but it is also narrower than the others I've seen, and much less grand. Angling my light back across the drawing room, I focus on Niall. I don't want to leave him there, not like that, but I came here for Lauren and I'm going to find her.

I'm breathing heavily now, a reaction to my fear and the exertion required to free Niall from his makeshift cocoon. I listen for telltale sounds of movement but there are none. How could he come so close to me and I not notice? He must move like a ghost or something. Edging my way into the corridor, I take every step as lightly as possible. Yes, my torch gives away where I am but moving through the lodge in the darkness would be crazy. At least if I see him coming, I'll have a chance.

At the door now, I'm keen not to leave anything unexplored behind me. I pause and listen; the waves breaking onto the beach can still be heard but the deeper I go into the house, the quieter it becomes. The air is stale, musty. No one has been in here in months. At least, not until very recently. I try the door and it opens easily, opening onto a cellar head with a narrow staircase descending away from it. The odour of damp carries up to me on a draught.

The walls are painted brick, but the white paint has flaked and is peeling away from the lower half of the staircase where the walls drop below ground. I shine the beam down the stairs, and there are signs of recent activity down below. An old oil lamp rests on top of a barrel, and the residue from burning oil through the wick has caught on the glass shade. I can almost taste the oil mixed with the damp in the air.

Movement behind me makes me turn; a shadow passes across the doorway. I bring my knife to bear but something clatters into me, and I drop my torch seeing the light dance as it bounces down the stairs into the cellar. I slash at the figure but my arm is blocked and a weight comes against me. And then I'm upended, falling through the air, my balance at odds with my vision. Air explodes from my lungs as I strike something hard, be it the stairs, the wall or the surface lining the cellar floor, but I crumple into a heap.

I roll onto my side. I have to get up again. Struggling to rise, a sharp pain lances my shoulder and I back away into the cellar, clutching my arm and trip on something unseen, stumbling backwards. Of my assailant, there's no sign. The door to the cellar head slams shut. My torch, on the floor, six feet or so away from me now at the foot of the stairs, flickers and then goes out, plunging me into total darkness.

Staring into the darkness I wait for a shape or to hear sounds as my attacker descends to the cellar, but there's nothing. It takes a few minutes for my eyes to adjust to the darkness. With one hand feeling my way through the gloom, I keep moving until I feel the cold touch of a wall behind me. Catching my breath, I stare into the gloom as shapes begin forming as my vision adjusts. My brain has to fill in the gaps though, because there's no natural light at all. What there is must be filtering in from the cellar head, casting an ethereal light down the stairs from above.

I hold my breath, desperate to become one with the shadows. Where is he? Why hasn't he come down the stairs? Can he see in the dark, like some kind of B movie horror villain? But I hear nothing, and I see nothing.

Once I'm confident that I'm alone, at least for now, I inspect my arm. I know it's not broken but I can't rule out dislocation and I may have broken my collarbone in the fall as well. Probing the area sends pain shooting down my arm as well as across my shoulder and up my neck. I can move it though, even if it's painful. I might have got away with it, but I'd rather not test myself too hard.

I dropped my knife when I fell. I think I'm stuck down here, alone and defenceless. He's playing with me. He must be. Setting out Niall's body like that to draw me in, distracting me enough for him to disarm me. Did he plan for me to go this way, leaving certain doors open to lure me in? That's possible. And I walked straight into his trap.

I still have my mobile. Fumbling in my pocket, I take it out and unlock the screen. The light display automatically dims but it still hurts my eyes to look at it. I'm aware I've just reset my vision too. They'll have to adjust all over again if I'm to move in the dark. I have no signal reception at all. Unsurprising, judging by how far underground I am along with the thickness of the walls.

I switch on the torch function, scanning the room with the white light. There are barrels lined up in one corner of the room; some storage racking is along the wall adjacent to my left. There are several plastic tubs on the shelves but upon inspection I find them empty. Looking down, I see that I caught my foot on some hessian sacks left in a heap on the floor. There is sand spilling from a stack of more sacks, sitting upon a pallet against one wall. Thinking how close we are to the beach, they must be sandbags stored here for use in the event of a high tide or possible flooding.

I am alone. I'm sure. There is only the one staircase and my heart sinks thinking that I'm trapped down here and I'll have to find a way to get through the door at the head of the cellar, and I don't fancy my chances of breaking through it. However, beyond the racking there's a brick arch which leads into another room. The ceilings of the cellar are open; wooden beams span the lengths between the exterior walls, resting on those dividing up the cellar.

I look around at the foot of the stairs, searching for my knife, but it's not here. Checking my torch, I can't switch it on. The wiring must have been dislodged when it struck the stairs. Chancing a look up towards the cellar head, I angle the light from my mobile that way, looking for my knife. If I dropped it up there, then it's gone now.

There is nothing in this room that can help me, and so I

move through the arch and into the next room. I find it's not one room but a passageway linking two rooms to this one. Both of them are smaller than the first, and other than a lot of cobwebs, some collapsible chairs and a metal table, also with folding legs, stacked against a wall, there's little of interest.

In the third room I find it must have been an original scullery or similar. There is an old bread oven built into one wall and a recessed area to one side where some cooking could have taken place along with a grate for an open fire. This clearly hasn't been used for decades. Now, there's a generator standing in the middle of the room, sitting on a brick floor. A diesel generator from the smell of it.

There must have been a leak at some point because the fuel has soaked into the cellar floor in the past, leaving a distinct odour hanging in the air. In the far corner are a line of jerry cans, six in all. Two are empty but the other four are either full or close to it.

Retreating from this room into the passage, I'm buoyed by seeing another set of stairs rising up to the ground floor from the far end. Looking around, I try and build a mental picture of the layout, and those stairs likely come up into one of the rooms towards the front of the house. Possibly another access point to ensure the servants stay below stairs and out of sight.

As quietly as I can, I walk up these stairs, switching the light off on my mobile when I come to another door at the top. There is no lock and, testing the handle, it opens easily enough. The hinges creak due to their age, and it sounds like an aircraft passing overhead in relation to the silence. Beyond the door is another room with dust sheets thrown over a U-shaped seating area before an ornamental open fireplace.

On the hearth is a basket for logs and kindling, with a small box of safety matches beside it. I was hoping to find a poker or something I could use as a weapon but the fireplace has a wood burner recessed in situ, so there are no such tools. A grandmother clock stands in the far corner, to the side of the forward-facing window, the ticking carrying in the dark.

I cross to the window and look out. Blair's pickup is still there, and I check that I still have the keys. I do, thankfully. Looking towards Craighouse, I see flashing blue lights. That can only be Ian McLean's patrol car. It is one of only two emergency vehicles on the island, the other a fire engine staffed by part-time volunteers. I wonder if the ambulance I called to collect Mhari Allen has made the crossing from Islay yet?

The white patrol car is visible through the shifting mist, tracking along the main coastal road of the island but it's not coming this way. My heart sinks, but there would be no reason for him to come here anyway. I could call him. Unlocking my phone again, I still don't have any signal which is really odd. I hold it in the air, close to the window but I have no reception at all. The screen states emergency calls are also unavailable, and they should work, especially this close to Craighouse.

'Kelly?' someone calls, drawing out the e sound in my name. I quickly hunker down behind a large armchair near the window. 'Kelly?' My name is called again, but I'm not sure where the caller is. The door into the atrium is open now, and he's moving through the house. His voice is carrying, reverberating off the polished and solid wooden surfaces. He's making no attempt at all to distort his voice. 'Where *are* you?'

His tone is light, as if we are playing a family game of hide and seek. He also sounds familiar, but I can't place him. He doesn't sound like Donnie, much older in fact. I try to melt into the shadows, become one with the furniture. I hear footsteps close by, and I think he must be outside the door. The sound of footfalls ceases. He's outside this room, silent. I realise I've been holding my breath, and my lungs are already starting to burn. The footfalls start up again, moving away from me, and I chance an intake of breath.

He must have gone back down into the cellar and found me

gone. Does he know the layout of the house? If so, he will have an idea where I am, but he didn't come in here. Is he waiting for me in the atrium? I'm not sure what to do. I hear squeaking floorboards nearby, but overhead. He must have gone upstairs. If Lauren is here, then she is probably up there.

I don't know what I should do. I check my phone again, but there is still no service. I swear internally. What the hell is going on? The floorboards squeak again, only this time it sounds like it's directly above me and my eyes drift up to the ceiling. *I have to find Lauren. She must be here, but where?*

My question is answered with a terrified scream from the room above me.

FORTY

'Mum!'

She's still alive. He wants to punish me, to scare me, possibly to chip away at me, piece by piece. Why else did he push me down into the cellar and not follow? I was at his mercy then. No, this is a game of cat and mouse. He's toying with me. Coming out from my hiding place and approaching the door onto the atrium, I pause, listening. There are no further sounds from above and I peer through the crack in the door, straining to see through the darkness up to the landing.

It's gone eerily quiet. I'm breathing as slowly as I can, trying to stay calm. My fight or flight reflex is in overdrive, but I'm not leaving here without my daughter. The plan must be to use Lauren as bait to draw me towards her, and into the next phase of this little psychodrama he's crafted. He has the upper hand in almost every aspect. There's only one way I can think of that sees me win. I can't allow myself to play by his rules.

Retreating from the door, hands raised in prayer to my mouth, I'm thinking hard. I have an idea, but it's risky and if I fail then it will cost me everything, including my life. I return to the passageway and make my way back down into the cellar. I'm sure I won't have much time, so I set about my task.

The jerry cans are heavy, fifteen kilos each, or more, I can't say for sure. They are also metal, and by the time I return to the generator room for the third the muscles in my arms are burning. I have to practically drag the can across the brick floor; the scraping and shrieking of metal lingers in the stale air. I'm sweating, hauling the last of the cans to the foot of the stairs beside the generator. I manage to lean it against the final tread of the staircase and unscrew the cap.

Whereas previously, the smell in the air was noticeable, now it is almost overpowering but only if you move into the passageway linking the cellar rooms. With luck, if my plan works, the odour in the generator room won't be too alarming. Making my way back upstairs into the front room, I peer around the door to make sure no one is waiting for me. It seems clear.

Moving across the room, treading lightly, I cautiously approach the atrium. Listening intently, I hear the floorboards on the upper level creak. My guess is someone is on the landing directly above me. Slipping out into the atrium, I hug the shadows with my back to the wall, keeping my eye on the staircase. Someone is definitely on the move above me, perhaps matching my steps. I'm at the beginning of the corridor now, making my way towards the drawing room. I'd like to arm myself with something from the kitchen before enacting my plan, just in case.

A flicker of movement to my right makes me stop in my tracks, and I stare down the hallway towards the drawing room, holding my breath. Was it a trick of the light or my overactive imagination? He can't be in there. He's upstairs on the landing, or am I mistaken? If he's in the drawing room, and not upstairs, then I'm walking straight towards him. Paralysed in situ, I realise I can't stay here. I'm out in the open. I'm vulnerable.

I listen, straining to hear any telltale sign to give away where

Donnie is, but there's nothing. Should I retreat? I don't know. A solitary note punctures the silence. The piano key, one depression of a top B, the sound carrying throughout the lodge.

'Oh, Kelly... come out, come out, wherever you are!' he calls playfully. He's not upstairs, and worse still, he's barely metres away from me. I know one more thing for certain too. This isn't Donnie. I'm sure of it. And I can't believe who I think it is. It's not possible. I have to breathe, trying to take small intakes so as not to give my presence away. I glance towards the passage linking to the kitchen. I might get there, if I'm careful.

The next step ruins any possibility of stealth. The floorboard squeaks under my weight and I stop dead, staring ahead of me. Could he have heard it? There's no sound of movement, no figure charging at me from the drawing room. Maybe I got lucky.

A figure steps into view, standing in the doorway, his form silhouetted by the almost imperceptible shafts of moonlight permeating through the shuttered windows behind him. It's not much, but it is enough. I know he's smiling even though I can't see him clearly. I would recognise the jawline anywhere.

'Hello, Kelly,' Hughie says warmly. 'How lovely to see you.'

I'm rooted to the spot. I should run. In my mind I'm screaming that command, but I don't. I'm frozen where I am. Is it shock, terror, or something else? Paralysed by the realisation of who I'm up against? I don't know, but I don't move and neither does he. 'Hughie?' I ask, but I don't need his confirmation. I know it's him, but I can't comprehend how we got here.

'Aye. Surprise!' he says, throwing his arms wide. He's grinning; I can see his teeth.

'W-Why?'

'Because it is no less than you deserve.'

'What did I do to you—'

'What did you do?' he screams and takes a step forward. I

flinch, but I still don't run. 'I lost almost everything! And you took what little I had left away from me!'

I shake my head. 'No, I didn't.'

'You did! Don't tell me you're not responsible because I know you are!'

'I-I don't understand—'

'You will, Kelly.' His tone changes, becoming measured but no less threatening. 'When all of this is over, you will understand *exactly* why I've done this.'

My hands are shaking, and I clench my fists to stop them but it's no use. 'What did I do to you? What could I have—'

'You let my daughter die!'

'Your daughter? No... I—'

'I read the transcripts! I know what happened and you let her die. You, a doctor, sat there and watched the life drain from my daughter...'

'Bonnie?'

'Don't you dare speak her name!' he screams, lurching towards me. Backing away, I bump against the wall and turn, running back across the atrium. I dare not look, but I know Hughie is following; I can hear his guttural snarling as he comes crashing through the door into the front room, almost stumbling, and making for the passage down into the cellar.

I feel a hand take hold of my shirt, but I'm running so fast, he can't get a good grip and I'm able to shake him off. I'm free again. My foot slips as I'm descending the stairs but the passage is so narrow I can use the walls to brace myself.

'Kelly!' Hughie screams after me, and I swear he's almost upon me, but the darkness down here is my friend. Knocking over the jerry can I positioned at the foot of the stairs, almost by accident rather than as I planned, the metal can offers a dead thud as it falls over, the contents gurgling as it begins pouring out onto the floor.

Not that I stop. My plan is at the forefront of my mind and I dash between the rooms, moving from left to right through the passage and into the larger of the three rooms. I sense Hughie is following, but he's dropped back, taking more care on the stairs. Reaching the far staircase, my shoes splashing through the contents of the other jerry cans I emptied earlier, I stop on the bottom step, turning back to the room.

There's no sign of Hughie. Taking out the box of matches I found beside the wood burner upstairs, I hurriedly open the box. My hands are shaking, but I place the end of the match against the side of the box and I wait.

I can hear footsteps in the darkness. He's walking slowly. I can hear him, but I can't see him. Glancing to my left, I see the old oil lamp on top of the barrel. Taking a chance, I remove the glass cover and adjust the valve, opening the flow of vapour from the sump. Striking a match, the cellar is briefly illuminated by the flare, dancing shadows cast onto the wall opposite. I still don't see Hughie.

Lighting the wick, I replace the cover but the flame is very small and I'm not sure how much fuel it has. I should have checked. Why didn't I check? I put it back down on the barrel. Fumbling with another match, I see Hughie standing at the far end of the cellar, watching me. I hold the box aloft, another match waiting to strike, so he can see in the light offered by the old lamp.

'Don't come any closer!' I yell at him. 'I'll do it. I swear I'll do it!' Undaunted, Hughie enters the room but only by a step. I can see the glossy shimmer of light reflecting from the pool of diesel at his feet. The smell down here is overpowering. So much for being subtle.

'I must admit,' Hughie says calmly, 'I'm impressed with your ingenuity. I wasn't convinced you'd follow all of the rules. I wanted you to realise what you are: a killer. Someone who thinks they get to decide who deserves to live and who should die. To admit it, finally, to yourself and the world. But let's not kid ourselves, Kelly. You're not going to burn this place down. Not with your daughter upstairs.'

'You think so?'

'Yes.'

'That's where you're wrong again,' I say defiantly. 'If my daughter is going to die, then she'll die my way. *Not yours!*' The lamp is burning better now, the light increasing, and I can see Hughie's expression. He looks less confident than he sounds.

'Okay.'

My gaze narrows. 'What do you mean, okay?'

He shrugs. 'Do it. Burn it down.'

'W-What?'

'Burn it down!' he says, taking a stride towards me. I raise the box higher still, emphasising my intent. Only, Hughie smiles.

'I'll do it. We can all go to hell together.'

'Your place is guaranteed, Kelly. And I'll be right there with you for an eternity, but Lauren? Does she deserve such a horrific end?'

'That's not your decision!'

'No, it's yours. Just like that day when you killed my daughter.'

'I didn't. It wasn't my fault what happened to Bonnie.'

He cocks his head. 'That's not what the police thought at the time. Or the General Medical Council.'

'I was cleared of any wrongdoing.'

'Aye, you were. And why was that, do you think?' Before I can answer, Hughie takes another step forward. He's in the centre of the cellar now, two metres from me. 'Was it because you did no wrong or was it because the girl who died was from the wrong side of the tracks?'

'I barely knew Bonnie—'

'But you knew she was shagging your husband! You knew

she was hanging out with your daughter, and they were taking drugs—'

'I knew nothing of the sort! Lauren doesn't take drugs, and never did.'

'Aye, because posh-arse Morningside kids don't take drugs. That's just what the council estate trash do, isn't it?' he says, snarling. 'It's why posh blokes from private schools can get away with snorting cocaine when a kid from a council estate would be sent to juvenile detention. It's one rule for the minority, and another for the rest of us.'

'Where the hell were you when Bonnie needed you, eh?' I hit back. 'That girl went from foster home to foster home, bouncing around in the care system because you let her down. And you've got the nerve to blame me!'

'I sat there,' Hughie says, his eyes gleaming, 'day after day, night after night, staring at the brick walls in my eight by six cell, thinking about nothing else other than what I was going to do to you when I got out.'

'Me! Then why pick on my daughter... why kill my husband?'

'Because I wanted to take what was special to you and squeeze,' he says, tightening a fist. 'Don't forget, tonight, this is all of your own making. All you had to do was kill one of your patients. Then this would have been over, but you couldn't follow simple instructions, Kelly. You had to do it your way!'

'Why? Why have me kill an innocent person? My patients have nothing to do with this—'

'And I had nothing to do with your life either! My life was simply collateral damage in yours. The whole point of any of this was to destroy your life, just as you've destroyed mine.'

'And you expect me to believe you would have given me Lauren back if I'd done what you wanted? You must think I'm an idiot!'

'Now you'll never know, Kelly. You'll have to live with knowing you've wrecked everything.'

'How long did it take you to dream all of this up?' I hiss at him. 'You think I'll care about any of this when I'm dead? There is no hell, there is no afterlife, no matter how much we want there to be. This is all there is.'

Hughie laughs. It is the creepiest of sounds. 'You think I intend to *kill you*? Far from it. You'll live with this night for the rest of your days, wondering whether there was anything you could have done differently. Could you have saved them, either of them.' He shrugs. 'And it will eat you up until the day you die.'

'Maybe that day,' I say coldly, 'will come sooner than you think.' I strike the match, the tip flares and, defiantly, I throw the match into the pool of diesel at Hughie's feet.

FORTY-ONE

The flame hits the diesel and is immediately extinguished. I can't believe it.

'Oops,' Hughie says, smugly. 'It's a shame you were so proficient in the study of medicine and not as gifted when it comes to chemistry, Kelly. You see, diesel has a far higher flash point than petrol. To ignite it, you need an enclosed chamber, a vapour and a slow burn.' He leans his head to one side, turning the corners of his mouth down and mocking me with fake sadness. 'Good for me. *Very* bad for you.'

Glancing at the box of matches in my hand, I'm stunned. Hughie moves slowly to one side, and then the other, mimicking Gene Kelly's *Singin' in the Rain* routine, coming ever closer with each step. I look up the stairs; I have to run, but how far will I get? To my left, the lamp is ablaze now, the flame flickering and dancing.

'An enclosed chamber?' I look at Hughie and he stops dancing, the smile fading as he follows my gaze to the lamp atop the barrel beside me. 'A slow burn, you say?'

Hughie moves a fraction of a second after I do, and I grasp the lamp at the base and I hurl it to the floor beside the empty hessian sacks on the floor at his feet. The glass shade shatters and the flames ignites the material which has been absorbing diesel ever since I emptied the jerry cans. Soaked in diesel, they light up with ease.

'No!' Hughie screams as the flames rapidly advance across the surface towards him. He tries to back away but he's standing in the middle of the room, where the pool is at its deepest. His dancing starts again, only this time it's a dark scene, far more macabre as he flails around, desperately attempting to put the flames crawling up his legs out. It's no use though. Soon they are at his knees. In minutes they'll be licking at his arms and face. Hughie is violently pitching from left to right, bouncing off the walls and racking, trying in vain to extinguish the fire.

The flames are unrepentant, though, growing larger, almost encouraged by the increasing intensity of his panicked shrieking. I turn my eyes away from the scene, and I run up the stairs.

Slamming the door to the cellar head shut behind me, I run into the kitchen and grab one of the wooden chairs pushed underneath the table. Returning to the access door to the cellar, I wedge the chair under the handle, just in case. Then I'm off and running, through the atrium and up the stairs, taking them two at a time.

'Lauren!' I repeatedly yell, but she doesn't answer. I go from room to room, throwing open the doors and scanning the interior. Although every room has furniture inside, all covered in sheets, I can't find my daughter. 'Lauren!' I scream, hearing desperation in my voice. She's here, and I have to find her quickly. The lodge is fashioned from stone, but the floors, joists and windows are made of wood. It's old, and once the fire in the cellar properly takes hold, the wood will burn, fast.

Throwing open the door to the last room, I'm dismayed to find nothing. Was it all a charade? Was he playing some kind of recording to me? Where is she? I'm ready to cry, panicking, and I don't know what to do next. 'Lauren!' I scream as loudly as I can. I'm about to leave, to restart the search all over again when I hear something. It's a scratching, scrabbling sound but it's muffled and faint.

Forcing myself to calm down, I close my eyes and listen, willing Lauren to tell me where she is. The scratching becomes a knocking, but there's a gap between each noise. It's coming from above me. There must be an attic room. Running back onto the landing, I try every door I see. There are two storage closets but the third I open leads to a narrow staircase.

The attic is in pitch darkness and, remembering my mobile phone, I reach for it but it's not there. I must have dropped it when I ran from the cellar. Hughie is downstairs, so I should have nothing to fear but I still climb the stairs cautiously. I wouldn't be surprised to find he's booby trapped something as part of his plans.

At the top of the stairs, I look around. There's a tiny circular window in the gable end wall, and two dormer windows facing the rear, across the beach to the sea. At the far end of the attic room I see a shape, writhing and squirming on the floor. Lauren! I run over to her, falling to my knees.

She's wrapped in plastic sheeting, in the same way as Freya and Niall, bound at the wrists and ankles but her head is free, with tape wrapped around her head and across her mouth and eyes.

'It's me, darling,' I say, touching her face. At first she recoils from my touch and I see the tape is also around her ears. She is almost completely barred from her senses. 'I'm here and I'm going to get you out.' She must be able to hear me because she stops struggling, although her breathing is rapid through her nostrils. It isn't as simple as pulling the tape away from her mouth or eyes; it's wrapped in multiple passes around her head.

I do my best though, eventually finding the end of the tape and unfurling it as best I can. Finally, I am able to pull the last of it away from her mouth.

'Mum!' she exclaims. 'It's Hughie! He's—'

'I know, baby. Don't worry, he can't hurt you anymore, but we have to leave.' Working on the plastic now, I'm trying to free her as quickly as possible.

'Mum, get me out of here, please...'

'I'm trying, I'm trying.' I'm clawing at the wrapping, but it is incredibly tight around her body. I get one arm free and she sets about helping me. Between us, we are making progress. I'm pleased to have found her, but I can't shake the thought of the fire below that I know is building.

'Kelly!' Hughie bellows from somewhere in the house and both Lauren and I stop.

'Shit!' I whisper.

'Mum, g-get me out of here, please.'

I resume my work, but I know he's coming. He'll know where to find us. I glance nervously at the stairwell. There's no way to secure it and even if I did, all I'd be doing is sealing our fate with the fire raging below.

'Come on!' I curse under my breath.

'Mum, he's coming... he's coming,' Lauren says, but I ignore her pleas, focusing on getting her out. Her second arm is free and if I can undo the tape around her ankles, she'll be able to wriggle free, I'm sure.

'Kelly! I've changed my mind!' Hughie yells. His voice echoes, and that means he can only be in the atrium or on the landing for his voice to sound like that. I'm hoping he's going to think we're outside already, and look for us out there, rather than risk coming upstairs. 'I've decided I'm going to kill your daughter in front of you. And then I'm going to kill you!' he shouts. Lauren meets my eye, and I can see she's terrified. I pull the last piece of tape clear and she shuffles her feet; between us we manage to free her.

'Come on,' I say, taking her hand and hauling her to her feet. But Lauren hasn't been able to move in some time. Her legs are stiff and the blood flow has been restricted. She almost falls when I drag her towards the staircase.

'I can hardly feel my legs,' she says. I hold her up, supporting her weight as we move across the attic and back to the only exit. At the top of the stairs we stop. I can see flames emanating from the atrium. The fire has engulfed the entrance to the house, and the flames have spread up the stairs and the landing is also ablaze. Smoke is carrying up the stairs past us and I can feel the heat upon my face. Worse than all of this though, is seeing Hughie standing at the foot of the stairs looking up at me, sporting a maniacal grin.

'We will all burn together,' he says before lurching forwards, clambering up the stairs towards us. Lauren screams, and together we move away. Thankfully, Hughie isn't moving well. Despite managing to extinguish the flames, he must be in great pain. I search the attic, but the only exit other than the stairs is out the dormer windows and onto the roof. It's not a great option, but it is the only one.

'Come on,' I say, half carrying, half hauling Lauren across to the window. She's crying now. The moment of relief she feels at her rescue is punctured, destroyed by the very real threat of being murdered. Propping Lauren up against the wall, I try the window. It isn't locked. There are no locks but it can't have been opened in years. The wooden frame appears to have warped or swollen in its constant duel with the Hebridean weather, and it's stuck firmly in place.

I'm wrestling with it, and I see Hughie reach the top of the stairs, collapsing in a heap on the floor and rolling onto his back, grimacing. Seeing him spurs me into life and I dig deep, wrestling with the window and it shifts, ever so slightly at first, before opening fully. The frame around the hinges is rotten, and levering it roughly aside sees one hinge break away from the frame. The glass feels heavy, swinging on one hinge and I shake it, bending and twisting. The second and final hinge gives way and the window falls away from the dormer, sliding along the slate tiles and disappearing from view.

Taking a firm hold of Lauren, I drag her to the window and she doesn't need any encouragement. Seeing Hughie in the attic is enough to motivate her and she clambers out onto the slates. 'Go right, go to the right,' I tell her. The pickup is parked that way, although I've no idea how we'll get down to it. Hughie groans, and as Lauren clears the window, I put one foot up on the sill, bracing both hands on either side of the window and haul myself up, feeling the wind gust over me, tasting the salt in the air and hearing the roar of the sea.

As I look back into the attic, Hughie rolls onto his front and with a snarl, pushes himself up with both hands beneath his chest. 'Kelly!' he screams at me. The flames are climbing the stairs behind him, licking at the attic floor. But I'm already out onto the roof. The tiles are slippery underfoot and, feeling my grip disappearing beneath my feet, I cling to the guttering along the side of the dormer.

Lauren is flat against the roof, already more than six feet away from me. I follow her example, lowering myself flat against the roof, distributing my weight as best I can. Lauren glances back at me and I force a smile, trying to reassure her. The flames are illuminating the nearby ground, reflected by the sea mist swirling around us, and turning the surrounding landscape into a truly apocalyptic scene.

'Kelly!' I look back to see Hughie poke his head out of the window looking both left and right. Upon seeing me, he also starts to climb out onto the roof. Is he simply pursuing me or has he also realised the only way to escape this inferno is across the roof? I don't care, and I hurry to catch up with Lauren.

In my haste though, I'm not paying attention, and I lose my footing as a slate dislodges under my weight. I find myself sliding, and my hands can't get purchase. 'Lauren!' I yell. I don't know why, there's nothing she can do to help me. It only takes a second for me to run out of roof and my legs are in free fall, only arresting my descent by grasping the guttering. The cast iron half-pipe comes away, and just as I expect to plummet to the ground, the movement halts and I'm left dangling from the roof.

Lauren's head peers over the lip, staring down at me from further along the roof. 'Mum!' Swinging myself to one side, gathering momentum in a pendulum action, I swing myself up and try to grasp the roof only for the slates I touch to shift under my weight, and I can't gain any purchase. Looking down, I see I'm over a pitched roofed, single storey lean-to extension at the rear. Probably a boot room or similar to avoid traipsing sand from the beach into the house.

Lauren retreats from view, and the metal edge of the guttering is digging into the skin of my fingers, and if they're not bleeding, I think they will be soon. Dangling from the roof, I contemplate how I can get back up, but I don't see how I can do it. My strength is failing, and my grip loosening. Movement from above draws my attention and I look up, half expecting to see my daughter staging some kind of misguided rescue attempt.

It's not Lauren, though. It's Hughie. He glares at me, leaning over the edge. Then he disappears and I think he's going after Lauren. I try again to get myself back up onto the roof, but I can't. The strain makes me wince; the pain in my shoulder is excruciating now, and my left arm has got to support the bulk of my weight.

The guttering moves, startling me. A booted foot is hanging over the eaves, striking the next fixture holding the cast iron gutter to the roof line. Hughie strikes it again and again. I can hear him grunting with each blow.

'Stop!' I yell. 'Please!' But, of course, he's not going to stop. He rams his heel against the bracket again and this time it breaks free. The guttering shifts again and I yelp, losing the hold I have with my damaged right arm. I'm swinging freely in the air now, holding on with one hand. Hughie scuttles along the roof; I can hear his movement above me, his boots scurrying across the slates.

His leg reappears, almost a metre further along, where the next bracket is located. He stamps down on it, the jolt jarring my arm, the one thing preventing me from a fall. 'Hughie, no. Please!' I plead with him, but I can barely get the words out, choking on my fear. He ignores me, glancing over at me with a twisted grin on his face as he stamps down again. The bracket moves, and another jolt threatens to shake me from the roof. 'Please...' I'm crying now. I clamp my eyes shut, praying for something, anything to rescue me.

The next blow doesn't come though. I look up just in time to see Hughie pitch forward over the eaves, falling headfirst past me at speed, arms flailing. He manages to utter one panicked shriek before impacting the ground below. Breathing hard, I look down. He's lying still beneath me, his head angled in an unnatural position. There's no recognition. No sign of the anger or hatred he's harboured for me all these years.

He's gone.

Lauren appears above me, reaching out and I'm relieved to see her.

'Mum! Give me your hand!' she shouts, extending her hand towards me. I raise my free hand to meet hers, but it's too late, my strength fails me, and I can't cling on any longer. Under protest, my fingers are wrenched from the pipe, and suddenly I'm falling through the air, chased down by the sounds of my daughter screaming.

FORTY-TWO

I'm cold, under water. I can't be, but that's what it feels like. Sounds are deadened, muffled. The voice is familiar, but different somehow. The sounds get louder, and the clearer they become, the more piercing and painful they are to my ear.

'Mum!' My eyes open. Lauren is above me, shaking my shoulders violently. 'You have to wake up.' She's trying to drag me from where I lie, but she's clearly struggling. I respond but my answer is incoherent, but enough to make Lauren pause. She looks into my eyes and the blurred shape coalesces into a vision of my daughter.

'Lauren,' I all but whisper. My left side isn't as cold as my right which seems at odds with what I expect. It's also brighter than it should be at this time of night. *It is night-time, isn't it?*

'Mum, you have to get up!' Lauren shouts, shaking me again. The noise level around me increases rapidly and I feel heat upon my face, dancing orange and yellow lights to my side. Rolling my head to the other side, away from Lauren, I see a body lying in the machair, where the beach sand meets the grassland. For a moment, terror grips me, and I grasp Lauren's arm, willing her to run, but Hughie isn't moving.

'The fire!' Lauren says, pulling me up into a seated position, supporting my back. Now I can see the flames. The Old Lodge has been engulfed in fire, spreading through old wooden floors and joists. Lauren's right. We are far too close. Gathering my senses, I look up at the pitched lean-to extension at the rear of the building. That's what broke my fall, and that's the only reason I'm not dead like Hughie.

Grasping Lauren's shoulder, I'm able to lever myself up with her support. The moment I put weight on my left leg though, pain shoots up my leg and into my hip. I swear, and Lauren shoots me a sideways look of concern. 'What is it?'

'My foot,' I say, wincing with each step. If Lauren wasn't here to support me, I wouldn't be walking that's for certain. 'A sprain... it could be broken.' I shake my head. 'I don't know.'

'Can you walk?'

'I'll crawl if I have to.'

Together, we make slow progress away from the building; the searing heat from the intense blaze is stinging my face. I angle our route away from the lodge but back around to where I left the pickup. The heat from the blaze is intense, and we need to get clear of it. I can see a car heading along the access track towards us. My first thought is it must be Ian McLean. He'll have seen the flames, and put two and two together, and made his way down here. But the blue lights are not on on his patrol car. I point towards the oncoming vehicle. We need help and I don't really care who it comes from.

'That way,' I say, and Lauren turns, my arm around her shoulder and we limp onto the access track, dispensing with the idea of taking the pickup. The car isn't moving quickly on the unmade road, and it's only a small hatchback. 'Here... this will do,' I say, panting at the exertion. We are clear of the building now, safe from the fire.

'Hey!' Lauren shouts, relieving herself of her burden and waving her hands in the air to attract the driver's attention. I put my hands on my knees, doubled over, trying to catch my breath. It's over. Not how I planned, but it's over.

The sound of the engine picks up. It's as if the driver is accelerating towards us. Lauren is still waving, but with less enthusiasm. 'What are they doing?' she says, backing towards me. 'D-Don't they see us?'

I react faster than I would've thought possible and shove Lauren aside two-handed with as much force as I can muster. She yelps at the unexpected push in the back, but I don't know if it's enough as the car strikes me at an angle below the knee and I slide up the bonnet, glancing off the windscreen and somersaulting up over the roof, coming down in a heap in the brush to the side of the track.

I've heard of this before, where the body goes into shock and delays the process of understanding what's just happened to it. I feel incredibly calm, lying on my back, hearing the brakes shrieking as the car comes to an emergency stop. Looking towards the car, I can see the red brake lights are illuminated. They go out as soon as I hear the engine switch off.

Then my body catches up. Pain explodes in my legs when I try to move. With only the glow of the nearby inferno to assist, I look at my legs, contorted as they are in an unnatural position. I scream. The sound brings Lauren running towards me. *How did she end up so far away from me?* Dropping to the ground beside me, she's in tears, likely in shock much the same as me. She doesn't know where to put her hands and they hover above me as she scans my body. 'What... what do I do?'

Neither of us notice the driver getting out of the car and approaching us, not even sensing her arrival at Lauren's side.

'Oh, Kelly dear... what have you done to yourself?' Ava asks.

Lauren looks round at her, scowling. 'Ava? What are you doing?' she says accusingly. 'Didn't you see us?'

Ava looks suitably contrite, but when our eyes meet I see something else. Satisfaction. 'Kelly dear—'

'You!' I say, snarling. 'It was you? I thought you were my friend.'

Lauren looks between us. 'What was... her?'

'In the messages... you called me *dear*, and I never picked up on it.'

Ava smiles, tilting her head to one side, and then glances back towards the lodge. Spotting Hughie's still form, the smile fades and she turns back to me.

'We had such grand plans,' Ava says. 'You know, they took Hughie and me over a year to organise everything. I had to encourage your predecessor to take retirement... and Hughie had to mock up everything to convincingly mimic the Highlands and Islands Enterprise initiative just to have you apply!' She shakes her head slowly. 'So much time. So much investment, and all to bring us here,' she says, looking at the lodge, flames dancing from the attic windows now. She looks back at me. 'All you had to do was to follow simple rules, Kelly. But you're not one to follow the rules, are you? That was our miscalculation.'

'You?' I ask. 'Why? What did I—'

'You took away my daughter!' she says, spitting the words at me. Lauren flinches but she's frozen to the spot. 'Mine and Hughie's. Did you think we would let you get away with it?'

'But... Bonnie was in the system,' I counter.

'And I was getting myself straight,' Ava argues. 'Hughie got himself involved in all that smuggling and left me alone with a wee girl. I couldn't cope. I tried,' she says, her eyes glazed. 'Damn it, I tried, but I was never a very tactile person... and not really cut out to be a mother.' She looks over me, off into some non-distinct point in the distance. 'At least, that's what I thought... until I came looking for her. I came to find Bonnie, only... she was gone.' Her expression hardens, and she looks down at me. 'And you killed her.'

I shake my head. 'I did my best, Ava. I really did—'

'Don't *lie* to me!' she screams and Lauren jumps. She's too scared to look at Ava, and I can see her shaking with fear.

'I'm not lying, I swear—'

'You murdered my little girl!' Ava screams at me. 'You took her away from me and now I'm going to break you just as you did me!'

'No, please, don't...'

'We did all of this to make you suffer, to feel the pain that we felt, but now I see it for what it is. A waste of time. I can make you suffer with one stroke.' Ava's hand snakes out and grasps a fistful of Lauren's hair, hauling her away from me. Lauren screams in pain, falling backwards as she's dragged off balance.

'No!' I scream at Ava, my voice breaking. 'Please don't hurt her. Don't take my daughter away from me!'

Ava, a few steps away now, pauses, holding Lauren upright but still on her knees. She produces a knife from her coat, holding it against Lauren's throat, but staring at me with a gleeful expression.

'You'll watch her die, and then you'll know what I went through. You'll know how much it hurts to not be there for your child when she needed you the most.'

'No, wait! Please!' I shout and I can see Ava is enjoying my suffering. I try to move, to crawl towards them but the pain is too much, and I howl with the first movement. This only makes Ava happier, the blade pressing against Lauren's throat. She's crying openly now. My baby is terrified and there's nothing I can do. 'Why Freya?' I ask, desperate to distract Ava from her task. 'Why did you have to kill Freya?'

Ava glares at me, her satisfaction evaporating in the blink of an eye. 'Because you chose to save her over my child. Why should she get to live, and my daughter gets to die? Answer me that?'

I shake my head slowly. 'I know it's unfair. If I could have saved them both, I would have!'

'Liar!' Ava screams, pressing the knife harder against Lauren's throat. She moans, a trickle of blood running from where the blade meets the skin.

'No, it's true!' I yell. 'But you're right. I should have saved them both. I should have done more... and if I had my time over, then I would do more.' The admission appears to throw Ava momentarily. Maybe I can get through to her, stop this before anyone else is hurt. 'I'm sorry,' I say quietly. Ava hesitates, and I see the knife lower fractionally. 'I'm so sorry for your loss. Bonnie was a great kid—'

Ava's scowl returns, and she jabs the knife into the air at me. 'Now I know you're lying. You hated my daughter—'

'That's not true. I didn't.'

'You hated her because she was sleeping with your husband,' Ava says. 'And he got what he deserved... and you may have cheated justice once, but not again.' I'm about to scream at her, Ava angling the knife to slice across Lauren's throat, when an explosion detonates to my left. The shock wave knocks all of us off balance, and I find myself flat against the ground, my ears ringing.

It feels like the earth is shaking beneath me, the sound of the sea muted. The propane cylinders. The fire must have reached them. The nausea is awful, the dull ache in my head, and I think I'm going to be sick. Lauren is lying face down, hands clamped over her head in the brace position, elbows to her face. Ava is staggering back to her feet, and already searching for something on the ground.

The knife. She's dropped it. I want to get up but the pain returns as soon as I try to move. There's nothing I can do. 'Lauren!' But she doesn't hear me. She's alive, breathing, but she's not running away. She has to run. Save herself even if that leaves me here alone with Ava. 'Lauren. Run, baby... please!' I shout.

She lifts her head, staring at me with bloodshot eyes. She's in shock. She can't process any of this. Ava is focused again, coming to stand over my daughter, the knife poised above her. I raise a hand, pleading with her but Ava only smiles at me.

A shape comes from the right, and something catches the light as it arcs through the air, striking Ava across the back of her head. It's like watching the scene unfold in slow motion. Ava stands still, seemingly frozen in time, surprised, and then her eyes roll up and the blade slips from her fingers as she crumples to the ground.

Blair is standing over her, sporting a shovel with a sturdy two-handed grip. He's breathing heavily, torn gaffer tape dangling from his wrists and ankles. He looks down at Lauren, who crawls over to me, and I draw her into my arms, ignoring the pain I'm feeling. Then his eyes meet mine. There are flashing lights visible in the direction of Craighouse now, the blare of sirens carrying on the breeze only seconds later.

I'm crying now, staring at Blair McInally. I silently mouth the words *thank you*, Lauren's head on my chest, and me, stroking her hair just as I did when she was sick as a toddler. Blair doesn't say a word, his chest steadily rising and falling, and he simply tosses the shovel aside, offering me a curt nod.

Now it's over.

EPILOGUE

SEVEN MONTHS LATER

The sound my heels make on the freshly varnished floor echoes in the empty room. Pausing in front of the ornate mirror still hanging above the fireplace, I examine my reflection, leaning on my cane. Black has never really been my colour. Yes, it goes with everything, and it is befitting of the day. A gentle murmur of road noise from outside sounds like that of a motorway to me having got used to what passes for traffic through Craighouse.

I dare say no one pays it any attention around here. If anything, it's quieter than normal. I hear footsteps from the lobby. Lauren pokes her head through the door.

'There you are,' she says, looking around the room anxiously. 'Are we about done?'

'Yes, I'll not be a minute.' My daughter senses my mood. She's been hyper-vigilant of late. Who could blame her? Although, she's fared better than I have with all of this. Crossing the room to me, I put my arm around her, and she does the same to me. The closeness we share now is very special.

'It's weird to be back here, huh?' she says and I nod. The postman climbs the steps to the front door, and we both see him through the bay window. 'I'll get it,' Lauren says, decoupling from me and leaving the sitting room.

Looking around the room, there are so many memories tied to this house and not all of them are terrible. Niall and I had good times here, too. Now, as I stand here, in a house devoid of any of our material things attached to those memories, it's just a shell. A ghost of what's gone before, I suppose. It doesn't matter anymore, the things that happened here.

I'm looking forward now.

Lauren returns with a clutch of letters, sifting through them. Most look like junk mail, flyers and the like, but she pauses on one in particular, fishing it out for me.

'This one is addressed to you, Mum.' She passes it to me, and I don't recognise the handwriting. Checking the postmark, I see it was stamped at a sorting office in Stirling. I don't know anyone in Stirling. I thought I'd updated all of those who needed to know our new address. I look up from the envelope as Lauren backs out of the room, and she smiles. 'I'm just going to check out my bedroom one last time. Okay?' I smile, nodding. We're both saying our goodbyes in our own way. Lauren hesitates at the doorway, one hand on the frame. 'It's fitting, don't you think?'

'What is, darling?'

'To be here, on today of all days.'

I incline my head. 'Yes, I suppose it is.'

Lauren leaves and my thoughts turn back to Niall. For his memorial service to be held in the same church we exchanged our vows in was strange, and to go from there to visit our familial home is fitting. I said goodbye to my husband properly this morning and now I'm saying goodbye to the last physical representation of our lives together, before handing the keys to the agents for completion day tomorrow.

The bank agreed a stay of execution in the repossession process following Niall's death. As his next of kin, because we were still married, it fell to me to tie up probate and I couldn't begin that process until I was able to leave hospital. I missed the funerals, both Niall and Freya's. Reconciling everything that happened, returning both Lauren and me to a healthy state has been a real slog at times.

Today brings closure. Lauren is right. It is fitting to be here. Walking over to the bay window, wincing at the ever-present pain in my right leg, I stand in the sunshine streaming in from a glorious Edinburgh day. It's good to be here, regardless of the circumstances that brought me back. This is my city, my home. And I'm not running from it anymore.

Next week, I begin another new chapter or should I say, I make a fresh start in an old chapter, taking up a new role at the Royal Infirmary. I never believed that I would be able – or allowed – to put the past behind me. In a perverse way our experience on Jura led to such an outpouring of compassion that I think people figured I'd suffered enough. It's a part-time position, but I'm still rebuilding my life as much as I am my body. We will see where it takes me.

Lauren will be heading off to St Andrews this coming September, taking up a place on her undergraduate course reading Marine Research. I couldn't be prouder of her. She won't allow herself, or me for that matter, to be a victim in our lives. She's turned a horrific experience into fuel to drive her passion forward.

She is an inspiration. She's my inspiration.

Leaning my cane against the window seat, I lower myself onto the cushions, glancing out at the trees upon hearing birdsong. I'm leaving the fabric cushions here. They were made to measure anyway, and I'll not need them in my apartment overlooking the Meadows. Using my thumb, I tear open the envelope and take out the folded paper inside. It is a handwritten letter.

My reflective mood dissipates, a knot of fear constricting my chest.

My dear Kelly,

You may thank me at your convenience for saving you from facing the mental torture of a trial with my guilty plea. I will be held behind these walls for what feels like an eternity, but I want you to know that I haven't forgotten about you. Everything I do from here on will be focused on one goal, the day where we meet again. A guilty plea reduced my sentence by one third. I am already one third of my sentence closer to the day where we will meet again.

You will never be rid of me. There are no walls tall enough. No cage secure enough. I will see you again, in person. For now, you can expect me to visit you in your nightmares. Look for me in the shadows, for one day, I will be there. On that day, you will pay for the decision you made and for what you took from me.

Take your daughter to a safe place. Live your best life. As for me, I have nothing else but time. And I am patient. As God is my witness, Kelly, you and everyone you love will suffer by my hand.

The letter is unsigned. How did she get this out of a maximum-security institution, let alone have it mailed to me here?

'Mum?' I look up and seeing Lauren at the door watching me with a curious expression on her face, I crumple the letter in my hand, forcing a smile. 'Are you okay?'

'Yes, why?'

'You were miles away. It's like you've seen a ghost or something.'

I scoff, shaking my head. 'No, not a ghost. Something else.'

'What is it?' she asks, crossing the room and sitting down beside me.

'Nothing, darling.' I tap her knee, and meet her doubting look with a broader, still artificial, smile. 'It's absolutely nothing, honestly! Do you have everything you need?'

She relents, and smiles. 'Yes, I'm ready to go. You?'

'Yes. Tell you what, you go and bring the car around to the front,' I say, 'and I'll be done in a minute.'

'Okay. Do you need help getting down the steps—'

'I'll be fine. Go on with you.'

Lauren gets up and walks out of the room. I lever myself up, feeling the stiffness of my weaker leg and grimacing, allowing my cane to support my weight when I stand. I walk slowly over to the fireplace.

Ava is correct. I'll never be free of her. She will be in prison for a very long time, but she didn't receive a whole life tariff. Should she do as she says, become a model prisoner, attend all of her rehabilitation sessions and remain focused on her goal, then she will be released from prison one day. It might be two decades from now. Three. Perhaps more. But I don't doubt her resolve.

She will do as she says. One day, I will see her leave the shadows.

I'll be waiting for her though. I'll be ready, because I know it will happen. If someone killed my child, I don't doubt I would feel the same. Tearing the letter into pieces, I lean over, awkwardly, open the door to the wood burning stove and toss the pieces inside.

Righting myself, I catch my own eye in the mirror once again. Staring at my reflection, studying myself, I look older. Forty years of age, and I'm starting again from scratch. *Almost.* Doctor Kelly Howlett, accepted into her old life once more. I wonder how Ava can be so clear-minded, so absolute in her assertion that I knowingly killed her daughter? I suppose I can't blame her. After all, I did make a choice that day.

Once I realised something suspect was going on at the barbecue, I paid more attention. There was a reason Bonnie wouldn't cast off her cut-off shorts and dive willingly into the pool along with her friends. She had no knickers on, seeing as they were still on the floor of my daughter's bedroom, courtesy of my husband. Seeing her casually hand something off to one of their friends at the party, I did some snooping, and when I got the opportunity to look in the bag she was so protective of that day, I found the ecstasy tablets.

I did make a choice that day. I chose to put a handful of those tablets into Bonnie's drink. It was impulsive, rather than premeditated. I had no idea she would share the drink with Freya, though.

A car horn sounds twice in quick succession. Lauren is waiting for me. Straightening my jacket and adjusting my hair in the mirror, I'm ready to face the world again.

It's true, I did make a choice. It's just not the one everyone accused me of.

A LETTER FROM JASON

Dear reader,

I want to say a huge thank you for choosing to read *Family Doctor*. If you did enjoy it, and want to keep up to date with all my latest releases, just sign up at the following link. Your email address will never be shared and you can unsubscribe at any time.

www.bookouture.com/j-m-dalgliesh

I hope you loved *Family Doctor* and if you did I would be very grateful if you could write a review. I'd love to hear what you think, and it makes such a difference helping new readers to discover one of my books for the first time.

I love hearing from my readers – you can get in touch through social media or my website.

All my best,

Jason x

www.jmdalgliesh.com

facebook.com/jmdalglieshauthor

x.com/jmdalgliesh

PUBLISHING TEAM

Turning a manuscript into a book requires the efforts of many people. The publishing team at Bookouture would like to acknowledge everyone who contributed to this publication.

Audio
Alba Proko
Sinead O'Connor
Melissa Tran

Commercial
Lauren Morrissette
Hannah Richmond
Imogen Allport

Cover design
Henry Steadman

Data and analysis
Mark Alder
Mohamed Bussuri

Editorial
Rhianna Louise
Lizzie Brien

Copyeditor
Jane Eastgate

Proofreader
Becca Allen

Marketing
Alex Crow
Melanie Price
Occy Carr
Cíara Rosney
Martyna Młynarska

Operations and distribution
Marina Valles
Stephanie Straub

Production
Hannah Snetsinger
Mandy Kullar
Jen Shannon
Ria Clare

Publicity
Kim Nash
Noelle Holten
Jess Readett
Sarah Hardy

Rights and contracts
Peta Nightingale
Richard King
Saidah Graham